First Case

Jersy Morine

Prologue

Everything around her was starting to get blurry. Her feet were no longer on the ground. She couldn't feel her body anymore. All she could feel was how fast her heart was racing and the tight grip his hands had around her neck. She had no idea how long she hadn't been breathing, but she could tell she was going to black out any minute. She could hear herself pleading inside her head. *Please, God. Please. Don't let me die tonight.*

She had her hands around his wrists trying to pull him off, but she wasn't strong enough. She had been trying to squirm out of his grip for what felt like hours, but she honestly had no idea how long he had been holding her up against this tree strangling her.

Finally, she felt her foot lightly brush something. *His leg.* She did the only thing she could think to do. She kicked her leg out as far as she could, hitting right between his legs. He cried out in pain and loosened his hands from around her neck. She took the opportunity and ran as fast as she could. She had no clue where she was going, it was too dark to see. All she knew was she had to get out of these woods. She had to find a house, a road - anything where she could get help.

She had been running for too long. Her legs felt as though they were jello. She could only feel fear and pain.

She was beginning to think the woods would never end, that there was no way out. She couldn't see a single thing. She could feel the damp grass under her feet. It felt like she was just running in a black hole. But she kept going, she had to. Until her right foot smashed against the side of a stump and sent her flying, landing on her face. She could hear the loud crunching of leaves getting closer. *He was coming.* She didn't take any time to feel the pain in her ankle or even think, she knew she had to keep running. But before she could even get up, she felt something hard hit the back of her head. Everything went black.

One

Anna Harvey was sitting in the backseat of her best friend's mom Meghan's car, on their way to the local mechanic shop. Her best friend Jordan was in the passenger seat flipping through some notes for their calculus test this morning.

"Were here girls." Meghan announced. "Go get your car, Jordan."

Anna looked up to see they were parked right in front of *Chad's Auto Clinic.*

"See ya, Meghan. Thank you." Anna smiled before closing the back door.

Anna used to call Meghan "Mrs. Embers" back in high school, but Jordan and Anna are now in their first year of university, so Meghan had insisted she started calling her by her first name. She had also used to joke that "Mrs" made her feel old.

Meghan nodded and gave Anna a wave. But, before she could begin backing out of the parking lot, the shop owner Chad Anderson began walking toward Meghan's *Subaru.* He was wearing a dark brown sweater and his faded jeans were covered in oil. He gave a nod to Anna and Jordan before smiling at Meghan.

"Hey, Chad." Meghan gave a soft smile back. "Busy morning?"

Chad nodded. "Seems to be the week of replacing rocker panels."

As the two kept talking Anna noticed the genuine smile on Chad's face, rather than a friendly one. She thought about it for a moment before shaking her head, erasing the thought. *Meghan and Chad? As if.* She had definitely just been watching too much *True Crime* lately and was itching for something mysterious to happen.

Snapping Anna out of her thoughts, she heard Jordan clear her throat impatiently. She saw Meghan give Jordan the *'Really?' look.*

Chad lightly chuckled and held out a set of keys towards Jordan. "Brakes are good as new. No more failing to stop at red lights."

"Thank you." Jordan sighed.

"You can pay inside," Chad told her. "Luka is in there for a little longer until he leaves for class."

"Luka?" Meghan raised her eyebrows. "I thought you had a receptionist?"

"I did." Chad nodded. "Well - do. Kind of. She failed to show up again today. I haven't seen her in a few days now."

Anna noticed Jordan was starting to walk up towards the entrance and began to follow her. But not before she heard Chad say, "I need to fire her. Do you want to replace her? I could use a pretty secretary to see everyday."

Anna stopped and thought for a moment. Was she overthinking? She tried to tell herself she was, but when she looked back toward the *Subaru*, she could see a kind of lust in Chad's eyes as he stared at Meghan. Maybe she wasn't overly obsessed with *True Crime*, maybe she was right.

Anna didn't realize when she stopped to think, she had actually stopped walking.

"Anna, you coming?" Jordan interrupted her thoughts.

Anna looked up to see Jordan had made it to the front doors. She began jogging to catch up. Jordan gave her a questioning look, but

Anna figured it wasn't worth discussing with Jordan right now, she would probably just call her crazy. Instead, she brushed it off and stepped in front of Jordan, opening the shop door.

Luka Anderson was spinning around in the secretary chair while what looked to be taking a video on *Snapchat*. He immediately stopped spinning once he seen them and cleared his throat. His cheeks turned as red as a stop sign.

Anna couldn't help but laugh. She hadn't seen Luka in nearly six months, since they graduated high school. Looks like he was still the same old guy.

"H-hey guys." He gave a slightly embarrassed look. "I didn't hear you two come in."

Anna looked over at Jordan holding back a laugh, "We can see that."

Jordan held out a hundred dollar bill in his direction. Perks of living in a small town are things can be a whole lot cheaper when you know the right people.

"I'm just here to pay for my car, then you can get back to whatever it is you are doing."

"Sure doesn't look like secretary work to me." Anna teased.

Luka put the hundred in the till as he looked up at Anna and smirked. "Yeah, doesn't seem like a good career path for me, huh?"

Anna let out a small laugh. "Clearly." She wished she hated the way he smirked at her and the way he always had some platonic snarky comment off the top of his head, but she didn't.

Back in middle school she had tried to hate Luka. If anyone had asked, she would say she didn't like him. He was too much of a try-hard. He always thought he had to be the coolest and better than everyone. He tried to live up that reputation in high school and mostly succeeded. By that point Anna had just pretended she didn't even know him. But, she couldn't resist starting at him back in high school when they used to have science class together.

With all these thoughts coming back to her, Anna knew she needed to get out of here. Fast.

"Well," She turned towards Jordan. "We should go."

Jordan nodded and headed toward the door. As Anna began following her, she couldn't help but give one more tease. "Considering your dad just told us you've got some heavy work to do at your trade school today."

She was lying, but she just felt like wounding him up. She didn't know why, it was just fun. They used to joke around in middle school before he decided he needed to be number one.

She knew Luka was half way through his first year of college planning to become a mechanic like his dad.

"Heavy work?" She could hear the panic in Luka's voice in the distance. "You're kidding, right?"

Anna laughed a little too hard once she was out the front doors. She knew he would believe her. She almost felt bad. Almost.

Jordan laughed along with her. "You really have a hate out for him, don't you?"

Anna held back the urge to laugh at that too. She knew she didn't hate Luka, no matter how hard she had tried to for years. She was far from hating him. Quite the opposite, really. But, she would never admit that to anyone. Not even her best friend. Instead, she smiled. "Something like that."

Anna stared out the window as Jordan pulled into the parking spot they park in everyday. Her and Jordan went to the same university at the edge of the small town they both lived in, Edgar's Cove. Most young adults from Edgar cove went there too. Everyone had always said it was "just in their backyard" and was the easier way to go, unless you were a teenager who just wanted to get out of this small town.

Anna was thinking pretty deeply about what she had seen at the shop. She couldn't help but wonder, was something really going on between Chad and Meghan or was Anna's life just boring and she was scraping for something exciting to happen around here? She honestly didn't know. Edgar's Cove was in one of those phases right now where nothing big was happening with anyone, and everyone was content. Anna hated these phases, she thought they were extremely boring.

"What is it?" Jordan asked.

Anna felt taken back for a moment and just stared at Jordan.

Jordan smiled, "I know that look, Anna."

Anna scoffed, "Fair enough."

She sighed, not sure if it was worth mentioning to Jordan. She decided to give it a shot anyway.

"Do you think your mom and Chad were being- I don't know- *flirty* this morning?"

Anna could see Jordan thinking for a moment. "Yeah, maybe a little. What about it?"

"Doesn't it freak you out?" Anna questioned. "I thought Luka's dad was married. I mean, your mom is too, but considering the situation I wouldn't exactly blame her for seeing other guys." Jordan's parents were still technically married. Her mom had filed for divorce, but her dad refused to sign.

"Woah, wait. You don't think they were actually *flirting*, do you?"

"Yeah?" Anna felt more confused than ever as she leaned back in her seat.

Jordan shook her head. "No, it's not like that, Anna. Chad has always done things like that. But it's totally platonic. Though I still don't think he should be doing it, considering he does have a wife. Not only that, but since she is sick too."

Anna wasn't convinced, but nodded anyway. It seemed more than platonic to Anna, but maybe that was from all the *true crime* she has watched over the years, that had made her focus more on little details.

Jordan probably just wasn't paying enough attention to the details like Anna always had. She had to pay attention to the details if she wanted to be a detective. Of course, Anna didn't want to be right. Luka's dad and Jordan's mom? That would be inexplicable for everybody.

However, a little voice deep inside Anna's head told her to keep an eye out, just in case.

As Anna was getting out of the car, she heard the rattle of a loud muffler. She knew exactly who it was, everyone did. When you live in a town as small as Edgar's Cove, you know who the boy driving the jacked up *Dodge Ram* with a muffler you can hear across town is.

She turned to look across the parking lot to the street and saw the black square body passing by the university, on his way to the trade school that was located in the next town over.

Anna turned to Jordan and they both shook their heads. Luka always had to be noticed. He craved attention. Anna kind of felt bad for him. It wasn't necessarily his fault that his dad was well known and he wanted Luka to live up to his reputation.

As they walked up toward the school, Anna kept her eye on the raven-haired boy through the passenger side window that was down, until he was out of sight.

She couldn't help but replay the conversation from this morning, trying to hold back a grin. She saw him look toward her last minute before he was gone down the road and got a jittery feeling in her stomach. She acknowledged it for a moment, before shaking her head and telling herself it was nothing.

Two

"Hey guys, wait up!" Jordan heard in the distance as she and Anna were walking through the halls to their shared chemistry class. They turned around to see the university's top football star, Owen Bentley. He had gotten accepted to Edgar University through a scholarship for football.

"Hey." Jordan gave him a smile, quickly dropping it when she noticed how sad he looked. "Are you okay?"

Owen shrugged hesitantly. "Yeah, I just wanted to know if either of you have seen my sister Chelsea around lately?"

Jordan gave Anna a confused look that she returned.

"No, actually." She thought for a moment. "Now that you mention it I haven't seen her in the past couple of days."

"Me either." Anna chimed in. "She hasn't been to psychology class for a little while."

Owen gave a disappointed nod that didn't go unnoticed by Jordan.

"Why?" She asked. "Did something happen?"

"My mom is really worried about her. She hasn't seen her in a few days. We were quiet about it at first because we assumed we were overreacting, but now we don't know what to think." He explained.

"When was the last time you saw her?" Jordan asked.

"Two days ago." He answered. "It's not like her to just run off."

"Has something bad happened to her?" Anna whispered.

Jordan nudged her, giving her a side eyed glare.

Owen's voice turned to a low saddened tone. "We're not sure. But that's what my parents think."

Jordan reached out and gently placed her hand on Owen's arm. "But we don't know that. Maybe she is okay and she'll turn up soon."

Owen titled up his head so he was now looking at the ceiling. Jordan could see the tears that wanted to form in his eyes, but he pushed them back. "Yeah, I know. But-"

Before he could finish, his phone rang.

Jordan stepped back a little, giving him space to take the call.

He looked up at her, his eyes full of worry.

"What is it, Owen?" Jordan asked.

"It's my mom calling."

"Answer it. Maybe they found her." She encouraged him.

Nodding, he put the phone to his ear.

"What if it's bad news?" Anna whispered.

Jordan shook her head. "I don't want to think that way."

"I know, but what if?"

Before she could argue anymore, she saw Owen's face drop. He was pale.

"No." Was all he said.

Jordan stepped back toward him. "What is it?"

"I knew it." She heard Anna whisper behind her.

Jordan kept her full attention on Owen. "Owen, what is it?"

He pulled the phone away from his ear, his eyes full of tears. "They found her."

"Where?" Anna asked.

He took a deep breath before speaking. "Her body washed up on the beach off of Crescent Avenue."

Jordan gasped. "Owen, I'm so sorry."

"Me too." Anna frowned.

"What happened to her?" Jordan asked. "You don't have to tell me right now if you don't want to."

He sniffled. "They're looking into it. But they're saying she was murdered. The police told my mom she has a large wound on the back of her head. That's all she knows."

"Chelsea was murdered?" Anna asked in disbelief.

Owen didn't say anything.

Jordan reached for his arm again. "I'm so sorry. We're always here for you, okay?"

He nodded as tears rolled down his cheeks.

Jordan didn't know what else to say to him. She felt the urge to reach over and wrap him in her arms, because she didn't know what else to do, but she didn't. She just stood there in shock like Owen. She watched as Owen looked up from the floor, tuning back into the world around him. Everyone else continued on as normal, since they didn't know yet. They were all talking and laughing with their friends, while she stood here and watched Owen fall apart.

"Owen." She said, snapping him out of his haze.

He cleared his throat as he looked down at her, his eyes glossy. "I really just need to get out of here."

Jordan wasn't going to protest and ask him to stay, she knew the outside air would be good for him right now. But more than anything, she wanted to go with him. She wanted to help him through this process. But, she also knew that he probably wanted to be alone right now and she could understand that.

Nodding, she let him go. She watched as he walked past her, keeping his eyes on the floor, careful not to look at anyone. She still wanted to run after him, but kept her feet firmly planted and watched him go down the hallway until he was out of sight.

Jordan sighed and turned back to Anna. "I can't believe this."

"Chelsea was murdered." Anna said again, clearly still not believing it.

"Maybe she wasn't." Jordan said, still trying to keep things positive.

"He said there was a gash on the back of her head, Jordan."

"Maybe she fell and hit her head on a rock or something." As soon as the words came out, she didn't even believe herself.

Anna shook her head, disregarding her conspiracy. "Chelsea goes missing and then turns up dead. That's not something that happens around here, Jordan. This is Edgar's cove. The smallest town in the state with a population of 90 people. Can we be real for a minute please?"

Jordan nodded. "I know. You're right. It's just so hard to believe something like this would happen here."

"I wonder if she was murdered and then dumped into the water." Anna suggested.

"I don't even want to think about it." Jordan shuttered.

"The question is, did the killer want her body to wash up and be found, or is this going to be a surprise for them too?"

Three

"**D**ammit!" I screamed as I threw my phone across the room, aiming for the wall. I heard it smash before it fell to the floor.

I was reading the online Edgar's Cove newspaper. The front page was titled "**Teen's Body Washes up on Beach**". It had a picture of the young girl, Chelsea Bentley. She was found late this morning, but the article didn't get put up online until 2:00 this afternoon.

I should have known this would happen. I should have known her body would wash up to shore. The brick I tied around her must have loosened and slid off, making it to the bottom of the ocean, leaving her body behind. I didn't put enough thought into what I was doing, I rushed things. All I could think of at the time was I had to get her gone before sunrise. Now look, it's all a complete mess.

I screamed a couple more times, punching the wall. I threw every beer bottle I drank so far today at the wall as hard as I could, releasing all my anger. But now, it's time to be cool.

I have to act like everything is normal. No one will suspect me. I can absolutely get away with this. It's a small town, but there's lots of terrible people living here. I could name a list of people in this town they would suspect before they ever suspected me to be a murderer.

Even if I technically was. I don't really like to call myself that, because I don't just go around killing random people.

I've never even killed someone before. The most I had ever done was get into a few intense bar fights and sent some guys to the hospital with some threatening injuries, but none of them ever died.

I never planned to kill Chelsea, I always thought she was such a nice girl. *Too nice*. Which is exactly why I had to do it, she left me no choice. I know I did the right thing. No one else would ever understand my reasoning. But I did. Which is all that really matters.

Well, that and no one ever finds out.

Four

Anna and Jordan were sitting on the kitchen counter, each with a solo cup in their hand. The upbeat music was deafening. There were people yelling and playing beer pong, some casually making out on the couch. Truthfully, Anna didn't know the guy throwing the party. She had just heard about it through a girl in her french immersion class and dragged Jordan here. Jordan was used to it by now, she had been doing it since their first week here and they were now just a couple months from their summer vacation.

"Your mom actually took that job offer?" Anna asked in disbelief. She had to yell a bit, even though Jordan was sitting right next to her.

Jordan shrugged. "I'm not that surprised. She'll take any job she can as long as it pays more than the last." She paused and took a drink from her vodka filled red solo cup. "Although it does seem a little gross to me that she now works for Luka's dad."

For some reason Anna still couldn't wrap her head around it. Probably because of what she had saw at the shop yesterday morning when Chad had offered Meghan that job. She still couldn't get that moment out of her head. She knew the drinking she would be doing at the party they were at tonight would make her even more curious.

"I honestly didn't think he was serious when he offered her that job."

It was true. Anna thought he was only joking about it so he could find a way to flirt.

Anna was about to mention how things with Jordan's mom and Luka's dad were slowly becoming more and more suspicious, when she caught the glimpse of a green sweater moving all too fast out of the corner of her eye. She whipped her head around to see Owen storming in, his face red as a tomato with a sour look.

"Jordan, look."

Jordan whipped her head around, brows furrowed. "What is he doing?"

"You!" Owen yelled, pointing his finger directly in Luka's face.

Luka, who was sitting at one of the tables with his friends doing shots of tequila, looked up at Owen with the same confused look as Anna.

"What is Luka even doing here?" Anna asked.

"You don't remember?" Jordan laughed. "He and Gage were good friends in high school."

"Who's Gage?" Anna's brow furrowed.

"The guy who's throwing the party!" Jordan yelled at her.

Before Anna could reply, she noticed how quiet the room became other than the music and Owen's booming voice.

"You had something to do with this, didn't you?" Owen began shouting so loud, everyone in the room began to turn their heads to see what was going on.

Anna watched as everyone around began pulling their phones out of the pockets and started filming the scene in front of them.

"Oh my god." Jordan got out before Anna could.

Anna couldn't take her eyes off the scene in front of her.

Luka put his hands up in defence. "Owen, look, I don't know what you are talking about. I didn't do anything. I'm just trying to have a good night."

Owen bit his lip as he held back tears. "The hell you didn't. We both know you were the last one to see her alive."

Luka silently stared at Owen for a long moment. "Who, Chelsea?"

"Don't even say her name." Owen roared. "You don't deserve to."

Anna was growing nauseous, and it wasn't from the vodka. She had a terrible feeling this was going to turn bad, fast.

"I didn't do anything." Luka repeated.

"The hell you didn't, Luka! You were the last one to see her that night."

"No I wasn't." Luka shook his head. "She never showed up."

Anna looked at Jordan confused. "What does he mean?"

Jordan shook her head and shrugged. "I'm just as lost as you are."

Owen looked to be taking that information in for a moment, almost believing it. "You expect me to believe that, Anderson?" He scoffed.

"Well it sure sounds more reasonable than me committing murder, Owen." Luka pointed out.

It had been confirmed in the Edgar Cove newsletter this morning that Chelsea had in fact, been murdered. The police are saying blunt force trauma and strangulation, due to the gash on the back of her head and the red marks they found around her neck.

Owen slapped the shot glass out of Luka's hand. The tequila spilt all over him as the cup flew across the room. "You're a liar."

This got a reaction out of Luka. He stood up, stepping closer to Owen so their faces were inches away from each other. "What the fuck, Owen?"

"Tell me what happened to her!" Owen demanded.

"Listen, alright?" Luka's neck began turning red from anger. "Because you don't seem to be hearing me. I did not hurt Chelsea. I would never do that."

Anna felt her stomach turn as she saw Owen's fist clench. She had a bad feeling this was about to turn into more than just an argument. "We need to get over there."

Jordan didn't say anything, but nodded in agreement. She jumped off the counter and began running toward the two angry boys as fast as she could.

Owen rubbed his other hand across his angry smirk. "Bullshit."

Just when Anna thought the two couldn't get any closer, Luka took another step forward. "Whether you like it or not Owen, I did care about Chelsea. I'm not the monster you're making me out to be. I would never-"

Without warning, Owen's fist collided with Luka's jaw. Luka went down hard. The whole room gasped and hollered. Anna did too as her hand flew over her mouth as she completely stopped in her tracks, staring at Luka, who was now on the ground.

She ran over to Luka as fast as possible, without thinking. He was about to get up, probably to throw a punch back, but Anna couldn't let him. She knelt down next to him, placing a hand on his shoulder. "Luka, don't. It's not worth it."

He looked up at her and they locked eyes for what felt like a good thirty seconds. She saw a spot of blood in the corner of his lip. She reached up and pulled her sleeve down, wiping it off for him. He seemed frozen, letting her do it.

"Just walk away." She told him.

She could see his head spinning, contemplating if he should get up and attack Owen or not.

He looked from Owen and then back to her. "Yeah. Yeah, I guess you're right." He began to stand and brush himself off.

Anna felt relieved that Luka wasn't going to fight Owen. After all, they're not in high school anymore. She thought Luka's fighting days were over. She wasn't sure why she felt the relief, or why she even cared. She didn't understand the nervousness in her stomach when she saw Owen hit Luka. She told herself it didn't matter that it was Luka. No matter who it was in that situation, she would help them because she is a kind person. She didn't believe it, but it made her feel better to pretend it was true.

Luka looked over at her for a moment, as if he was going to say something. Probably ask her why she came over to help him, but he didn't. She was glad he didn't, because she honestly didn't have an answer.

Five

Owen wanted to go in for more. He wanted to finish Luka for what he had done to his sister. Of course, he had no proof Luka did anything, except for the fact he had been casually dating his sister for the past two months and the last their mom knew, Chelsea was supposed to see Luka the night she died.

He tried to take a step forward to go back over to Luka, but stopped in his tracks when he felt two hands on either shoulder. He looked down to see Jordan looking up at him. Her face was full of worry and her eyes were pleading for him to stop. Just looking at her face was enough to get him to stop, it was enough to stop the whole world around him. But she didn't know that.

"Owen, don't. Please." She pleaded.

The concern in her voice made his heart ting with pain. He couldn't say anything, he just looked in her eyes and nodded. For a split second, Luka and the world around him didn't matter, he was only focused on Jordan and it brought him comfort. He wanted to tell her how he felt about her for some time now, but was too afraid he would ruin their friendship and lose her forever.

"Relax, okay?" She cut into his thoughts. "Let's go get some air. Maybe some ice for your hand too."

Owen hadn't even noticed the pain in his hand until she pointed it out. He looked down to see her gently holding his hand while inspecting it. His knuckles were a little bloody and would definitely be bruised later.

Jordan nodded her head toward the direction of the door. He could still hear people laughing and yelling at both him and Luka.

Owen watched as she guided him to the ice freezer. He had wanted to be with Jordan for nearly three years, since the first day of tenth grade when he met her in their shared math class. The way she wrapped the ice carefully and put it on his hand, even the way she was caring for him in general, made his heart ache. Not the kind of pain he had felt just a moment ago trying to fight who he believed killed his sister. But the kind of pain when you knew you needed somebody. And he did. He needed Jordan.

Once they were outside, she cut into his thoughts again. "Owen."

He looked down at her, barely able to speak. "Yeah?"

Her voice was soft and it made his heart flutter. "What happened back there?"

He took a deep breath, scared how she would react to what he believed. "I think maybe Luka had something to do with Chelsea's death." His heart sank when he saw the genuine fear in her eyes. She probably thought he was crazy. But if she did, she didn't say it.

"What makes you think that?"

"The police who are investigating Chelsea's murder took her phone and went through it to see if they could find any leads." He explained. "They came by earlier today and told us Luka was the last person she texted."

Jordan seemed genuinely interested in what he was saying, that made him feel a lot better, like maybe he wasn't crazy after all.

"What did she say?"

"That she would be at his place in fifteen minutes. They said the text was sent the same night she was killed, possibly within the hour." Owen realized he sounded like he was begging her to believe him. He was, though. He wanted her to believe him because he knew how hard this would be to prove. But he didn't want to show her how much he wanted her to believe him in case it scared her off.

Jordan gave him a small pitiful smile as she reached out to lightly touch his arm, but she didn't say anything.

Owen couldn't stand the silence. "I know that I might totally sound out of my mind-"

"No, no. I'm not saying that at all." Jordan cut in. "I just think you should wait a little longer, let the investigators find more evidence."

Owen still didn't seem satisfied. He didn't want to stop, he needed to know the truth. The police could take months to figure out what happened to Chelsea. He needed someone's help to figure out what happened to his sister and he wanted it to be Jordan. Even though she didn't think he was crazy, she still wasn't convinced of his theory. Maybe he just needed to find something more that would convince her.

Six

Anna was sitting in the library when she got a text from Jordan telling her to meet her at her jeep as soon as possible. Curious, she packed up her books, threw her bag over her shoulder and dashed out the front doors.

Jordan held out a pineapple mango smoothie. "Took you long enough."

Anna wrinkled her brows. "Hey! I thought we were going to go get smoothies together."

"I know, I'm sorry. I had a lot on my mind after talking to Owen and decided to skip English class. I'm sure I'll hear about it from the professor later, but that's the least of my worries right now."

Anna could sense something was wrong. She knew Jordan long enough to know that look on her face. She closed the jeep door fast and turned in Jordan's direction. "What happened?"

"Okay, first, we've talked about this. No slamming my jeep doors. I've saved up for this baby since I was ten." It wasn't a newer jeep, a 2008 Jeep Liberty to be exact. But, it was still Jordan's baby.

"Sorry, sorry. Get to the story."

Jordan sighed. "After the fight yesterday, I talked to Owen. He said something that I can't stop thinking about."

Anna pressed her lips together so she wouldn't say anything. Every time she thought about Owen punching Luka she felt angry at Owen. But, then she immediately feels bad for him when she realizes how much pain he must be in from losing a sister. Anna couldn't even imagine losing one of her little siblings. They were everything to her.

"What did he say?" She asked.

"The last text Chelsea sent before she was murdered was to Luka."

Anna froze. "What did it say?"

"That she would be at his house in fifteen minutes." She explained.

Anna felt her heart sink as she thought back to what Luka had said during the argument with Owen. *She never showed up.* That was proof that Chelsea was on her way to Luka's. Could Luka have done something? No, of course not. Luka could never do something like that, that wasn't who he is. Sure, he'd ended up in a couple fights between middle school and high school trying to keep up his father's reputation, but that still wasn't who he is. He wasn't a bad person.

"Anna?" Jordan cut into her thoughts.

Anna looked over to see Jordan was looking at her with concerned eyes. She must have been staring off for too long thinking about Luka. "What if Chelsea really did never make it to Luka's house?"

"You're saying something could've happened to her on the way there?" Jordan asked for clarification.

"I-yes?" Anna stuttered. "Couldn't it have?" She felt stupid for asking that. Of course that was a possibility, but so was something happening to her at Luka's. She didn't think Luka could hurt anyone so that's why she didn't want to believe it.

Jordan looked at her with worry. "You're not picking sides are you? Luka or Owen?"

"Of course not!" Anna said a little too fast and Jordan noticed. "No, okay? I am not taking sides. We don't know enough yet."

Truthfully, Anna didn't know if she really was taking sides or not. Maybe she was. Was she? She wished she wasn't. Owen was going through one of the worst times of his life, she couldn't blame him for lashing out, but she hated seeing Luka get hurt. Deep down, she knew why. It had something to do with that tingling feeling she got whenever she saw him ever since sixth grade.

"Exactly." Jordan nodded. "I told Owen that too, before he goes accusing someone again."

Anna took a sip of her smoothie right as she got an idea. "This is it. This is my moment."

"Oh no." Jordan turned her body, giving Anna her full attention. "What now?"

"We are going to solve this case!" Anna yelled and immediately threw her hand over her mouth when she realized they were in the small town *McDonald's* parking lot, it was the one on the corner just down the street from the university. You could usually find it packed with eighteen to twenty-five year old's there nearly all day long grabbing lunch before a exam or midterm.

Anna had been obsessed with *Nancy Drew* her entire childhood, so it was no surprise she was now obsessed with anything true crime related. She couldn't even come up with a number for how many true crime cases she has watched and tried to solve while watching. She even still owned every *Nancy Drew* book she has ever read. She was even studying criminal justice at university this year and would be for the next six, to work her way up to become a detective. *Detective Anna Harvey*. She liked the sound of that. She figured this could be her test to know whether she was made to study real crime cases or not. Of course, she would have to hide this from the real investigators on Chelsea's case.

"We?" Was all Jordan asked.

"Yes!" Anna exclaimed. "We both know the police in this small town are either too busy or too lazy. They don't really care about what happened to Chelsea, but Owen does." Anna could tell since tenth grade Owen and Jordan had feelings for each other. Now they were first year university students and those feelings were still there, even if neither of them would admit it. She knew if doing this would help Owen, Jordan would be in.

"You really want to get Owen's hopes up?" Jordan asked.

Anna knew doing that could be a bad idea because it had only been three days since Chelsea's body was found on the beach and it is still extremely fresh for Owen. But, she also knew Owen wanted to know the truth about what happened to his sister, and that's why he hit Luka.

"But what if we did find the truth? Or at least something that would lead us to the truth. We could end Owen's misery." *And Luka's*, she thought.

Anna could see Jordan was thinking really deeply on this as she stared out the windshield, not really looking at anything, but just lost in her thoughts. She felt relief when she saw Jordan nod her head. "Okay, where do we start?"

"With that." Anna felt her heart pain at what she saw in front of her. It was Luka, with a coffee in his hand, still grease on his clothes from trade school, standing with two men in long trench coats, both wearing a badge and gun on their hips. *Investigators.*

"Those must be the investigators on Chelsea's case." Jordan guessed. "The one on the right's name is Marvin."

"How do you- oh, your mom?" Anna asked, knowing full well about Jordan's mom's history with men. She reminded Anna of *Blanche Devereaux* from *The Golden Girls.*

Jordan nodded. "You guessed it."

Anna shook her head in disgust before focusing back on what going on in front of her. Luka kept looking from the officers to the ground. Anna noticed the way he began to look around to see if anyone was watching what was going on. She knew people were watching. That's the type of thing people were looking for to distract them from studying from their midterms and exams and thirteen page essays, when they went to grab a coffee that they told themselves would make them get work done. She felt bad, but she kept watching, eager to find out what was going on over there. She could only see the side of all their faces, but the officers looked to be really grilling him.

"It doesn't help that we can't hear what they're saying." Jordan sighed.

Anna's jaw dropped when she saw the three of them start walking together toward the police car. "Are they-?"

"Taking him in?" Jordan finished for her. "Yeah."

Anna felt like she could burst into flames. She had so many questions. Why were they taking Luka in? There's no way he actually killed a person. He was stupid and rebellious, but he wasn't a psychopath.

As if Jordan could read her mind, she began trying to comfort her. "I'm sure they're not actually tossing him in county jail, Anna. They probably just need to do a proper investigation because they know Chelsea was on her way to Luka's house that night."

Anna nodded, forcing herself to believe that what Jordan was saying was true. It had to be, right? She didn't like this. The police were clearly wasting their time. *That's it*, she thought, *I'm going to find out what's really going on.*

Seven

Luka was led into the interrogation room with the two officers who brought him here behind him. The room was dark and gloomy. He looked over at the one way mirror, taking in his reflection. He assumed there were other officers on the other side watching what was about to happen.

"Take a seat, Luka." Said the officer who had introduced himself as officer Marvin.

Keeping quiet, Luka took a seat in one of the chairs at the interrogation table. He hated to admit it, but he was a little nervous. He didn't know what was going to happen in here. Truthfully, he wasn't even sure why he was brought here. Why wasn't the quick interrogation in the middle of the parking lot enough?

The other officer, named officer Baldwin, was the first to break the silence. "We'd just like to ask you a few questions, Luka."

"You already did in the parking lot." Luka was already growing tired of this. It was Monday afternoon and he had just gotten out of his mechanic class. All he wanted was to go home and take a nap.

Ignoring Luka's point, Baldwin started with the questions. "When was the last time you saw Chelsea?"

"I already told you." Luka grumbled.

"Well, remind me." Baldwin shrugged.

"Tuesday."

"So nearly a week ago." Baldwin added up.

"Just two days before she was murdered." Marvin piped up.

"I told you, I didn't do anything to Chelsea." Luka raised his voice.

"Let me remind you of the texts." Marvin offered, walking towards him. He placed two laminated photos of text message conversations between Luka and Chelsea in front of him.

Luka looked down at them, rereading them.

Chelsea: I thought you loved me?

Luka: Loved you? Chelsea, we're not that serious.

Chelsea: What the hell are you talking about?

Luka: It's just a party that my friend is hosting. You're over-reacting.

Chelsea: Overreacting? How stupid are you?

Luka: I'm not the stupid one here. You're the one who can't seem to understand we've only been together for two months.

Chelsea: We're still in a relationship, Luka. You make it sound so casual.

Luka: It is casual. You can't keep controlling my life.

Chelsea: I'm not controlling you!

Chelsea: If we're so causal, why'd you buy me that bracelet?

Luka: Because I like you! Just because I bought you a bracelet doesn't mean we're married.

Chelsea: You're pathetic.

Luka closed his eyes in embarrassment. He now understood how bad those texts looked. He didn't think they would be brought up again, but he should have. Now he has to deal with it.

"You don't sound too happy in those texts." Marvin stared at him.

"I wasn't." Luka sighed.

"In fact, you sound angry." Marvin continued.

"I was angry. It was an argument."

"An argument that really got to you?" Baldwin asked. "Perhaps she got under your skin and really angered you?"

"So I was pissed off. So, what? It was just an argument."

"Or maybe you took it further than an argument." Officer Marvin put out there as he set another laminated photo of text messages in front of Luka.

Chelsea: We need to talk about this.

Luka: I can't keeping living like this.

Chelsea: We need to talk, Luka.

Luka: Fine. Come over to my house.

Chelsea: I'll be there in fifteen minutes.

"Those texts were sent Thursday night. The day Chelsea was murdered." Officer Baldwin told him.

"She never came to my house that night."

"Then where did she go?" Marvin asked.

"I don't know, okay?" Luka was now yelling. "I never saw Chelsea that night."

"Right. You said you saw her Tuesday." Marvin reminded.

Luka nodded. "I did. Tuesday afternoon after she was done all her classes for the day."

Marvin nodded. "Right. Chelsea was enrolled in Edgar University. Do you know what she was taking?"

"A biology major." Luka answered.

"It's a shame she'll never get that." Baldwin frowned.

Luka could feel his anger rising, but stayed quiet.

"You wanna know what I think?" Marvin offered.

"You're going to tell me anyway, aren't you?"

Marvin raised his eyebrows.

Luka gestured his hand, giving him the go ahead.

"I think you're lying to us. I think Chelsea did make it to your house Thursday night."

"I'm telling you, she never showed up!" Luka sighed.

"She showed up and continued the argument. Perhaps you wanted to be free of her so you could be with someone else, since you felt as though she was controlling your life." He said, referencing the text.

"You sound crazy." Luka rolled his eyes. "None of that is true."

"Maybe things got out of hand during the argument," Baldwin continued the story for him. "Maybe you hurt her and dumped her in the ocean."

"I did not kill Chelsea!" Luka yelled. "I'm not a killer. I would never hurt her."

Officer Marvin sighed as he crossed his arms. "But it seems you did hurt her. Emotionally, if not physically."

"You have nothing against me right now." Luka's voice was stern.

"Not yet." Baldwin said.

"Nor will you."

"We'll see, Luka." Officer Marvin shook his head.

"Can I go?" Luka asked. "If you two are done coming up with your crazy theories."

"They might be theories now, Luka. But we'll prove it." Officer Baldwin told him.

"You can leave." Marvin gestured to the door. "But don't go far. We're not done."

Luka stood up from the hard chair and began walking toward the door. Once he reached the handle, he turned. "We're done."

Sighing, Luka opened the door and walked out of the station feeling more anger than he had felt in his entire lifetime.

Eight

Anna was growing impatient. She had made Jordan stay parked in the parking lot, skipping their chemistry class to wait for Luka to come back so she could find out what happened at the station.

"You know we had that paper due today." Jordan sighed.

"But I don't need chemistry to become a detective."

"No, you just need it to pass."

"I need real detective experience to see if I'm set out for this." She grumbled.

Jordan shook her head and took a sip of her second smoothie. Anna had offered to buy them another since she figured they would be waiting a while.

"Anna." Jordan groaned. "We've been sitting here for over an hour."

Anna didn't look at Jordan, but continued to scan the road for any sign of Luka coming. "I know, I know. Just a little longer, okay? He'll definitely be here soon."

He had to, she thought. He was taken from the *McDonald's* in a police car. His truck was still sitting in the parking lot, he had to come back for it.

The truth is, Anna was growing impatient too. Luka had left at 3:18 and it was now 4:30. *Come on, Luka.*

As if on cue, a red *suv* pulled into the parking lot. "Is that him?" Anna asked eagerly.

Jordan nodded. "Looks like Chad's vehicle."

Anna leaned closer to the windshield to try to get a closer view, not caring if they saw her staring. They probably had, considering there were only five vehicles in the lot now.

"That's definitely Luka in the passenger seat." Anna confirmed.

"Mmhm." Jordan agreed. "Looks like a pissed off dad in the driver seat to me."

Who cares about Chad? Anna thought. If he was angry at Luka because he was scared this would ruin his reputation then he should be disgusted with himself, his son didn't ask to be taken in. As soon as Luka was out of the truck, Chad sped off.

"So what's the move, *Drew*?" Jordan asked, never failing to remind Anna of her *Nancy Drew* days.

Without hesitating, Anna began opening her door. "We go over there and talk to him."

"What?" Anna heard Jordan ask faintly, but she already started heading toward Luka before he got the chance to speed away too. She heard the jeep door slam as Jordan's quickened footsteps walked beside her. "We're just going to go over there and start questioning him?"

Anna thought for a moment about how silly that sounded, but she realized that's exactly what she was doing.

"Yes." She nodded.

As they approached closer to Luka he had one foot on the step to get in his truck, but stopped moving once he looked over at them. Anna nearly laughed when she saw how confused he looked.

"What are you guys doing here?" He asked.

"Looking for you." Was all Anna said, letting his confusion rise. She didn't know why she got such a kick out of it, but she did.

"Okay." He sounded worried. "What for?"

Anna decided to get straight to the point. "What happened down at the station?"

Luka's eyes widened like he wasn't expecting anyone to talk to him about this today. Anna assumed he didn't. He was probably going to lock himself in his room for a week other than school. Word spreads in this small town fast, everyone would know by tonight.

"Uh, just some questions." He began to answer, but then hesitated and stopped. "Why are you asking?"

Anna scoffed, "What, is it a secret or something?"

"No." Luka sounded defensive. "I just don't understand why you're asking. Do you guys think I killed Chelsea too?"

"Luka, no." Jordan denied before Anna got the chance to. "We don't believe you did anything to Chelsea."

Luka sneered, "Everyone else does."

Anna felt her heart sink at the pain in his voice. She couldn't believe people actually thought Luka killed Chelsea. "But *we* don't, okay?"

Luka looked at them silently. But Anna could see in his eyes that he didn't believe her.

"Why are you guys asking then?" He asked, his wall of defence still up.

Anna wasn't sure how to say it without sounding crazy. She also couldn't tell people she was beginning to try and solve a murder case. But, she figured with the amount of people blaming him, she could trust Luka with this. Of course, unless he really was the killer, then she would be screwed. But, she still didn't believe he did it.

"We're trying to find out what really happened to Chelsea." She explained.

Typical Luka, he had no idea what they were talking about. "Yeah, everyone is."

Anna looked over at Jordan who was looking back at her and sighed. "No, Luka. We're actually looking into it. You know the cops aren't going to do enough."

He stared at them for a minute until the information set in. "You mean you're going to try and solve the case?" He asked, loudly.

"Shh!" Anna looked around to make sure no one heard him. "Not everyone needs to know."

Luka apologized with his eyes and put a hand over his mouth.

"Yes," Anna continued. "We are actually looking into it."

He seemed to be trying to process what had just been said. "If you guys really don't think I did it, why are you questioning me?"

Jordan shrugged. "We have to start somewhere."

Anna looked at Jordan displeased with the way she said it. "We just want to know what happened so we know where to start."

Anna felt her heart race as Luka kept his eyes on her. "Let me help." He said, finally.

Anna furrowed her brows. "What?" She honestly didn't think she heard him right. He wants to join them on their investigation? Luka Anderson? No way.

But, he repeated it. "Let me help you guys."

Jordan let out a small chuckle. "Luka, really?"

To Anna's surprise, he nodded. "Really."

Anna made eye contact with Jordan as they both thought about what to do. Should she say yes? Everyone thinks that Luka had something to do with Chelsea's death, this could be a way to prove himself innocent and Anna didn't want to take that away from him. But he could also screw up and get them caught.

She thought for a moment, "Okay."

Jordan's eyes grew wide, "Anna?"

Anna looked at her and shrugged, "Maybe he's good at something."

Jordan scoffed, "What could he possibly be good at?"

Luka wrinkled his nose. "Thanks, Jordan."

Her jaw dropped as if she just remembered Luka was there. "I-sorry." She said quietly.

Luka put his hand in the air to stop her, letting out a small chuckle. "Don't even worry about it, we're good."

Anna watched Jordan give him an apologetic smile. Luka returned a friendly one. She hated herself for it, but Anna felt herself becoming a tad angry. Was she jealous? *Get a grip, Anna*, she thought to herself.

Jordan sighed, snapping Anna out of her thoughts. "I just don't see how you're going to help us. I'm not even sure the two of us know what we're doing."

Anna grinned. "We could let him join us."

Jordan looked skeptical. "Anna, what are you thinking?"

"It could be fun." Anna shrugged. "Maybe he really won't be a good help. But, we could watch him make a fool of himself."

Jordan couldn't help but laugh. "You may have a point."

Luka rolled his eyes. "Does that mean you guys will let me join your little detective gang?"

Anna wrinkled her nose. "Detective gang?"

"Okay, okay that's a terrible name, I know." Luka tapped his chin. "I'll work on coming up with a better name for us."

Luka began walking back toward his truck when Jordan stopped him. "Hang on."

"Yeah?" Luka turned. "You thought of one?"

"No!" Jordan shook her head. "You can come up with a name all you want, but no one finds out what we're doing, got it?"

Luka saluted her. "Yes ma'am."

Jordan turned to look at Anna, "What have we done?"

Anna didn't say anything. She just stared at Luka and laughed. This was going to be fun.

Nine

Jordan was on her way to her English class, but stopped when she noticed a group of students gathered in the foyer. Curious, she walked a little closer to get a better view of what was going on. She saw a few of the girls in the group were holding hands while tears rolled down their faces. That's when she noticed a table with a framed picture of Chelsea and a few lit candles perfectly displayed. She stood there for a moment and watched everyone bow their heads remembering their dear friend. She couldn't imagine the pain and loss they must be feeling. She imagined herself in their shoes for only a second, before she couldn't handle even thinking about it anymore. She would never make it without Anna.

Jordan looked away when she felt a pair of eyes on her. She looked up to see Owen watching her as some tall brunette she had never seen before looked to be giving her condolences. Jordan kept her eyes on Owen as he nodded to the girl in front of him mouthing a "Thank you", before beginning to walk towards her. He flashed her a smile. Jordan didn't know it, but her stomach filled with butterflies.

Jordan smiled back. "This is really beautiful."

Owen hummed. "Yeah, I think she would have liked it."

Jordan let out a soft laugh and nodded. "Definitely."

It fell silent for a moment as Jordan stared back at the memorial display. What she didn't notice was Owen staring longingly at her.

She was the first to break the silence. "How's the hand?"

"Not so bad." He told her, bringing his hand up closer to look at it. "The swelling has gone down anyway."

Jordan looked down at his bandaged knuckles. She still winced a little at the thought of the pain. "That's good. How are you, though?"

Owen took a deep breath thinking about how to answer. "It never really gets any easier, does it?"

Jordan frowned. Her heart ached for him. She wished there was more she could do. She assumed there was nothing she could do to help ease his pain. Little did she know about Owen's feelings for her.

"My mom and dad are still in pretty rough shape about the whole thing." He admitted.

Jordan nodded. "It can't be easy losing a child."

"I try to be there for them as much as I can. But I'm still hurting too, you know?"

Her heart shattered at the crack in his voice. "You're allowed to take time to heal your own heart, Owen."

He nodded and gave her a saddened smile. "Yeah, I know."

Not knowing what to say, she returned the saddened smile and reached out, placing a hand on his arm, rubbing her thumb back and forth.

He looked down at her hand for a long time before saying anything. "I'll be okay." He finally looked up at her, giving her a soft smile.

Jordan honestly didn't know what to say. "Yeah, you will." She didn't know it, but just her presence was enough to comfort him.

"I am however suspended for the next couple days. My Human Biology professor is pissed that I'll have to make up the exam."

Jordan frowned. "That's not so good, I'm sorry." She wished things were easier for Owen. He lost his sister and the entire university thinks he's crazy for punching Luka at that party.

Owen shrugged. "It's not so bad. Maybe the time away from here will be good for me. Besides, I'm lucky enough that they're letting me stay."

Jordan hadn't thought of it that way, maybe he was right. Maybe some time to himself would be good for him. It can't be easy having to get up and come here everyday with people who say they feel sorry and care, but they really don't.

"Maybe you're right," she started. "Just don't let those really sad thoughts come through when you're alone, okay? And if they do, call me. Please." Jordan knew she cared about Owen, but sometimes she wasn't aware how much.

Her heart beamed at Owen's genuine smile.

"I will." He said. "I promise. That means a lot, you know. The boys don't really know how to talk to me anymore after losing Chelsea."

Jordan's heart sunk. The boys Owen was talking about were the football guys. That was the friend group Owen usually hung around everyday. She felt terrible for him not having any friends to lean on during this difficult time.

"Well, I'm always here." She offered.

"I know." He smiled. "Thank you."

Jordan returned the smile before she let out a sigh. She wasn't dealing with a death or anything close to that, yet she felt like she too needed a break from this place. Her sigh didn't go unnoticed. Either that, or Owen could read minds.

He lowered his head so he could face her more clearly. "You look tired. You want to get out of here? You're already late for class."

She smiled, checking the time. "You're right, I am. So much for English class today."

"We can go to that coffee shop at the end of fifth street I know you love." He suggested.

Jordan looked surprised. "You remember my favorite coffee shop?"

Owen looked away, then back at her shrugging. "Of course."

She smiled. Even her own mother couldn't remember her favorite coffee shop. Although, sometimes Jordan felt like her mom didn't care about any of her favorite things.

"Yeah." She said finally. "I'd love to."

Owen held the door for her as they began walking down the parking lot to his car.

As Jordan sat in her favorite booth, she let out a sigh of relief. She came here often, it was her escape place. She loved how peaceful it was and how it felt so homey. Their caramel coffees were pretty good too. She had only been seated for a second before her phone chimed. It was Anna.

Anna: Meet me at our apartment at 7:00. Luka said he would meet us at the deli and tells us what happened at the station.

Jordan: Will do.

Finally. They had tried to get Luka to tell them earlier this afternoon, but he wouldn't budge. He claimed he had to get home before his mom killed him. Jordan really hoped the three of them would find something so she could bring Owen some closure.

"Everything okay?"

The sound of Owen's voice startled her. She hadn't even realized he came back from getting their drinks.

Jordan nodded. "Yeah, of course."

Owen set down her caramel coffee in front of her.

Jordan smiled. "Thank you. You really didn't have to pay for mine."

Owen blew through his lips gently, "No, no don't worry about it."

Jordan smiled slightly before she looked down at the table. She felt bad for leaving Owen out of her and Anna's investigation, especially since they were letting Luka join. Jordan knew since Owen and Luka were not on the same page about things, the four of them investigating would never work. But even still, deep down she had wished they let Owen in on it, rather than Luka. Although, she really didn't want to hurt Owen.

Breaking her thoughts, she noticed Owen looking at her concerned, out of the corner of her eye.

"Are you sure you're okay?"

Jordan let out an embarrassed laugh. "Yeah, sorry. I think I'm over-tired."

Owen looked at her silently. He wasn't buying it.

Shit, she thought. Now she had to tell him something.

"You seem like something else is on your mind." He said softly. "It's me, Jordan. You can tell me."

Jordan knew she could tell Owen anything. They had been close friends for years. They never became inseparable or anything like that, but they have always been good friends.

She pursed her lips thinking about what to say. "It's no big deal. Something strange happened earlier today."

Owen furrowed his brows giving her his full attention.

Jordan hated to bring up anything about Chelsea to Owen. But, maybe he didn't know about Luka being questioned. Owen deserved to know everything going on in his sisters murder case. Jordan knew how close they were, only being eleven months apart.

"Anna and I saw a couple detectives doing some questioning in the *McDonald's* parking lot."

She could see confusion flood across his face. "Do you know why?"

Not wanting to mention Luka's name, she shook her head. But she knew he would ask why. So, she took a deep breath and got it over with. "They were there to question Luka."

She frowned as she saw Owen's face turn into a serious expression.

"At least I think they did," She continued. "They left with him."

After she said it, she instantly regretted it. Even though she really believed Owen should know everything, he probably brought her here to talk about anything but.

Owen's shoulders relaxed. "Oh."

Jordan could've swore he seemed physically relaxed by the thought of Luka being taken in by the police. She gave him a saddened smile. "Owen."

He looked as though he was going to say something, but didn't.

"Do you really believe Luka is capable of murder?" Jordan hated to ask.

"No- I mean, I don't know, okay? I don't know."

She knew Owen was going through a lot and was probably extremely overwhelmed. He definitely was not thinking clearly. Even though Jordan was an only child, she still knew the pain of losing a sibling must be one of the worst kinds of pain you could experience. However, Owen needed to realize, even though Luka can be a bit much, that doesn't make him a murderer.

"Look," Owen sighed. "All I know is my sister is gone and I want to find the monster who did this."

Jordan reached her hand across the table and grabbed Owen's, giving it a squeeze. "I can understand that. I'm sorry I brought it up. I just thought you should know."

Owen shook his head. "No, don't be sorry. Thank you for keeping me in the loop. No one else has ever since I punched Luka."

She gave him a mournful smile at what he said next.

"I only mentioned his name because I had to."

Now, she felt even more confused. "What are you talking about?"

"The detectives," he began. "When they were asking my family questions. They asked if she was seeing anyone, I mentioned Luka."

Jordan relaxed when she realized Owen was just doing what he needed to cooperate with the detectives. "And that's it?"

She could see Owen thinking for a moment. "I mean," he paused. "I might have told them to pay close attention to him."

Jordan almost couldn't believe him. But after watching him punch Luka and call him a murderer in front of a great majority of the university and Luka's friends, she could.

She kept quiet and continued drinking her coffee, staring blankly at him. She understood his sister's death had to be hard on him, it would be on anyone. But she was starting to think it was really taking a toll on him. He has been so obsessed with Luka lately, it was starting to worry Jordan. She really cared about Owen and didn't want him to get too caught up in his idea, and take things too far. She knew what she had to do. She had to find some evidence that leads them closer to finding Chelsea's real killer, for Owen.

Ten

A s Anna took one last glance in the mirror, she saw a flash of headlights through the window. Her and Jordan's apartment was on the first floor and the parking lot was right across from her bedroom window. It was still just the beginning of spring, so it still got dark fairly early.

Grabbing her purse, she dashed out of their apartment. She could feel the jittery feeling inside her stomach. She couldn't seem to contain herself. She knew this was a big step in her first ever case.

Jordan's eyes were wide as Anna slipped into the passenger seat. "I have to write this on the calendar."

"What?" Anna asked, fastening her seat belt.

Jordan shrugged. "You've never been on time. Shouldn't I be coming inside right now finding you crying in your closet?"

"Yeah, yeah." Anna rolled her eyes. "But tonight is our first step to my first ever case solving. This is a really big deal, Jordan."

Jordan laughed. "Someone's eager."

Anna nodded. "Now let's go."

The deli was only ten minutes from the their apartment that was directly in the middle between the university and the main part of town. It was small and didn't have a designated parking area, so Jordan pulled into the alleyway everyone used. Anna always found it creepy at night, especially when she got off her shift at midnight and had to walk to her car. It was always so dark. The only light was the street lamp at the end of the alley beside the road.

"I don't see Luka's truck." Jordan said, killing the engine.

Anna quickly looked around before sighing. "I don't either. It seems like him to be late though."

"You're right on that one." Jordan nodded. "Want to head in and get a booth anyway?"

The deli was practically empty, per usual on a Monday night. Besides them, there was just a lonely teenager sipping a milkshake, with her hood up, blasting music from her earbuds so loud Anna could hear she was playing the song *Smells like Teen spirit* by *Nirvana,* and an old man having a slice of pizza with a picture across from him that Anna assumed was his passing wife. Her heart ached for the man.

"Hey, Anna!" Mindy, her favorite co-worker yelled.

Anna waved excitedly. "Hey, Min!"

"Two shakes?" She asked.

Anna nodded. "You know it."

"Want to sit in the booth at the back?" Jordan asked when Mindy slipped away to make their milkshakes. "Considering the conversation we're going to have if Luka does show up."

Anna nodded. "Good choice." *Where the hell is he anyway?*

Once they sat, Mindy came over and placed two vanilla milkshakes in front of them, each with a cherry on the top.

"Thanks, Min." Anna smiled.

Mindy smiled back. "Not a problem."

Once she returned back to the counter, Anna turned to Jordan. "You don't happen to have any *Bailey's* on you, do you?"

Jordan scoffed. "Are you kidding me? You know I always keep a small bottle in my purse for emergencies."

Anna beamed. "You are the greatest person in the universe, you know that, right?"

Jordan rolled her eyes as she discretely handed Anna the mickey sized bottle of *Bailey's*. "Yeah, yeah."

Anna poured a quarter of it into her milkshake before handing it back to Jordan. She watched as Jordan put only a splash in hers, given she would be driving later.

Anna looked down at her *apple watch*. It was now nearly 7:30. Where the hell was Luka?

"What time did you tell him to meet us here?" Jordan asked, clearly also wondering about Luka.

"I figured he would be late." Anna took a sip of her drink. "So I told him 7:00."

Jordan laughed. "Safe move. Do you think he'll show?"

Anna honestly didn't know. "He better."

She was dying to know what happened at the station. For Chelsea's case and to see if he was okay after whatever the hell happened down there.

"It's not like were accusing him. We just asked for his help and he said he wanted to."

You better not bail on me, Luka Anderson.

As if on cue, they heard a loud muffler. Anna smiled. "He's here." She watched the door as she heard the engine cut.

Anna felt butterflies when the little bell above the door rang as she caught a glimpse of the raven haired boy. She watched him nod to the waitress before scanning the place. She felt nervous, but managed to lift her hand in the air to wave him over. He sat in the side across from her and Jordan.

"Nice of you to join us." Jordan joked.

Anna nodded. "You're late."

Luka looked at the time on his watch. "Only a half hour past the time I was told? That's early for me."

They all laughed. Anna was surprised how easy it felt as they all sat together. She hated to ruin it by bringing up him getting questioned about his ex-girlfriend.

"So," Luka said, as if he was eager to get started. "Where do we begin?"

Anna hadn't really thought about that. "You tell us."

"Well," Luka began. "I was walking to the front doors of-"

Jordan raised her hand. "No boring stuff unless it's important."

"Well then you guys are going to have to help me out." Luka grumbled.

Anna rolled her eyes. "How about why did they decide to take you to the station?"

Jordan nodded. "Yeah, why couldn't they have questioned you in the parking lot?"

"One question at a time." He complained. "They took me down because they thought they had something on me."

"What do you mean?" Anna asked, feeling uneasy.

"The night she was," he paused, taking a deep breath. "Killed."

Anna started to feel bad. Luka already looked like he didn't want to talk about this.

"She was on her way to my place." He continued.

Anna looked over at Jordan, she could tell they were thinking the same thing. Owen wasn't lying about the text saying she was on her way over to Luka's. Anna felt her heart sink.

"The officers investigating her case found the texts," he paused again like he was hiding something. "And some other ones."

At first Anna was grossed out thinking about what he meant, but she could tell by the look in his eyes that wasn't what he meant at all. "What other texts?"

He sighed. "We got into a fight that night right before she was supposed to be at my place. I sent some angry texts. They thought of course that was the motive. That I did it."

Anna could see his fists clenching with anger. "But you didn't."

He seemed to relax a little just hearing those words. "Exactly."

"Why didn't you take things more seriously?" Jordan blurted.

"What do you mean?" Luka asked.

Jordan looked as if she was nervous to ask Luka her question. "The night Owen hit you. You seemed more angry at him than anything, rather than being upset that your girlfriend isn't here anymore."

Anna had no idea where Jordan was going with this, but she didn't like it. Was she accusing Luka?

"Of course I was angry at Owen. I still am. He's calling me a murderer." Luka roared.

"What about that night?" Jordan asked. "Why didn't you spam call her, or go out and look for her?"

As much as Anna hated to admit it, Jordan had a point. Why didn't Luka do more?

Luka looked offended. "I don't know, okay? I was angry and I wasn't thinking straight. You're turning this into a replica of what happened down at the station."

Jordan swallowed. "I'm sorry. But there's a lot were going to need to figure out if were really going to do this."

Anna nodded. "It's true. We're not trying to accuse you, Luka. We just need to understand."

Jordan grabbed her phone when she heard it vibrate. "I have to go."

"What?" Anna asked. "We're not done here."

"I know, I'm sorry. But, I have to go meet Owen." She told her. "You two can handle being alone with each other, can't you?"

Anna grumbled. No, no they couldn't. However, a little part of Anna was excited to be alone with Luka. "But you're my drive back home."

Jordan smirked at her. "I'm sure Luka wouldn't mind driving you home. Right, Luka?"

He grinned. "My pleasure."

And there were those butterflies. *Damn you, Jordan.*

"Well, looks like it's just us." Anna said. *Really Anna? That's all you could think to say?*

He nodded but Anna could tell he wasn't actually paying attention to her. He was focused on something behind her.

"Luka." She groaned. "Just because Jordan left doesn't mean were done here."

Luka held up his hand. "Just wait."

Slightly offended, Anna crossed her arms. "Don't tell me to-"

He rolled his eyes. "Look behind you."

She whipped her head around to see what all the fuss was about.

"I meant slowly." Luka groaned, his voice a whisper.

Why was he whispering? The only thing Anna saw was a blonde headed boy who looked to be about twenty-one ordering a slice of pizza for his brunette girlfriend, who looked a little too young for him.

Anna turned back around at a loss. "What about them?"

"You want to know what I think about who killed Chelsea?" He asked, keeping an eye on the two at the counter.

Intrigued, Anna simply nodded.

"That," Luka pointed low so that the boy couldn't see. "Is Chelsea and Owen's older brother."

Anna's jaw dropped. Chelsea and Owen have another brother?

Luka could tell what she was thinking and nodded. "I know. It surprised me too."

"Are you sure?" Anna asked, not believing him. "Or is that some guy you think is Chelsea's brother?"

"It is." He grumbled. "I've met him once."

"Why hasn't anyone ever heard of him?" Anna was eager to know more.

"He's not a good kid." Luka explained. "He's big on drugs. I don't mean smoking weed, either, I mean the real hard stuff. He never graduated. Chelsea told me he landed a job for some guy who smuggles drugs in across the water."

"He's a drug dealer?" Anna asked, invested.

Luka widened his eyes telling her to keep her voice down. "Yes. But I think there's more to him."

"What do you mean?" She asked.

"His name is Jarid. He's got bad anger issues. Real bad. Half the reason he couldn't graduate high school was because he got suspended too many times for throwing kids in the hospital. Eventually he was expelled and decided to drop high school altogether."

Anna couldn't believe what she was hearing. "How do you know all this?"

He shrugged. "Chelsea complained about him once when he came home to their mom's looking for a place to crash for the night. So, I asked about him. She said he only comes home from time to time."

Anna shook her head. "Okay, but I still don't see where you're going with this."

"Chelsea got scared when he came around. She never wanted to be alone with him. I think he killed her."

This might have been the first time Anna had ever been speechless. "That's a big accusation." She warned.

"So is Owen claiming I did it." He argued.

She nodded. "I can't argue with that. But, what about the motive?"

He shrugged. "He's short tempered. Maybe he didn't mean to kill her, but couldn't control his anger.

Anna looked over and watched as Jarid and the young girl made their way from the counter over to a booth further up from where she and Luka were sitting.

"Or," Luka added, "She did do something that put him over the edge and he did mean to kill her."

Anna couldn't believe it, but she felt like Luka's conspiracy might be possible.

He looked down at her trying to read her expression. "Do you think I'm crazy?"

She shook her head. "I hate to say it, but no."

He smiled. "Just for the record I haven't told anyone that theory."

She smiled back, feeling special. "We are, however, going to need to find proof."

Eleven

Jordan pulled into her favorite coffee shop off fifth street almost five minutes after leaving the deli. Owen had texted her saying he could use some company. She was glad having her around meant something to him, rather than staying all alone, letting his sister's death ruin him. But, she still wasn't aware just how much having her around meant to him.

Getting out of her car, she pulled her grey cardigan tighter around her as she felt the chill spring breeze. She looked around the place to find Owen sitting at the back window booth where they had sat last time the two of them were here. He smiled when he saw her and she couldn't help but feel warm inside.

As she sat, she noticed a cup of caramel coffee already sitting on the table.

"I already ordered." Owen grinned.

Jordan smiled at him. "Thank you."

He nodded. "You got here fast."

Jordan took a sip hoping she wouldn't have to go into any detail tonight. "Yeah, I was just down at the deli."

Owen looked apologetic. "Oh, I'm sorry. I didn't mean to interrupt anything."

Jordan quickly shook her head. "No, you didn't. I'm happy to be here with you. Besides, I told you to text me whenever you needed."

Owen nodded. "I thought about heading over to the bar to drink my pain away. But, I figured a coffee and being here with you would be the safer bet."

Jordan frowned. "Well, I'm glad you're here instead."

Although, if she was being honest, part of her was wondering what was happening on the other side of town where she left two people alone, who should probably never be alone together.

Perhaps Anna was missing her too. Jordan hadn't even been gone from the deli for ten minutes and Anna had texted her.

Anna: Luka just told me the craziest theory. You've got to hear it.

Jordan: Interesting. Did it make any sense?

Anna: LOL. I honestly think he might be onto something even though it's a bit of a long shot. Let me try to get more out of him.

Jordan found that hard to believe. Luka having a valid theory? That never happened.

"Is everything okay?" Owen asked, catching back Jordan's attention.

She felt embarrassment flare up her cheeks. She came here to give Owen come company, yet here she was on her phone. "Yes, sorry. It's just Anna."

Owen laughed. "I figured. Don't worry about it."

Jordan smiled. Most people did. Anna and her were practically inseparable.

Jordan tried to ignore it, but her phone kept vibrating from Anna's spam messages.

"You didn't leave her at the deli or something, did you?" Owen joked.

Jordan let out a fake laugh, not sure what to tell him. But before she could decide, she let a little bit slip. "Yeah, I actually did. But she has other company."

Owen raised his eyebrows as he took a sip of his black coffee. "You and Anna hangout with other people?" He laughed.

Jordan smiled. It was good to see him in a good mood. She missed this Owen. "Crazy isn't it?"

"Who would've thought?" He smiled back.

"You seem a lot lighter tonight." Jordan pointed out.

He shrugged, "Things do lighten up when you come around."

Jordan felt her cheeks turn warm, unsure what to say. But before she could think of anything, her phone continued to vibrate four times in a row.

"You might want to get that." Owen told her.

"I'm really sorry." She said, reaching for her phone.

Anna: You need to get back here.

Anna: Like, right now.

Anna: I just learned so much from Luka.

Anna: This could be our first ever breakthrough in the case. You need to get your ass back here, now.

Jordan rubbed the back of her neck, unsure what to do. Part of her wanted to stay with Owen and keep him company, but the other part of her wanted to go back and help Anna with her investigation.

"Jordan," Owen snapped her out of her thoughts. "What's wrong?"

She shook her head. "Everything is fine."

"You don't look fine."

She sighed. "Owen, I really have to go."

He furrowed his brows. "Jordan, what is going on?"

"It's really nothing for you to worry about."

"I worry about you, okay?" His voice was stern.

She stayed silent and looked up at him.

"If something is going on I want to come with you." He demanded.

"Owen." She tried to protest.

He shook his head. "Jordan, come on. You don't have to hide anything from me."

She felt more confused than ever. Should she bring Owen? How would Luka react? Better yet, how would Owen react to Luka? She knew bringing him would cause so many problems, but she could tell he wasn't going to stand down.

She took a deep breath. "We're taking my car."

Owen nodded, grabbing his coffee and dashing out the front door.

Once they were in, Jordan broke the news. "I have to be honest with you so you don't freak out when we get there."

He frowned. "What is it?"

Jordan took a deep breath. "Luka may be at the deli when we get there."

"You guys were with Luka?" He shouted.

"It's not like we were hanging out with him." Jordan yelled back. "We were asking him what happened during his questioning earlier."

"That doesn't help." Owen snapped.

They were a minute away from the deli now. "Yes it does, Owen." She whined. "We are trying to figure out what happened to Chelsea."

"What the hell are you talking about?" Owen swiped a hand roughly through his golden locks.

"Don't you want to know what happened to your sister?"

"Of course I do!" He yelled,

"Then trust me." Jordan begged. "Because I promise you I am going to try to do everything I can to give you some peace."

Owen didn't say anything, but Jordan could feel him staring at her. But out of the corner of her eye she couldn't read his expression.

"You guys were questioning Luka, not taking his side?" Owen asked, calmly.

"Yes." Jordan looked over at him. "I'm not taking anybody's side, okay? I am simply digging for the truth."

It was silent for a few moments before Jordan spoke again. "This is Anna's investigation, by the way."

"I figured." He snorted. "To her favour, I know how obsessed with *Criminal Minds* she is. She'll make one hell of a detective one day."

Jordan laughed. "No kidding."

Twelve

As Jordan pulled back into the alleyway, she saw Luka's truck was still here. She figured he would be, but now she felt more nervous about going inside with Owen.

She turned to Owen. "Are you sure you are going to be okay seeing Luka?"

He didn't look certain, but nodded. "Yeah, I'll survive."

"That means no yelling or punching him tonight."

Jordan saw his cheeks heat up. "I won't. I promise."

She reached across and squeezed his hand. She let go of the door handle when she noticed Owen keeping his grip on her hand. She looked over to see him already looking at her. She couldn't exactly read his eyes, but the small smile he wore gave her comfort. Before Jordan could have an opinion about what was happening, Owen quickly dropped her hand, opening his door.

Jordan waited a moment before opening her own. *What the hell was that?*

Not wanting to make things awkward, Jordan didn't ask. She jogged up to Owen as they walked to the front of the deli.

As they rounded the corner, Owen came to a sudden stop.

Jordan furrowed her brows. "Owen?"

He stayed silent. She looked up to see him looking through the window at the couple who was sitting at one of the booths. Jordan had never seen either of them before.

"Owen." She said again.

He shook his head before looking over at her. "Yeah?"

"Do you know those people?"

He looked away from her and at the ground. "Yeah. I used to know him, anyway."

"What do you mean you used to know him?" She asked. "Did you and that guy used to be friends or something?"

He shook his head as he looked back up at the guy with long curly hair. "He's my brother, Jordan."

Jordan was frozen. "What?"

He sighed. "I know."

"You have a brother?"

"I used to. He's not exactly around anymore."

Jordan looked back up at the guy Owen claimed was his brother. Other than the blond hair, they looked nothing alike.

"Look," he closed his eyes. "Can we talk about this later? I'll explain everything."

Jordan thought for a moment before nodding. "Sure."

Owen turned and began walking into the deli. Jordan didn't fail to notice how he turned his body away from the booth his brother was at, making no contact. He wouldn't even look at him. Jordan couldn't help but wonder what had happened between them. Why did Owen not want his brother to see him?

"It's about time." Anna complained when she saw Jordan.

Anna's eyes got big when she saw Owen. She looked at Jordan as if to ask her what he was doing here.

"I know." She whispered. "But he promised to behave."

"Actually." Anna said, "It's a good thing you're here."

Owen raised his eyebrows.

"Because I just found out that is your brother." She told him, looking over at Owen's brother.

Owen glared over at Luka. "Oh good." He said sarcastically.

Jordan saw the look on Owen's face and put her hand on his shoulder, motioning him to sit down with her in the booth, opposite to Anna and Luka. Jordan couldn't help but notice how at some point Anna had moved to sit in the same side as Luka.

"So," Jordan broke the silence. "What's this theory you were texting me about?"

Luka's face turned pale. "Anna."

"Oh," Anna chuckled. "We don't have to talk about that right now."

"It's okay, Anna." Owen shut her down. "I can handle it."

"Well," Luka leaned forward, taking a sip of his sprite. "If you set down the idea of me being a murderer for a second."

Owen gave a sarcastic nod. "Right."

"You can open your mind and think about-"

"Luka," Jordan cut in. "Get to the point."

He looked down at the table and sighed. "Maybe Jarid killed Chelsea."

Jordan looked over at Owen to see his leg now bouncing. She reached under the table and gently placed her hand on his knee.

He snapped out of his trance and looked over at her.

She smiled at him before looking back to Luka. "What reason do you have?"

"Well," Anna spoke up before Luka could.

Luka sighed and leaned back in the booth, letting Anna talk for him.

"It has been proven he isn't the most friendly, right? He's got a past of anger issues and a lot of bruised faces to prove it."

Jordan was worried Owen would get offended, but felt relaxed when she saw a smile appear at the corner of his mouth.

"Chelsea always told me how scared of him she was." Luka looked directly at Owen. "She always said she only had one brother."

Owen looked back at Luka expressionless.

"Are you going to tell me I'm wrong, Owen?" Luka asked, hotly.

Owen shook his head. "No."

The other three in the booth all looked over at Owen, mouths agape.

"I think you might have a point."

"I am so reminding you that you said that." Luka joked.

"Jarid is a dangerous guy." Owen said, keeping his voice down so Jarid wouldn't hear. "For all we know, Jarid went home to my mom's that night from a failed drug deal and took it out on her."

"That's exactly what I'm saying." Luka nodded. "But how do we prove that?"

Owen leaned back in his seat, "That's going to be the hard part."

"So you don't think I killed her anymore?" Luka asked.

Owen kept his eyes on Luka and let out a long sigh. "I think you're a dumbass that might be too dumb to be able to commit a murder."

Luka let out a loud belly laugh that made the rest of them laugh. "I might have to agree with you on that one."

"Yeah, that really sounds like you." Anna inquired.

Luka looked over at her unamused. "Hey, it's only funny when Owen says it."

Anna put her hands up in defence. "Just being honest."

Luka stuck his hand across the table, "So we're good?"

Owen looked down at it before looking back to Luka. "Yeah, we're good." He reached over and shook his hand.

Jordan looked over at Anna and smiled.

Owen picked up his coffee he had brought from the shop. "Can I ask you something, though?"

Luka raised his eyebrows. "What's that?"

"Why didn't you do anything more that night?"

He sighed, "Honestly I thought she ghosted me like any of my other exes."

Anna snickered. "Yeah, I'm not surprised."

Luka glared over at her while Owen burst into laughter.

Jordan's eyes widened, "Anna, serious situation here."

Anna stopped drinking her shake and dropped her jaw, realizing what she just said. "I-yeah, right. Carry on."

"Thank you." Luka said sternly.

Owen frowned, "Chels wasn't like that."

Luka's eyes went dark as he looked down at his lap, "No, she wasn't. I wish I hadn't thought that way of her. I guess I was too damaged from the past."

Anna looked over at Luka and was about to say something, but Jordan noticed.

"Anna." She whispered.

Anna quickly looked at her and pursed her lips.

Before anyone could say anything else, a loud phone rang. Jordan looked across the room and saw Jarid reaching in his pocket, before placing his phone to his ear.

"Hello?" He said. "I'm on break. Just let me know when another shipment comes in."

Luka shook his head. "Drugs."

Owen nodded.

"We already dealt with that. She's gone." Jarid lowered his voice.

Anna looked over at Owen. "What the hell?"

"We took care of it. It's not going to come back to you." Jarid shook his head. "Besides, it's not like you did it, anyway. You were just asked to help."

Jordan felt her chest tighten.

Jarid sighed. "Alright, alright. I'll be there in fifteen." He said before hanging up the phone.

"What the hell just happened?" Anna asked, before anyone else could.

"That sounded like an interesting conversation." Luka said.

"A little too interesting." Owen carefully looked over his shoulder at his brother.

"What are we going to do about this?" Anna asked.

Luka snapped out of his haze. "About what?"

Anna looked over at him, coldly. "Really?"

Luka looked at all three of them for an answer.

"Wow." Owen murmured, looking over at Jordan.

Jordan didn't know whether to laugh or pity him. "Oh, you're serious."

Anna took a deep breath. "About Jarid's conversation, Luka."

He closed his eyes. "Oh, right. My bad."

"Yeah," Owen began. "Who knew all I needed was to sit in a booth with you for half an hour to realize there is no way you could have killed my sister."

Luka shrugged. "What can I say?"

Jarid stood up from his booth. "I've gotta go, okay?"

His brunette friend nodded.

"You'll be alright?" He asked her.

"Of course." She smiled at him.

"Alright." Jarid nodded, before leaning down to kiss her.

"I think we should follow him." Anna suggested.

Owen took a deep breath. "That's a dangerous game, Anna."

"He's right." Luka inquired. "So he and I will go."

"No," Anna shook her head. "I want to go."

"Why can't we all go?" Jordan asked.

"I think we should split up. Two of us follow him, two of us stay and keep an eye on the girlfriend." She explained.

"She's like sixteen, Anna." Jordan scoffed. "What do you think she's going to do?"

Anna shrugged. "If she's caught up with Jarid, who knows what else she could be caught up in."

Jordan nodded. "Fair point."

Luka looked at her for a long moment waiting for her to change her mind. "Are you sure?"

"Positive." She nodded. "You and I should go."

Jordan raised her eyebrows and smirked at Anna jokingly. She could tell there was some serious tension between the two.

"Me?" Luka sounded alarmed.

"You just said you wanted to go." Anna asked, puzzled.

"Yeah, with him!" Luka pointed to Owen. "He looks tough. Plus, it's his brother."

"Oh, you think I'm gonna protect you, huh?" Owen laughed.

"If you didn't know, I'm a bit of a coward."

Owen nodded. "I'm starting to get that."

Anna scoffed. "Come on, Luka. If you do it well enough, he won't even realize he's being followed."

"And these two just get to stay here?" He cried.

"Yes, just hangout and keep and eye on her."

"Sounds good to me." Jordan said.

"And safe!" Luka whined. "Why are you putting my life at risk but not theirs?"

"You will be fine, Luka." She rolled her eyes. "We need to leave now before he's gone."

Luka let out a shaky breath. "I hope he's already gone."

"Keep us updated." Owen said. "Be careful out there, Luka. Anna's life is in your hands."

"Come on, Owen. That's a lot of pressure for a coward." Jordan joked.

Owen smiled down at her, sending butterflies through her stomach.

"Ha ha." Luka said sarcastically. "Take a picture, Jordan. This coward is going on a mission."

Anna smirked before grabbing Luka's arm, pulling him out the door.

Thirteen

Owen crossed his arms and laid back in the booth, smirking.

"It's really good to see you two on good terms." Jordan smiled.

Owen nodded. "Yeah."

He hated to admit it, but he couldn't help but wonder if he had made the right decision. He and Luka were never friends. Owen honestly didn't know what to think of Luka. They had gone through school together since primary, but only talked a handful of times. All he really knew was he played girls better than he played basketball, and he used to be one of the best players their old high school had. So, when Owen had found out Luka was dating his sister, he didn't know how to react.

There wasn't any evidence that said Luka did kill Chelsea, but there also wasn't any that said he didn't. Although, there really wasn't much evidence at all. It had only been three days since Chelsea's body was found.

"You really did mean it, didn't you?"Jordan asked, as if she could read his mind.

Owen thought for a moment. He honestly didn't know. He wanted to tell her yes, but he also didn't want to lie to her. More importantly, he didn't want her to think he was crazy.

"Yeah," he shifted in his seat. "He seems like a pretty cool guy."

"You promised you would explain later." Jordan reminded him. "About your brother."

"Right." Owen sighed, looking over at the booth Jarid's girlfriend was still sitting in.

Jordan seemed to read the look on his face. "Only if you want to."

Part of him didn't want to. His family was a lot more hectic than he wanted to admit to the girl he liked.

"No, it's okay." He shook his head. "Jarid isn't a good guy. He left home when he was sixteen after he got expelled from school and decided to never go back."

"Why don't I remember him?" Jordan asked.

"He's six years older than us." He answered.

"Oh."

"Apparently he landed a job for some guy who imports drugs and sells them to people around here." Owen continued. "I don't really know much about it. Chelsea told me sometimes he comes over to our mom's place to crash for the night. I don't know where he stays the rest of the time."

Jordan nodded. She honestly seemed a little startled. He really hoped he didn't scare her.

"Do you think he could have murdered Chelsea?" She asked quietly.

Owen took a deep breath. "Honestly?"

She nodded again, waiting for an answer.

"Ever since Luka brought the idea to my attention, I don't know why I hadn't thought of it. Jarid is a really dangerous guy, especially during withdraws.

She gave him a sympathetic smile.

There was something really bugging Owen. "Can I ask you some-thing?"

"Of course."

"Knowing what kind of person my brother is, does that change your perspective on me at all?

She looked at him like he was crazy. "What? No of course not."

He relaxed a little, really hoping she was telling him the truth.

Before he could reply, the little bell above the deli door rang. Owen looked up and saw a girl with long blonde hair, who looked to be about sixteen walk in. She immediately walked over to the booth Jarid's girlfriend was sitting in and sat across from her.

"I wonder who that is." Jordan whispered.

"Maybe just a friend." Owen shrugged.

"Finally." Jarid's girlfriend said.

"What's going on?" Her friend asked her.

"I think Jarid got caught up in something bad." She explained. "You're the only one I know I can tell this to."

"What do you think he's involved in?"

"He had blood on his hands a few days ago, Claire. Literal human blood."

"How do you know it's human?" Her friend asked.

"Well he doesn't hunt." Jarid's girlfriend groaned.

"I told you dating him was a bad idea. He's twenty-four."

"Hey, I'll be eighteen in two months."

Jordan looked over at Owen. "Wow."

"I called you here as my friend, okay? Not for some intervention."

The blonde sighed. "Okay, sorry."

"Did you see the news? About that nineteen year old girl who was murdered?"

Her friend nodded. "Yeah, she was found on the beach. They said she was strangled and then hit in the back of the head."

Jarid's brunette girlfriend nodded. "I think Jarid was involved in it."

Owen felt his body tense.

"You think he killed her?" The blonde asked.

"I think he at least helped with her body."

"What are you going to do?" Her friend asked.

"I don't know. I need some time to think."

Jordan turned to look Owen in the eyes, face full of fear.

"What the hell did we just hear?" She asked.

"Sounds like we aren't the only ones who think Jarid is guilty."

Fourteen

As Anna climbed up into Luka's truck, she saw a blue civic across from them with Jarid in the driver seat. "There he is."

"Oh good." Luka said sarcastically.

"Oh, hush. This could give us answers, you know."

"It could also be the end of someone's life if we make one wrong move." Luka argued.

The sound of Jarid starting the engine, grabbed Anna's attention. Quickly putting the car in drive, Jarid spun out of the alleyway and down Main street.

"Wait until he gets to the lights and then start to follow him." Anna instructed.

Once the car stopped at the lights, Luka turned on his truck. Anna winced at the sound. They better not get caught because of this truck.

They followed the car for about fifteen minutes. Jarid was going fast, usually about twenty over every speed limit. They went on the highway for most of the time.

"You don't think he spotted us, do you?" Luka worried.

Anna sighed, unsure. "I hope not."

Finally, the civic turned off at exit 13. Luka followed, keeping a good distance between them and the civic. The car drove up the street for only a minute before turning left down some unmarked gravel road. It was hard to see at the hour of 8pm, but the little bit of moonlight helped them just enough.

Waiting a moment, Luka turned down the road. "Where does this lead to?"

"I don't know, but I have a bad feeling." Anna admitted.

The gravel road seemed to be a shortcut to somewhere. About a mile down, they turned left again, onto a paved dead end road. Once the car parked at the bottom, Luka pulled his truck off to the side, shutting down the engine. They couldn't quite see what was at the bottom of the road they were on, but Anna could swear she saw water. The headlights of the civic were still on, shining bright against an old red shack, blocking the rest of the view.

"We need to get a closer look." Anna suggested. "I can't see anything from here."

Luka's eyes went wider than ever before. "You want to get out of the safety of the truck?"

Anna nodded.

"Are you out of your mind?" Luka demanded. "We could get spotted and killed. We don't know who else is down there."

Anna rolled her eyes. "You're such a coward."

Anna reached for the door handle and opened it, stepping to the ground.

"Anna!" Luka whispered. "Get back in the truck."

Ignoring him, she quietly shut the door.

"Dammit," he muttered, opening his door. "Wait up."

Anna smirked. "Stay if you want. I'll survive."

"You're fucking insane." He told her. "I'm not letting you go down there by yourself."

She smiled at that, as butterflies surrounded her stomach.

They relied on the moonlight to see, not wanting to blow their covers. It worked for the most part.

"What the hell is this?" Luka asked.

The old red shack had a rusted door that sat open, giving them a crack to look inside. Anna squinted, trying to get a better view. She could've swore she saw a small pile of bags full of white powder. Across from the shack, was water, with a small motor boat sitting in it, tied to the wharf. The rest of the area was surrounded by pine trees and long grass. The area seemed to be very well hidden.

"It's a wharf." She answered.

"Move a little faster will ya?" A voice from the boat yelled.

Anna and Luka quickly ran behind the old shack.

"I'm trying, alright? You're the one who called me here when I nearly went to jail for you last week." Another guy yelled.

"That's definitely Jarid." Luka stated.

"Because of me?" The other man yelled. "Boy, I saved your ass and gave you a life. You should be thanking me."

"Hey, I helped you and your friend with your dirty business, even though you knew who she was to me." Jarid growled.

"You said she didn't mean shit to you, kid."

"She didn't. But still."

"Shut your mouth and finish unloading."

"Are they talking about Chelsea?" Luka asked.

Anna shrugged. "We need to get closer."

"Anna, you are going to get us killed." Luka shook his head.

Without a word, she began to move forward toward the edge of the shack. She still couldn't see who was behind the truck with Jarid. She continued to move forward, when her foot didn't lift because she was too focused on not getting caught and slid it across the pavement that led down to the dock, making a large scraping sound. Anna closed her eyes and held her breath.

"The hell was that?" The other man yelled.

"I don't know, I'll check it out when we're done." Jarid told him.

Shit. Now she really needed to hide. She could not let Jarid find her, he would kill her. Apparently, Luka was having the same thought, as he slid up beside her.

"I need to see who that other man is." Anna whispered, curious.

"Peek around the edge, you should be able to see." Luka suggested.

Anna quietly took two steps to her right to the end of the shack and peeked around. Luka was right, she could see both Jarid and the other man. The other man turned around, getting the final small box off his truck, handing it to Jarid. Anna squinted trying to see what they were loading. She couldn't be certain, but she figured it was some type of drugs. This was the guy Jarid worked for, selling drugs.

Finally, the other guy turned back so Anna could see him from his side angle. He was older, as she figured he would be. He looked to be about forty-five or fifty. He had short, greasy hair and a stubby black and grey beard. Anna could have swore she had seen him before. Maybe not in person, but at least a picture.

She quickly and quietly took two steps back toward Luka.

"Did you get a look at him?" He asked her.

Anna nodded. "I've seen him before."

"That's it, kid." The man said. "Get out of here while I go across the water and get Marty the money for this."

Jarid nodded. "Sounds good."

Luka and Anna stood quietly, listening to the sound of the boat engine start and make it's way across the water. Jarid began to walk back toward the driveway.

"Follow him." Anna muttered.

Luka began to walk slowly behind Jarid, with Anna beside him. Anna felt her heart sink into her stomach when Jarid suddenly stopped in his tracks. He lifted his head toward the sky and slowly turned around. He was now facing the shack Luka and Anna were standing behind.

"I know you're here." He said, calmly.

Anna felt like she was going to puke. Luka looked over at her, eyes equally as scared.

"Just come out." Jarid suggested. "So we can get this over with."

Anna swallowed hard. Was Jarid going to kill them?

She heard the sound of a knife flipping open. *Yes, he was going to kill them.*

Anna's mind went blank. What were they going to do?

She noticed Luka quickly step so he was in front of her. She was still terrified, but that gave her a slight feeling of comfort.

"Come on." Jarid whined. "I just want to have a little fun."

Luka closed his eyes tight. He looked like he was trying to think of a plan.

Jarid began to walk closer to the shack. Anna could hear her heart pounding in her ears. Was this her last moment?

"I just want to teach you not to waltz into places you're not welcome." Jarid let out an evil laugh.

"Luka." Anna whispered, her palms full of sweat.

He shushed her, not realizing how close Jarid was to them.

Until his hands were on the side of the shack as he peeked around the corner, "Boo."

Without warning, Anna screamed.

Fifteen

Jarid didn't even flinch. He gave them a smile that could have been mistaken for an evil clown. He sure looked like one. His teeth were dirty and his front bottom teeth were pointy, like vampires.

"Wrong place, wrong time." He said as he raised the knife and began to lunge at Luka.

"No, Luka!" Anna screamed.

Luka grabbed Jarid's wrist that had the knife in it, attempting to keep it away from his throat. But Jarid looked to be stronger than he thought.

Anna's mind shut off and her reflexes kicked in and she began to lunge at Jarid, smacking him.

This seemed to anger Jarid. His flaming eyes fell on her as he tossed Luka into the side of the shack so loud it echoed.

Anna's hand flew over her mouth. "Luka!"

He lay on his side and groaned.

"Luka," Anna yelled. "Can you hear me?"

But, Jarid was already on his way to her.

Without thinking, Anna ran. She ran along the edge of the water until she reached the tall pine trees. Running as fast as she possibly could, she ducked behind one, holding her breath. Like a horror movie, she waited.

"Come out, come out wherever you are." He laughed.

What a psycho.

Jarid slapped his hands against the other side of the tree. "Gotcha."

She screamed again and tried to run, but this time he grabbed her arm, yanking her back. He pushed her up against the tree placing his face as close to hers as possible. She held back vomit at the smell of his breath.

He placed his knife against her throat, "What are you gonna do now?"

Convinced this was the moment she was going to die, she closed her eyes. *Please no.* She tried to squeeze out of his grasp, but he kept pressing the knife harder to her throat. She swore she could feel it beginning to cut the skin as tears made their way to her eyes. "Please."

"No begging." He smiled. "This is your own fault."

This was it. He was going to slit her throat. So much for solving her first case. Anna closed her eyes and waited.

She heard a loud voice beside her. "Jarid."

Luka. He's alive.

Jarid moved his attention toward Luka. "Oh look, someone's awake."

Luka bit his lip glaring at Jarid. "Let her go."

"I wish I could man," Jarid flicked his tongue. "But I can't."

He put the knife back up to Anna's throat.

"Luka." She pleaded.

He looked back to Luka. "You know, I never really liked you."

"Right back at you." Luka growled.

"You were never good enough for Chelsea. You didn't treat her right. I mean, could you even call what you guys had a relationship?"

Luka let out a deep sigh. It looked like he was holding back a lot of emotions. "Jarid, you do not have to kill us."

"But where's the fun in that?" Jarid teased.

"Jarid," Luka warned. "Let her go."

"I'm going to kill her just like you killed my sister."

It was pitch black now, but Anna could see the red in Luka's face.

"You and I both know you killed her, Jarid." Luka snapped.

"Excuse me?" Jarid asked. "I-"

But before he could finish, Luka grabbed a large rock beside his foot and lunged at Jarid.

Jarid's grip on Anna released as he fell to the ground along with his knife.

Luka raised his arm and slammed the rock directly over Jarid's head. Anna winced at the sound of his cracking skull.

"Luka." She whispered.

He didn't even budge. He stood over Jarid, looking down at him.

Anna looked down to see the rock still in Luka's hand. Her stomach flipped when she saw the dark spot on the rock. Blood.

"Luka." She repeated, taking a step closer.

Her jaw dropped and she felt her body go numb. She thought she was going to puke. Jarid lay in front of them with a puddle of blood pouring from the top of his head. His arms were spread and his was knife by his side. Anna couldn't see him breathing.

"Is he alive?" She managed to choke out. She knew he wasn't.

Luka snapped out of his haze and looked over at her.

"We have to get out of here." He said, bending down to pick up Jarid's knife.

Anna stood still, not understanding how he was so calm about this.

"Take my hand." Luka told her.

"No." Anna said, stubbornly.

"Look, I'm not asking you to marry me, okay?" He shouted. "I'm trying to save you."

Anna swallowed hard and took his hand. She couldn't help but notice how soft it felt and how good it felt to be in her own hand. She looked down at their intertwined hands, but wished she hadn't. She felt the vomit in the back of her throat when she saw the slight bit of blood from the rock on his hand.

Luka tightened the grip on her hand as he began running back to the truck. He had slipped Jarid's knife into his pants pocket and the rock in his sweater pocket.

When they reached the front, he released her hand and they both went to their separate doors climbing in as fast as they could. Luka locked the doors as he turned on the engine.

Anna felt the insides of her stomach curl at the sound of the doors locking. She shifted her knees to face the door and couldn't bring herself to look at Luka. Her mind was spinning. *What the hell just happened?* Luka just murdered a man. She turned her head to look out the window and closed her eyes, holding back tears.

She still couldn't believe Luka was some cold blooded murderer. She kept telling herself in her head that if Luka hadn't hit Jarid over the head with that rock, she would be dead. She tried to find comfort in that thought but couldn't.

Luka put his truck in reverse and sped out the gravel road and back onto the paved roads as fast as he could.

"Hey," he said lightly, looking over at her. "It's okay."

Her chest felt heavy and she couldn't find her words. It didn't feel okay. All she managed was a slow nod.

"He's gone now, okay?" He forced a smile. "We are alive and every-thing is going to be alright."

Anna began biting the nails on her right hand, she always did when she was nervous. "But, he's dead, Luka. You killed him."

"Maybe he's not dead." Luka sighed. "Maybe I just knocked him out."

"You didn't hear the sound of his skull cracking?" She snapped.

Anna stared at him for a while. Jarid was definitely dead and Luka definitely killed him. In the moment of silence Anna couldn't help but wonder about Chelsea. She hated just the idea that Luka had anything to do with it. But after watching his plain reaction after hitting Jarid over the head, she wasn't sure what to believe anymore.

"Besides," she suddenly felt like she couldn't breathe. "If he wasn't dead, that would mean he would come back for us."

"You're right." Luka nodded. "He's probably dead."

"You killed a man." She continued to bite harder, until she drew blood.

"I had to, Anna." He pleaded. "You would have died."

Anna remained silent. She told herself he was right and that he really did save her life back there.

"It was self defence," he said low, "self defence."

Anna looked over at him, not sure if he believed himself or not. "It was self defence?"

"Yes," he nodded. "It was self defence."

Anna nodded too, forcing herself to believe it at least for right now.

Luka tightened his grip on the steering wheel. "You can't tell anyone about this. Not even Jordan."

"Look, I get keeping quiet about this, but Jordan-"

"Not even Jordan." He repeated.

"She won't do anything, Luka." Anna pleaded. "She'll understand."

"I'm sure she will." He nodded. "But then she'll tell Owen. Owen won't understand."

She bit her lip and looked over at him. She hated to admit it, but there was the possibility of Owen finding out.

"Owen won't take it well," he continued. "He'll use it as leverage, go back to saying I killed Chelsea."

Anna felt the weight on her shoulders. She needed to tell her best friend. "I'll tell her not to tell Owen."

"But she will," Luka shook his head. "Everyone knows they have something going on, even if they don't know about it."

If she didn't feel like she was going to cry, she would have laughed. He was right. Jordan and Owen have been into each other for years. Yet neither of them can figure out the other one likes them back.

"You can't tell Jordan, okay?" He asked.

She nodded. "Okay."

Anna's whole body felt heavy, it was all too much for her to take in. Worst of all, she couldn't even have her best friend to help her through it. All she had was Luka. She wanted to laugh at that. All she had to help her through this was *Luka*. She looked out the window at the darkness and couldn't help but let the tears roll down her cheeks.

Sixteen

A**nna** had gotten a text from Jordan saying her and Owen had gone over to the local bar to wait for them since the deli closed at ten. Anna honestly hadn't realized how long they had been gone chasing down Jarid.

Luka pulled his truck into the parking lot and Anna could see the neon "Edgar's" sign. She let out a shaky breath before reaching for the door handle. She jumped when she felt Luka place a hand on her arm, stopping her.

"Sorry," he said, furrowing his brows. "I didn't mean to startle you."

He must've noticed Anna jump. Part of her was embarrassed, considering it was just Luka. But another part of her felt nervous after watching him hit Jarid over the head with that rock, but she didn't want to show him that.

Anna shook her head. "You didn't scare me. Just a lot happened back there."

"Yeah, I think we could both use a drink."

"Then let's stop sitting here and go in and get one." She said, eager.

"I just want to make sure we're on the same page first." Luka shrugged.

"What do you mean?"

Luka sighed. "We shouldn't tell Jordan and Owen everything that went on tonight."

Anna scoffed. "You want me to lie now too?"

"Well," Luka started, "A little. But not completely."

"Mind informing me of what I am allowed to tell them?" Anna snapped.

Luka looked out the windshield and sighed. "Let's just not mention he's dead, okay?"

Anna stayed quiet.

"We can say we saw him and followed him," Luka continued, "We can even tell them where we ended up. Just not that he's dead."

Or that you killed him, Anna thought. She sighed. She knew she wasn't thinking straight right now and there wasn't enough time to weigh the pros and cons of Luka's suggestion. But, with the little part of her that was still functioning after all of that trauma, she figured he was probably right. If Jordan and Owen knew Jarid was dead that would bring up question she couldn't answer and that would create a whole new problem.

"Fine." She nodded. "Can we go?"

Luka didn't say anything, but opened his truck door. Taking that as a yes, she opened her door and jumped down. Luka always had to have the town's attention and get his truck jacked up way too high for Anna's liking.

They made their way inside, looking around the crowded bar for Jordan and Owen. It wasn't packed, but it was definitely busy enough. The place was loud and Anna had to squint her eyes to get used to the mix of smokey haze and neon lights.

"I think I see them." Luka pointed over to a table at the back of the room.

Anna looked over and saw them sitting at a table for four. They were sitting side by side, each with a bottle of *Bud Light* in front of them. They were longingly looking into each other's eyes, as Jordan laughed while Owen was telling her what must have been a funny story. Any other day, Anna would point this out to Jordan. But, after the night she just had, she wasn't in the mood for love.

Anna and Luka headed over to the bar first before going over to Jordan and Owen's table. Luka had ordered a *Budweiser* while Anna ordered a *Corona*. Luka placed ten dollars on the counter. As she began to head toward the table she took a swig. She closed her eyes, letting the alcohol hit her system, instantly beginning to wash away her stress.

Luka was walking ahead of her, but neither Jordan or Owen seemed to notice them.

Luka cleared his throat, "Hey, guys." He had to speak fairly loud so they could hear him over all the shouting voices in the place.

Owen looked up at them, "Hey, you're back."

He didn't sound enthusiastic. Clearly he had forgotten all about the mission Luka and Anna had went on and simply wanted more time alone with Jordan. Although, she didn't entirely blame him. She was probably a good distraction for him to stop reminiscing about his sister.

Jordan turned around and reached to squeeze Anna's hand. She had no idea how much Anna needed that right now. But, at the same time, it made her want to break down and cry. Anna wanted to just spit out everything she witnessed tonight, but she knew she couldn't. As scary as she found Luka tonight, she didn't want to ruin his life. So, she took another swig of her beer to keep herself quiet.

"Any luck?" Jordan asked.

"Please tell me you guys found him." Owen pleaded.

Anna nodded, "We did."

Owen's eyes lit up. "That's great."

"But where is he now?" Jordan asked, clearly noticing they showed up fairly early with no Jarid or police.

"We lost him." Luka spoke quickly.

"What?" Owen roared, "You guys lost him?"

"Maybe you should have gone then." Luka barked.

Anna smacked Luka's arm. "We lost him, yes. But we followed him to some wharf."

"Wharf?" Jordan repeated.

"I don't know of any wharf's around here." Owen said. "Where'd you find this wharf?"

"It's a really secluded area. I think it was about fifteen minutes from the deli." Anna explained.

"Secluded?" Owen hummed, "As in hiding drugs?"

Luka nodded. "Smuggling them in to town by boat."

"Was he alone?" Jordan asked.

Anna found herself making eye contact with Luka as if she was asking him whether to answer or not. She hated that. She has always been the lead girl. She always made her own decisions and never let anyone tell her what to do. But after tonight she felt so small. She felt as if she couldn't make any decisions right now.

Luka nodded, giving her the go ahead to tell the truth.

"No," Anna finally said, "He was with some older guy."

"Any idea who it was?" Owen questioned.

Anna bit her lip. "No, but I've definitely seen him before."

"What did he look like?" Jordan asked, nervously.

"He was probably about fifty. I think his hair was grey, but the dark made it hard to tell. He had a small scruffy beard that was black with some grey strands." Anna explained, not thinking much of it.

Jordan stayed silent. She looked down at the bar's wooden floor boards and crossed her arms.

Owen seemed to take notice of this, "You're not cold are you?"

"No." Jordan spit out. There was no way for her to be cold. She was in a sweater and they seemed to be getting good weather for April. Besides that, they were in a crowded bar.

Owen's question seemed to draw the attention of both Anna and Luka.

Anna leaned her hand across the table, reaching for Jordan. "Are you okay?"

Jordan let out a small laugh, "I'm fine guys, relax. I'm just trying to piece everything together like you guys are."

None of them seemed to believe her, but they agreed to let it go.

"So you said you've seen this guy before?" Jordan questioned.

"Definitely." Anna nodded, "I've almost got it. I just can't place a finger on it."

Jordan began to shake her leg under the table. "Interesting."

"You got any ideas?" Owen placed his hand on her shaking leg.

"No." She replied too quickly.

"You sure?" Owen looked over at her.

"Yes." Jordan looked back at him. "It's always possible if Anna has seen him before, I have too."

Anna nodded. "Good point."

Anna could tell there was something going through Jordan's mind. She might have pieced something together. But Anna couldn't understand why she wouldn't tell them, or her at least.

"What happened after you guys followed him?" Owen asked.

Anna felt her stomach sink. Here comes the lying.

"He took some drugs off the boat and stored them." Anna explained, trying to continue telling the truth.

"That's it?" Owen squinted his eyes as he looked over at Anna.

She couldn't help but wonder if he could tell how nervous she was. Did he know she was about to lie? She hoped not.

Anna looked over to meet Luka's eyes. He was glaring at her. She took that as a sign not to talk and let him instead.

"He got on the boat." Luka lied.

"Yeah, he went off to pay some guy." Anna sighed, backing his story up.

She felt Luka watching her. She didn't want to look at him, but she couldn't help it. He kept his stone cold glare and nodded, approving of her answer.

Anna still didn't feel right. She hated lying to her best friend. On top of that, she still hadn't processed what happened to Jarid back there.

"What about you guys?" Anna asked, eager to change the topic.

"Yeah, actually. Something interesting happened." Owen nodded.

"She called one of her friends over to the deli to tell her she thinks Jarid was involved with Chelsea's death somehow." Jordan explained.

"Did she say how?" Luka asked.

Jordan shook her head. "Not exactly, but I think she meant as in dumping the body."

Anna whipped her head toward Luka. "That's what Jarid meant."

"What are you talking about?" Owen demanded.

"Jarid was talking to the older guy about how he had helped him even though he knew what the girl meant to him." Anna told them.

"That's what he said?" Jordan asked for clarification.

Anna nodded.

"He meant as in his sister." Owen's voice was stern.

"This proves my case." Luka said.

"But what if all he did was dump her body?" Anna pointed out. "That still doesn't say who killed her."

"The older guy we saw." Luka shrugged.

Owen nodded. "We need to find Jarid and get him to talk."

Anna felt a lump in her throat as flashbacks of Jarid hitting the ground flashed through her mind. Finding Jarid would be easy, but getting him to talk would be the impossible part.

Seventeen

Jordan had excused herself to the bathroom, leaving the other three at the table. She was glad the bathroom was empty rather than filled with the friendliest drunk women like it usually is each time she comes here. Not that she doesn't like making friends and telling strangers not to text their ex, but she needed to be alone right now.

She stood in front of the mirror staring back at herself. She was feeling extremely claustrophobic, and not just because the local bar's bathroom was small. She looked down and noticed her hands were shaking. She could feel vomit rising in her stomach.

There's no way it's really him.

Jordan didn't want to believe she knew someone who was attached to this whole thing, but she couldn't help but wonder. When she heard Anna describe what the older man at the wharf with Jarid looked like, she couldn't stop her mind from spinning. She had no proof, but by the sounds of the small drug importing she would bet money that she knew exactly who it was. She only knew one person in this small town who imported and sold drugs and owned a wharf.

Randy Embers.

Her father.

She had to keep reminding herself that there was no evidence to prove that Jarid was the one who killed Chelsea, but it was very likely.

Even so, there was no evidence saying her father had helped Jarid, if he had killed her. Maybe Jarid did this all on his own.

Jordan knew she was fooling herself. They had all discussed it at the table back there. Jarid was talking about helping move a body, not killing someone. Jarid most likely didn't kill Chelsea. Jordan's father probably did. She knew her father was a drugged out dead beat. He was capable of anything. That included murder, especially if someone got themselves involved with his dealings that weren't suppose to.

She closed her eyes and bowed her head, holding back tears. She already hated her father enough her entire life, she didn't need to hate him more. She had always been the daughter of a man who imported and sold hard and deadly drugs. She would hate to see that upgrade to the daughter of a murderer.

Jordan was trying to piece everything together in her head, when she thought about Owen. *Oh god*. If he found out that it was her father who killed his sister, he would hate her for the rest of his life. She couldn't imagine the pain of that. She really cared about Owen. The last thing she wanted was to lose him.

She took a deep breath and pulled herself off the counter when she heard the door start to open. She looked up and saw some tall blonde girl. They gave each other a smile before the girl walked into the stall.

Jordan felt her stomach fill with knots. She had a terrible feeling about where this investigation was headed. But, she knew she needed to help Owen find answers. She thought about Anna and how she had said she had seen the older man before. She knew Anna was smart and good with detail. It was only a matter of time before she figured out exactly who she saw.

Eighteen

Owen had walked Jordan to her political science class this morning. She thanked him and rubbed his arm, telling him she would see him later. He couldn't help but feel warm inside as he left the hallway and headed back out the front doors.

He was supposed to be heading to his science class, but decided he wasn't in the mood to get back to class yet. It had only been five days since Chelsea's body had been found and his head still wasn't in the right head space yet.

He couldn't help but feel like Jordan was a little bit off this morning. After she had gone to the bathroom at the bar last night, she seemed like a whole different person. She didn't laugh as much, she barely even talked. He made a mental note to ask her about it later when they met up.

It was only 11am, but Owen decided to head to the bar anyway. One drink wouldn't hurt as long as it was only one. He did have a habit of getting carried away sometimes and turning one drink into eight, especially since his sister died, but he told himself today was not going to be one of those days.

He hopped in his car and drove a little further into town where the bar was located. He parked the car up front before walking up to the front door. When he pulled it open he was hit with the smell of smoke and bourbon. Shaking all his worries off, he walked up to the counter. He was met by a bartender he had seen many times here since he turned nineteen seven months ago. He gave him a nod and ordered a beer.

Owen decided to just sit at one of the bar stools this morning since he was all alone. He looked around the room and took everything in. It wasn't filled in here like it was last night, there was only a handful of people. All the guys in here were older and have all been regulars for twenty years.

Once he was about halfway through the bottle, he felt his phone vibrate in his pocket. Assuming it was Jordan, he pulled it out with a smile on his face. He looked down at the name and saw it was his mom.

You need to come home. Now.

Getting a sinking feeling in his stomach, Owen put a five dollar bill on the counter, left his beer and jogged out the door to his car. His mom's text was extremely vague, leaving his mind to wander down every path and possibility. He couldn't help but wonder if the police had found Chelsea's killer and that they would finally get their peace.

When Owen pulled up to his mom's house, he took notice to the police car that was parked in her driveway. He wanted to believe it was for a good reason. That they were going to tell them they had Chelsea's killer locked up. But, his gut told him that was not what was going to happen.

Nervous, he made his way to the porch door, opening it. When he stepped inside he saw his mom sitting at the round kitchen table, accompanied by two police officers. They looked to be the same ones who came to their door when they told them Chelsea was dead.

Owen's mom smiled at him as she got up to pull him into a hug. Full of questions, Owen hugged her back. When they pulled away, Owen could see the tears in her eyes.

"Mom, what's wrong?" He asked.

She took a deep breath. "Honey, they found Jarid."

Owen squinted. "What do you mean?"

His mom reached out and rubbed his arm soothingly. "I'm sorry, Honey."

Owen couldn't process what was going on. "Jarid is dead?"

One of the officer's spoke up. "I'm afraid so. He was found on the shore, just like your sister."

Owen felt his chest get heavy. Both of his siblings were dead? How could this happen?

"What happened to him?" Owen asked.

"Looks to be blunt force trauma as well." The officer spoke again. "We think he was hit with a small to medium sized object."

Owen couldn't breathe. "He was murdered?"

The officer stayed silent, but nodded.

Owen couldn't feel anything. He wanted to go back to the bar and drink until he couldn't walk. He couldn't understand this. Both of his siblings were murdered days apart. He felt his anger rise. He and Jarid were never close, but that was still his brother. He was going to find out what happened.

"Owen," the officer began, "We'd like to talk to you."

Owen looked up at him. "Sure."

"Let's go to another room. I'd like to do this privately."

Feeling uneasy, Owen followed. The officer lead them into his childhood bedroom, gesturing for Owen to have a seat. He sat on the edge of the bed and waited.

"Talk to me about Jarid." The officer said.

Owen shrugged. "We honestly weren't all that close. I barely knew him."

The officer nodded. "Quite the opposite of your relationship with Chelsea?"

Owen nodded.

"Did you or either of your siblings ever get into any extreme arguments?"

Owen furrowed his brows. "I haven't talked to Jarid in five years."

"What about Chelsea?"

"Sure, we've gotten in quite a few arguments, as siblings do."

"Did you ever get violent with her?" He asked.

Owen glared at the officer standing in front of him. "Where the hell are you going with this?"

"I'm just trying to find answers, Owen."

"It sounds a lot like you're trying to accuse me of murder to me." Owen barked.

"I'm just wondering." The officer said, calmly.

"Wondering what exactly?" Owen could feel the sweat pouring from his forehead.

"I've been told your sister was quite popular. That she had a good reputation in this town, even in university."

Owen nodded. "She was very well liked, yes."

"Maybe you were jealous of that." The officer put out there. "Maybe she constantly overshadowed you and you got tired of it."

Owen could hear his heart pounding. "You're fucking crazy. You're wasting your time."

The officer shrugged. "Chelsea took all the spotlight from you, Owen. In high school, your parents, even everyone in town liked her more."

"So what?" Owen screamed.

"So maybe you wanted to get rid of her so you could have some of that light."

Owen slammed his jaw tight as he felt his muscles tense. "I'm done talking to you."

"Just one second Owen." The officer held up a hand for him to stop.

"I'm not going to sit here and listen to you tell me I killed my sister."

"Let's talk about Jarid, then." He offered.

"I didn't kill him, either."

"I just want to know what you know about him." The officer told him.

Owen shrugged. "Not a lot. He was a high school drop out, got into some hard drugs. That's all I really know."

The officer nodded. "So it's not exactly a surprise he turned up dead."

Even though Owen had assumed Jarid would turn up dead someday, he didn't like hearing it from this officer. That was still his brother.

"We all thought he would overdose someday. Not be murdered." Owen explained.

"Right." The officer sighed. "So you knew nothing about Jarid's death until you walked into this house?"

"Not a thing." Owen gritted his teeth. "Are we done here?"

The officer nodded as Owen stood up from the bed and stormed out of the house, slamming the front door behind him.

Nineteen

Luka still had a couple of hours to kill until class, so he decided to head over to his dad's auto shop and pick up his tools he used for class that his dad had borrowed yesterday.

Luka cruised down the highway letting the wind mess up his hair. He couldn't help but picture Jarid's lifeless body. He tried to feel some remorse, but couldn't find any. Each time he thought about what happened he pictured Anna's face. He saw how terrified she was with Jarid's knife against her throat. He wrapped his fingers tight around the steering wheel and gritted his teeth. He couldn't explain what he was feeling, but he felt this protectiveness over Anna. He felt like he had to save her. He felt like it was his fault she was out in that danger in the first place. If he could go back, he would have grabbed Jarid right from the beginning and beat his face until his body became lifeless.

Deep in his thoughts of Jarid and Anna, Luka hadn't noticed the exit creep up on him, or that he was going thirty over the speed limit. Luckily, Luka turned at the last minute, making it onto the exit 7 ramp.

Luka drove five miles down the road before turning into his fathers auto clinic. He was quick to notice that there weren't any cars in the parking lot besides the employees. Taking advantage of the empty spaces, he drove up to the side so he didn't have to walk as far.

He dragged his boots along the dirt still feeling the anger he had felt on the drive here. Looking for his dad, he made his way over to the bay door first. It was halfway open. Luka crouched down to squeeze through. He saw there was a red *Honda* on one of his dad's hoist systems.

"Dad?" Luka called.

The room stayed silent. Luka furrowed his brows. Why would his dad leave a car half finished? Luka continued on his journey walking through the bay as he made his way to the door that entered the building. He thought maybe his dad was inside dealing with a client. Luka reached for the knob, but stopped just as his fingers grazed it. He could swear he saw something moving. He figured it was just his dad going through papers at the front desk, but couldn't help but notice the knots in his stomach telling him otherwise.

To be safe, Luka leaned forward to look through the small glass window. He felt his heart drop to his stomach. His dad was not going through receipts. He was standing over some woman who was sitting on the desk with her hands ruffling through his hair.

Luka felt his anger grow. That woman obviously wasn't his mom. His mom was barely mobile anymore. She was diagnosed with bone cancer six months ago, right before Christmas. The cancer seemed to spread quicker than the doctors could get her treatment. Whoever that woman was, it wasn't his mom.

Luka wanted to open the door and walk straight to his dad and punch him. But at the same time, Luka should have seen this coming. His dad used to work away and only came home every so often Luka's whole life, before he had opened his auto shop. Even at age twelve Luka could tell his father wasn't a loyal man and had other girlfriends in the town he was staying in when he worked. It's no surprise he would run and find someone new once his mom could barely walk anymore.

He shouldn't have, but Luka leaned down to look in once again. This time the woman stopped kissing his dad for a short moment and leaned back just enough that Luka could see her face. He could have puked. He forgot his dad had a new assistant. More importantly, he forgot that his new assistant was Meghan Embers. *Jordan's mom.*

He couldn't help but wonder if this was something his dad had been doing with Meghan for a while or if this was something he did with each of his assistants during the time they worked for him.

Luka didn't have time to process what he had just saw. He jogged back to his truck, leaving his tools behind.

For the first time, he winced at how loud his truck was. He really hoped his dad didn't hear it, and if he did he hoped he didn't catch on that it was him or that he had been there. But, he figured he was too busy with Meghan to pay attention to anything else. The last thing Luka wanted for his dad to find out he knew. He needed to find a way to handle this differently. For once he wasn't going to barge in and blow up at him. Luka knew that would bring him no luck anyway. He had no proof. But, he knew someone who might believe him.

Feeling more eager than ever, he drove straight to Anna and Jordan's apartment.

Twenty

Anna jumped when she heard a rapid knocking at the front door. Quickly making her way from the kitchen where she was cooking bacon, she peeked through the peep hole. She felt her heart do a little flip when she saw Luka Anderson standing outside her front door. But, she didn't know if the flip was from fear, or if it was those same old butterflies.

Taking the risk, she opened the door. "Luka?"

He opened his mouth to speak, but nothing came out.

"Luka," Anna squinted, studying him. "Are you okay?"

He pursed his lips and shook his head.

Anna noticed the dried tear on his cheek. Had he been crying?

"Oh my god, Luka." Anna reached out and grabbed his hand, pulling him into the apartment. "What happened?"

"Is Jordan here?" He asked.

Anna shook her head. "No, she has class right now."

He stayed silent for a few moments as Anna sat him down in one of the chairs beside the counter and poured him a glass of water.

"Thank you." He muttered, taking the glass.

She nodded and headed back to the frying bacon. "Can you tell me what happened?"

He closed his eyes and let out a deep sigh. "I-I saw something today."

"You saw something?" Anna repeated, not understanding where this was going.

He nodded. "Something I didn't like."

"Luka." Anna sighed, placing the bacon on a plate in front of her. "Can you please elaborate?"

"My dad." He spat out. "I caught him."

Anna stood there for a moment trying to understand. She was about to bite off a piece of bacon when she remembered when her and Jordan were at the auto shop. It was when she noticed Luka's dad getting a little too close with Jordan's mom. Anna hadn't let that go, she just hadn't found anything else to prove it.

"What do you mean you caught him?"

"He's having an affair, Anna." He looked deep in her eyes. "With Jordan's mom."

Anna felt relief in her chest. "I knew it."

As bad as the situation was, she couldn't help but feel some appreciation for herself. She had read all the right signs that day and came to a suspicion that turned out to be true. Maybe she was made to be a detective after all.

"What?" Luka shouted. "What do you mean you *knew*?"

Anna bit her lip, realizing she should not have said that. *A real detective would act as if they knew nothing, Anna. Come on.*

"I mean, what are you talking about?" She crossed her arms. "You sound crazy."

Luka's eyes widened as he threw his hands in the air. "Anna, please. I'm asking for your help here."

She sighed, stealing another piece of bacon off the plate before sliding it over to share with Luka. "Fine, talk. Tell me what you saw."

Luka explained all about how he looked through the window and saw his dad dry humping Jordan's mom at the front desk.

"Oh, okay." Anna put her hand up. "That was a visual I didn't need."

"How do you think I feel?" Luka sobbed. "I'm mortified."

"That's what you get for creeping in the window, you perv."

Luka dropped his jaw with his mouth full of bacon. "Would you have preferred I walked in on them?"

"Fair enough." Anna rolled her eyes. "I still can't believe I was right."

"Yeah," Luka shouted, "You never told me what you meant by that."

"It's my little secret." She joked.

"You have to tell me, Anna. I am a hero after all."

"A hero?" Anna raised her brows. "Since when are you a hero?"

"Since when I saved you last night." He answered.

She felt her heart stop for a second when she realized what he was referencing. It shocked her, but she knew Luka must want to joke about it as a way of coping.

"You are literally the last person I would ever want to save me." She rolled her eyes, deciding to play along.

"Well it sucks to be you, doesn't it?" He smirked.

Anna nodded as she took a sip from her glass of water.

"But really," Luka's expression turned serious. "Tell me."

Anna sighed. "Jordan's mom dropped Jordan and I off at your dad's auto shop that day you were playing secretary and I couldn't help but notice the way they looked at each other."

Luka thought for a moment. "Was this the same day he offered her that secretary job?"

Anna nodded. "Yeah, because you weren't very good at it."

"And they were already looking at each other like that?" Luka asked, ignoring her joke. "Before they even had the chance to spend endless hours in the shop together."

"Yeah." Anna sighed, throwing some more bacon in her mouth, clearly not processing what Luka had just put out there.

Luka kept staring at her, silently telling her she was missing some-thing.

Anna suddenly stopped chewing and looked up at him realizing what he meant.

"They could have been together before she took that job." Anna said in disbelief. "How long has this affair been going on?"

Luka shook his head. "I don't know. But we need to find out."

Anna nodded, mentally adding it to her list of crimes to solve in this small town.

Twenty-one

Her limp body lay in front of me. I lost count of how long I stood there staring at her. I found myself lost in the way the blood was oozing out of her head and how I could see a small glimpse of her skull where her skin had torn. Her blonde hair was now half red with only the bottom half left with her natural color.

I looked around and realized how deep in the woods we were. Had I really chased her this far and no one heard her scream? I considered myself lucky for that and pulled out my phone. I knew exactly who I had to call.

I sat there with Chelsea's body beside me for what felt like too long. I couldn't help but be worried that some animal would smell her blood and come try to eat her body.

My thoughts were discarded when I caught myself looking back down at her and her blood stained shirt. I hadn't done this before and I was worried about how calm I felt. I couldn't stop myself from staring down at the blood around her body and the red marks I left on her neck. The body I had made lifeless. I had done the right thing, hadn't I?

I snapped myself out of my thoughts as I looked around the room, taking in the walls around me. I blinked hard trying to focus on the reality around me. I noticed the fact I was sitting in a chair with a drink in my hand and was not back in that moment in the woods I had lost myself in. It had only been five days since Chelsea's body had been found and so far no hard evidence. They still haven't been able to figure out what I had used to hit her over the head with. That didn't mean I wasn't scared, I had never done this before. For all I know I could have left some trace of myself on her. I prayed with everything in me that I hadn't. Even if I had, I hoped the water had washed it all off before she was found. I did what I had to do to save myself. It wasn't my fault she had gotten in the way. She showed up at the wrong time. I know I did what I had to do, even if no one else would see that. It was for everyone's sake. Now, I just had to make sure no one suspected me. So far so good.

Twenty-two

Anna had texted Jordan she would catch a ride to the deli with Luka, so Jordan didn't have to drive back to their apartment to pick her up. Before she was able to see Jordan's reply, which she knew would be a tease, she quickly put her phone in her pocket.

Jordan had called Anna earlier panicked, telling her Owen had found out earlier this morning that Jarid was dead. Anna had done her best to act surprised, but she hated lying to her best friend. But, they were this far into it, there was no going back now. She was glad Jordan had called instead of telling Anna in person. She honestly wasn't sure she would have been able to hold it together.

A news article had already been released with the minimal details they had about Jarid's case so far. The four of them were planning to meet at the deli and read the article to see if there were any loose ends or anything that matched to Chelsea's case.

Anna was eager. She needed to know what that article said. She knew they most likely hadn't found any evidence of her on Jarid's body, but she needed to be sure.

Sitting in Luka's passenger seat, she couldn't stop the flashbacks from the night before. She felt her heart begin to race thinking about Jarid lying on the ground. Knowing his body had been found made her break out into a nervous sweat. Since it had only been less than twenty four hours since Jarid's death, Anna still hadn't had time to recover.

After the interaction with Luka in her kitchen, she didn't feel as nervous to be alone next to him. However, she couldn't help but notice the small anxious feeling in her stomach and the little voice in her head saying *"What if?"*

"Do you have any Kleenex?" She asked, noticing her nose had started running.

He looked over at her and nodded. "There's some in the glove box."

Anna leaned forward and opened the glove compartment. Right away she noticed a small box of Kleenex and grabbed it. As she lifted the box, she noticed a small gold bracelet at the back of the compartment. She assumed it must have been Chelsea's. For a second she could have swore she felt anger, but then snapped herself out of it as fast as it came.

Her lips moved faster than her mind could. "Is that Chelsea's?" She closed her eyes in embarrassment.

He looked over at her and then down into the compartment. "Uh, yeah. I found it the other day."

Anna stopped. *The other day? He found it?* "What do you mean the other day?"

When he looked at her she could see the panic flash across his eyes.

"Luka," she said slowly, "Where did you find it?"

He took a deep breath. "On the shore."

"What?" She yelled. "The shore where Chelsea was found?" She would have done anything for him to say no.

He didn't say anything, but nodded.

Anna didn't believe him. "You're telling me, you went back to the shore where Chelsea washed up?"

"Yes, Anna. I did." He roared.

Anna felt the same panic she had felt in his truck just last night. "Why would you do that?"

"I don't know, okay?" He shrugged. "I needed to wrap my head around things. I couldn't process that she was...dead."

The truck grew silent as they continued down the road. Anna was trying to piece things together. Why was Luka being so honest with her lately? Or was he really? She found it hard to distinguish whether he was just being honest and trusted her, or if he was lying about every little thing.

"You took that bracelet from the beach?"

"Yes."

"So you just took it?" She asked. "Without thinking?"

Luka kept his eyes on the road. "Yeah, so what?"

"I don't know," Anna sighed. "It could be evidence."

He looked deep into her eyes. "How?" She could have swore she heard a hint of panic in his voice.

She shrugged. "I don't know, I'm not a real detective yet."

"Well you seem to be well on your way." He smiled. "I'd credit those *Nancy Drew* books you used to read everyday in elementary school, though."

She felt her lips curl into a smile. She couldn't believe Luka remembered that. There were those damn butterflies again. How could Luka make her go from anxious to a stomach full of butterflies in just a few minutes?

"Well," she thought for a moment. "There could be some kind of DNA from her attacker on it."

Before Anna could come up with any other explanations, the truck pulled into the side of the deli.

"Looks like Jordan and Owen are already here." Anna pointed.

Luka nodded. "Probably having a little date before we arrive."

Anna laughed as they made their way inside to find Jordan and Owen sitting in the same booth they had all sat in last night. The two were sitting across from each other, but Anna couldn't help but notice how close their hands were from touching. "Hey, guys."

Jordan looked over, startled. "Oh, hey."

Luka and Owen stayed silent, but nodded at one another. Anna could swear she felt the same tension from the day Owen punched Luka at the party. The room fell awkwardly silent.

"Well guys," Jordan moved over to sit next to Owen. "Have a seat."

"Thanks." Luka muttered, throwing himself into the back of the booth. Anna sat next to him.

"Have you looked at the article?" Anna asked.

Jordan shook her head. "We were waiting for you guys."

"My mom said there isn't a ton of detail in it," Owen started. "But there must be enough since she's trying to shield me from it. She made me promise her I wouldn't read it."

"But you're going to break that promise." Luka's voice was stern.

Owen nodded. "I need to know what happened."

"Ready?" Jordan asked and everyone nodded. She was quick to open her laptop and pull up the Edgar Cove's newspaper. She flipped to the first page and saw a picture of Jarid's face. The title was "**Another Body found on Cove's beach**". Jordan positioned her laptop so they could all see. They all took a few moments to read it to themselves before anyone said anything.

Anna took her time reading the article. She wanted to see if there were any similarities to the article released about Chelsea. Ever since Luka killed Jarid, she couldn't help but question him. She knew just because she watched Luka kill Jarid, that didn't mean he killed Chelsea. But, she was hoping to find some differences in this article, so that she could decide Luka had no part in Chelsea's death.

"It says he was hit with a small to medium size object to the back of the head." Jordan pointed out.

Owen nodded. "Just like Chelsea was."

"Yeah, but read here." Anna pointed. "It says the wound was closer to the top of his head than the back, unlike Chelsea's."

"Hmm." Jordan said. "You're right. But, what if it was because Jarid was taller? Perhaps the killer couldn't get as good of a hit."

Anna felt her stomach drop. "That could be true."

"You don't seem to be buying that theory." Jordan stared at her.

Anna shrugged. "I can't help but wonder if were looking at two separate killers."

"I mean, yeah." Jordan nodded. "That could be possible."

"I think it's possible." Luka spoke quickly.

The other three all looked at him with the same confused expression.

He shrugged. "Just trying to bring some brains to the group."

Jordan couldn't help but laugh. "You think you're the brains here?"

"I-"

Owen cut him off. "Pretty sure that's Anna, buddy."

Anna forced a smile. She really did enjoy the compliment, but she was forcing all her strength right now to keep a straight face. She couldn't help but notice how calm Luka was as they were reading the article. It was like he had no reaction at all.

"Either way," Jordan started. "Both Chelsea and Jarid were killed by a blow to the head with a small to medium sized object. We could be talking about the same weapon here."

Anna nodded, but stayed silent, letting her thoughts consume her. She looked over at Luka who had just finished reading the article. He leaned back in his seat and shook his head slightly, before leaning back the booth and crossing his arms. Anna couldn't help but think he was disapproving of the article. As if the forensics had gotten it wrong or something. Luka held no emotion what so ever, just like when he stared down at Jarid's body after he hit him. Anna felt a shiver go up her body.

"If we are looking at two different killers though," Owen leaned back in his seat. "I just want to focus on the one that killed my sister."

Jordan looked over at him. "Are you sure?"

He nodded. "Yeah. Jarid and I might have gotten along when we were kids, but we fell out a long time ago. But, I really cared about Chelsea."

"Okay." Jordan placed her hand on his. "Than we'll do that."

Owen looked down at her and smiled, seeming to forget Anna and Luka were sitting across from them.

"Anyways," Luka rolled his eyes. "I would agree. I think we should place our focus back on Chelsea."

Anna held her breath. *Of course you do. You killed Jarid.*

She looked directly at Luka. "We still need to rule out whoever killed Jarid isn't the one who attacked Chelsea."

Luka nodded, keeping his stern eyes on her. "Right."

Anna didn't know what she was doing, but she didn't know if she could trust Luka or not. During their time in her kitchen she believed she could. But, after finding that bracelet she didn't know what to believe anymore.

Owen looked back at the article. "It says here forensics think he was killed at least an hour before he ended up in the water."

"So someone hit him over the head and then dumped him in the water." Jordan concluded.

Anna felt her heart sink. She wasn't sure why. She knew this was coming.

Luka nodded. "It could have been that other guy Anna and I saw that night."

Or you killed him.

Anna did wonder how Jarid's body got into the water. Had the older man she recognized at the wharf found his body and just dumped him?

Jordan nodded, uneasy. "That could be true."

Luka shrugged as he kept a calm face. "As far as I see it, these murders aren't tied together. I think it's possible that Jarid and the other guy got in a fight and something went wrong so he dumped him in the water."

Anna stared at Luka, every inch of her being wanting to reach over and grab him by the collar and ask him what was wrong with him.

"We should just focus on Chelsea's case for right now." He finished.

Anna couldn't rip her eyes from Luka. What the hell was he doing? She pictured Luka hitting Jarid over the head and how it was so similar to Chelsea. Two murders. The same M.O. Both victims are from the same family. Luka looked over to meet her eyes. Maybe there was a serial killer in town.

Twenty-three

Anna hadn't listened to the rest of the conversation the gang was having. She found herself too lost in her thoughts. She knew being a detective would be a difficult job, but this case felt impossible. Part of her felt awful for thinking Luka had been Chelsea's attacker. But, the signs were there. She thought they were at least. Sometimes she didn't know if she was making them up so she could get to the bottom of this case or not.

Jordan turned to face Owen. "I'm really worried about you, though."

He shook his head. "I told you. You have nothing to worry about."

"Both victims were from your family, Owen." Jordan pointed out. "How do we know someone isn't after you too?"

"Like Luka said," he began. "We could be looking at two separate killers."

"But what if we aren't?" She whined.

"You sound like my mom, Jordan." Owen complained.

Anna paused. She hadn't thought about that. Even though she realized the victims were from the same family, she hadn't thought about Owen.

"You should probably take precautions, though." Anna spoke up.

"Or," Luka started, "We solve this case faster and put the killer away so Owen doesn't have to worry about a thing."

"You got any ideas?" Anna asked. "Because I'm stumped."

Luka slouched his shoulders. "I don't know where to go from here either."

Jordan's face lit up. "Maybe we should go to the wharf."

"What?" All three others spoke at the same time.

She shrugged. "It's most likely the crime scene. The police just don't know that and are looking on the beach instead. But from what the two of you have told us, I'd bet money."

"I don't know, J." Anna was the first to speak. "It was scary enough the first time."

"It could be dangerous." Owen agreed.

Anna felt relief knowing she wasn't the only one who didn't want to go.

"Yeah, that guy could have things tightened up now." Luka inquired. "You know, if he really did kill someone."

Or you did.

Jordan shrugged. "I guess that just means we'll have to be more careful."

They all sighed as they thought about what to do.

"Owen, your car is smaller than my dick." Luka complained.

Anna glared over at him somewhere between disgusted and not surprised.

"Oh." Jordan whined in disgust.

"Well we couldn't take your truck there. We'd get caught." Owen pointed out. "I've never heard anything so loud."

Luka rolled his eyes as he leaned back to look out the window. "Anna and I made it through last time."

"That really surprises me." Jordan said.

"Yeah." Owen agreed. "How'd you not get caught?"

If only you knew we did. Just not with the truck.

Luka shrugged. "Beats me."

Anna closed her eyes as she felt her frustration build. She wasn't entirely sure how she got talked into this. The wharf was one place she never wanted to step foot in again. She couldn't help but grow nervous the closer they got.

"It's the next left up here." Anna directed.

"That small gravel road?" Owen sounded like he didn't believe her. Anna couldn't say she blamed him. When she first saw it, the last place she expected to end up was a wharf that was owned by a man who imported and sold drugs.

"Yeah, just trust us." Luka grumbled, clearly tired of Owen's small backseat.

"You make it hard to trust you, Anderson." Owen's voice was stern.

Anna looked up to see Jordan already looking at Owen. There was that same odd tension. What was with the last name calling? Anna couldn't tell if he was joking or not. She found herself wondering if Owen had really meant it when he shook Luka's hand.

Anna wished she could lean up and say *"Yeah actually Luka is a murderer. He killed your brother."* But, she couldn't bring herself to do that. She couldn't deny the little speck of hope left inside of her that whoever killed Chelsea, wasn't Luka.

The small *Honda* pulled into the gravel road and continued down until they found the same wharf Anna and Luka were at three nights ago.

"It's right up there." Luka pointed. "You should park your car over by the trees."

Owen listened and pulled the car over to the right. He parked it so it was extremely close to the trees and some of the longer branches from the odd willow tree drooped over the car. But, Anna knew if that guy did see the car, this tree wasn't going to be much help.

"Owen." Anna grumbled. "Jordan and I can't get out on this side."

"Not unless we want to get eaten by trees." Jordan joked.

"Don't whine, Anna. You'll both just have to climb across." Luka said, holding out his hand to her.

Part of her didn't want to take it. But the other part of her still really wanted to hold Luka's hand. She couldn't understand herself right now. After watching Jordan take Owen's hand and climb over the driver's seat, Anna took Luka's. She couldn't help but notice his firm grip as he carefully helped her out. When she looked up at him, he gave her a small smile. She missed this Luka. The version of Luka she couldn't resist. The one before he killed a man in front of her.

"This way." Luka pointed, leading the pack.

The four began walking down the trail Anna had found herself on just yesterday. She wished she could go back and warn herself to just run.

Once they got closer to the clearing, Luka stopped and held a hand back, scanning the area.

"Looks to be clear for now." Luka whispered. "But there's no telling for how long."

Anna nodded. "Maybe we should split up."

Jordan raised her eyebrows. "Are you sure?"

No, she was not. She didn't exactly want to be alone with Luka again, but she knew from last time if someone appeared Luka could just grab a rock and hit them.

She nodded. "We can cover more space in a quicker time." She was trying to think like a real detective here. She needed to let go of what happened here last time and focus on what future *real* detective Anna would do.

"You know that never went well in *Scooby doo*, right?" Luka hesitated.

Anna couldn't help but smile. There was that same old scared Luka.

Owen rolled his eyes. "You and Anna head that way. Jordan and I will stay to the right."

Luka threw his hands up in defence. "Okay fine, but don't say I never told you so."

Anna let out a small laugh as her and Luka began forward. She really hoped this was the right decision.

Twenty-four

Jordan and Owen continued to keep right as they made their way closer to the water. They were standing really close to each other. Their arms brushed one another lightly here and there. But Jordan secretly wished Owen would reach over and hold her hand.

Not the time or place, Jordan. You're on a mission here.

As they continued down, they came across the small red shack. Owen walked directly over to it and opened the wooden door that was barely hanging on. He looked back at her before they stepped inside. It was nearly pitch black, since there wasn't any windows, but the light from the open door gave them just enough to see. The only thing inside were a few piles of white bags. *Cocaine.*

"Wow." Owen looked around, slightly poking one of the bags. "So this was my brother's life."

It's also my dads, she wanted to say. But she couldn't bear to think how Owen would see her if he knew her father was the person his brother worked for and possibly had something to do with his death.

Instead, she nodded. "It's crazy."

"I guess this really is rock bottom. It's hard to believe my brother ended up like this. He was a normal kid until he turned ten."

Jordan couldn't help but find herself curious. "What happened when he was ten?"

"We don't entirely know. He went out on a hunting trip with my uncle one time. When he came back he just...he wasn't the same." Owen looked to the floor.

Jordan nodded. She felt bad for asking. She should have left it alone.

To her surprise, he continued. "It wasn't even a week after that he started killing the neighbourhood animals. I don't mean wild animals either. I'm talking about cats, dogs. One time he even broke into a house to steal a kids hamster. All so he could brutally kill it."

"Wow." Was all Jordan could manage.

"Yeah." Owen let out a small mirthless laugh. "That's why when Luka brought Jarid to my attention as a possible suspect, I felt like I should have thought of him. It's just hard to imagine my brother killing a person. Not only that, but our sister."

Jordan walked over and placed a hand on his shoulder. "Don't beat yourself up. It's a really stressful time. Besides, we don't know Jarid did kill Chelsea."

"I really hope it wasn't him." Owen sobbed. "It'll kill my parents. And they're already hurting enough."

Jordan stayed silent and leaned her head on his shoulder.

"Jarid turned out to be a scary guy, though. When my parents divorced I went to live with my dad so he wasn't all by himself, I couldn't help but worry about my mom and little sister. I should have thought about Jarid possibly hurting them one day."

"Owen," Jordan wrapped her arms around his torso. "You can't blame yourself."

In a matter of seconds Owen pulled himself together. "I know."

"Maybe we'll find something here that tells us Jarid didn't kill her."

They exited the shed and walked further down toward the water. They continued down until they got to the edge. There was a small white and blue motor boat at at the edge of the water, tied to the dock.

"The boat is still here." Owen pointed out.

Jordan nodded. "I guess we're in luck. Looks like he's not out picking up anything right now."

Jordan's mind found it's way back to her father. This looked exactly like the place her mother had pulled her from when she was five. It was the day her father had brought her here because he was behind on deliveries. It was also the day her mother was finished for good. Jordan knew her parents break up had a big impact on her mom. That's why she was always out with other men. It wasn't easy growing up with parents like that. That was part of the reason she went to college and got an apartment. That way she could get away and get invited to parties, which was an excuse to drink her problems away.

Jordan wondered if she would see her father today. Or if she would ever see him again for that matter. Not that she ever wanted to.

Owen's voice snapped her out of her thoughts. "Hey, what is that?"

Jordan looked ahead to where he was pointing in the distance. There was something small lying by the edge of the water. The shiny emerald green color gave it away.

Jordan walked over and picked it up. "It's a ring."

Owen furrowed his brows and made his way over. Once he got close enough, his jaw dropped.

Jordan felt a sick feeling in her stomach. "Owen, what is it?"

Owen clenched his fist as red began to form on his neck. "That ring. It's Chelsea's."

Jordan couldn't feel her body. "What?"

"It's Chelsea's." He repeated. "My mom gave that ring to her for her middle school graduation." He took it from her hand.

Jordan didn't know what to say. Why the hell was Owen's sister's ring at her father's wharf? Had Chelsea been here before she died?

"Why would Chelsea's ring be here?" Was all she could manage.

"I don't know." Jordan could hear the anger in Owen's voice.

"What would Chelsea even be doing here?" Jordan asked. "From what I knew of her, she was nothing like this. Sure, everyone knew her, but she was still a nice girl."

Owen shook his head. "She would have no reason to willingly come here."

Jordan couldn't help but hear the way he emphasised on the "*willingly*"

"Do you think somebody forced her here?" She asked.

He shrugged. "Maybe."

Jordan's heart sank. She was never close with her dad. He never wanted to be. His business was more important to him. If it flopped, he'd be out of money. Or in prison.

But, the thought of him possibly being the one who killed Chelsea left her feeling extreme anxiety. But not because of her dad, but because she was afraid of how Owen would react.

"Jordan." Owen's voice was stern. "We need to find out what the hell Chelsea was doing here."

Before she could reply, she heard tires against the gravel in the distance. Jordan had thought she couldn't get more anxious, but she was wrong.

"Owen," Jordan whispered. "Do you hear that?"

He nodded. "Yeah, someone's here."

Jordan felt her stomach turn into a carnival ride.

A large grey truck drove across the concrete. The back end had a couple large garbage bags with what Jordan assumed were filled with more small bags of cocaine. The driver backed the truck up in front of the water before pulling it in park. He quickly opened the door and stepped out of the truck.

Jordan sucked in a breath when she saw him clearly.

"He's here to put those on the boat. He must have a delivery across the water." Jordan acknowledged.

"Or he's taking them back." Owen suggested.

Jordan nodded.

She felt Owen lightly grab her arm. "Duck behind this tree."

Owen guided her with a gentle hand on her back, she moved her feet quietly until she was behind the large pine tree, out of sight.

She stepped over to the end to be able to peek around the side.

Jordan could feel herself sweating. He was exactly who she thought he was. Her father was standing just a few feet in front of her.

He began taking the bags off the truck and walking over to the boat before throwing them in. Jordan was beginning to feel sick. She didn't know how much longer she could keep hiding. She was feeling so light headed that part of her wanted to jump out from behind the tree and ask her father herself if he was a murderer. But, she knew she couldn't do that. Who knows what her father would do to her. Or worse, to Owen. She would never want to risk Owen getting hurt.

"Do you know that guy?" Owen whispered.

Jordan couldn't bear to tell Owen the truth. But she couldn't lie to him either.

"What about your car?" She asked, attempting to distract him. It seemed to work.

He shrugged. "I'd be very surprised if he hadn't seen it."

She nodded, wondering if her dad had spotted Owen's car and knew someone was here. But if he did, why wasn't he searching?

She looked back to get another glimpse at him and saw he was still calmly walking back to his truck. He gave no indication he knew someone was here. But, Jordan knew not to trust him. He wasn't always what he seemed. She knew she had to be ready for anything.

Jordan could feel the wetness on her palms. Did her dad know they were here? Worse, had he spotted Luka and Anna? She began to feel extremely worried for them. They probably had no idea her dad was even here.

Jordan assumed he hadn't spotted them since he just got here. She hoped it stayed that way and he would just leave.

After he had the last bag on the boat, he closed up the tailgate. But, instead of getting into the boat, he leaned against the tailgate and let out a loud sigh.

Jordan could feel in her stomach what was coming next.

He pushed himself up straight so that he was now standing behind his truck, looking out at the water. There was no way he knew which tree they were behind, but if you knew someone was here, it would be a good guess.

"Alright." Her dad shouted.

Jordan jumped at the sound of his voice.

"I know someone is here." He announced. "I'll give you one chance to show yourself."

Jordan leaned the back of her head against the tree. *Please, no.*

"And if you don't," He continued, "Then I'll have to find you myself. And I promise you, you won't enjoy what'll happen when I do."

Twenty-five

Anna and Luka found themselves in the exact area they were in last night. Anna tried not to think of the details, but her brain betrayed her. She could feel the anxiety rising back in her stomach the same as when she was running from Jarid. She could see his lifeless body lying in front of them as blood seeped from his head. She could feel her hands beginning to tense up, letting her fingernails press deep into her palms. Until something finally snapped her out of her thoughts.

"Anna?" She heard lightly. "Hello?"

She shook her head as to physically shake off the weight that was placed on her shoulders less than twenty four hours ago. "Huh?"

Luka stopped walking and looked down at her, eyes full of worry. "Are you okay?"

She laughed. "Yeah, sorry. What were you saying?"

"I asked you what exactly we should be looking for." He explained. "You're the detective here."

Anna looked up and smiled. "I'm trying."

"Well," he shrugged, "I trust you with this. And with the secret of what happened here last night."

Anna felt surprised that he would bring that up. "I didn't really have a choice though, did I?"

Luka stayed silent for a while. "I suppose not."

Anna kept walking, looking for anything that would help her find who killed Chelsea. She found herself praying that if she did find something that it didn't lead back to Luka.

Luka spoke up again. "But everything is going to be okay."

Anna couldn't tell if he was trying to convince her or himself.

"Because I took the evidence," he continued. "And that guy we saw. He looks like he wouldn't really care if his employee died."

The rock.

"Where is that rock by the way?" Anna asked.

"I took it home with me." He replied, shoving his hands in his pockets.

"What did you do with it?" Anna was scared to hear the answer.

"I left it in the truck when we were in the bar. Then when I got home I cleaned it off. I put it with the other rocks my mom has around her garden." He explained.

Anna nodded. She couldn't help but feel like Luka knew exactly what he was doing. As if that rock was just some minor inconvenience that he could easily handle, even though it was attached to something much bigger. Something much more gruesome.

"The point is, it's over." He sighed. "I'm sorry you had to see it. I just...I didn't want you to die."

Anna sucked in a breath. Did he really just panic in the moment? Did Luka just want to protect her? Or was killing something he got off too? She needed to know.

"It's okay." Was all she could come up with. "I understand."

She didn't really. She didn't understand any of this. She needed answers.

They continued down the gravel road in silence seeing nothing but water and trees. Once in a while they would find the odd pipe or cigarette packet, but nothing special.

"Look for anything that would attach to Chelsea." She finally said.

"What?"

"You asked what we should look for." Anna reminded him. "Look for anything that may lead back to Chelsea. If not, than anything about this guy that may scream 'murderer'."

"This guy doesn't exactly look like he has a clean slate." Luka pointed out.

Anna kept her head to the ground, looking for any clues, when she came upon a pair of black boots standing in front of her.

"Anna." Luka whispered beside her.

She stopped in her tracks noticing the dark blue jeans that were attached to the boots.

"Got ya." A deep voice boomed.

Anna looked up and saw the same familiar man. She could have cried at the sound of his loud, evil laugh.

"Whatcha gonna do now?"

Anna lowered her eyes to see the lowered pocket knife in his hand.

The sound of the booming laughter filled Anna's body. She couldn't tell if he was laughing for a really long time, or if the sound was so loud it was planted into her head.

Luka walked up so he was a step in front of Anna. He raised his arms in surrender. "We're sorry, okay? Just let let us go." Luka began trying to compromise.

The man laughed again. "Let you go? Now why would I do that?"

Anna felt frozen. She couldn't find the courage to speak.

"So you don't have to kill us." Luka explained. "We're good people."

Flashbacks of Luka standing over top of Jarid flashed in Anna's mind. Was Luka a good person?

"Good people?" The man boomed. "I'm guessing you two had something to do with my friend's death."

Anna felt her heart get caught in her throat. *Jarid*. He was talking about Jarid.

Luka shook his head. "I have no idea what you're talking about. We just stumbled upon this place today. Now we know we shouldn't have. So just let us go."

The tall man in front of them pretended to think. "Hmm. How about...no." He began raising his knife when Luka stepped directly in front of Anna.

"Anna, run!"

Without a second thought, she felt her feet beginning to lift off the ground. She ran until the two were out of sight. The only sound she heard were birds chirping in the distance and the sound of her feet smacking against the gravel.

She noticed she wasn't being followed. She knew she should get help, go find Jordan and Owen. But, she felt like she owed it to Luka. She couldn't leave him there to die. After all, he saved her. He killed a man for her. At least she hoped it was for that reason. Anna needed to save Luka too. She didn't intend on killing the man, but she at least needed to get Luka away.

She began looking around trying to find something, anything to defend herself. She saw a rock and recalled the way Luka had hit Jarid over the head. She didn't think she had that kind of strength. She needed something better. She continued scanning the ground when she finally came across a large stick. She quickly grabbed it and made her way toward Luka.

As she got closer she heard grunting. Were they fighting? Panicked, she picked up speed while hanging onto her stick. She needed to hurry. She couldn't let Luka die.

The first thing she saw was the large man's hands around Luka's neck. Without hesitation Anna ran up behind him. She made quick eye contact with Luka who's eyes grew wide at the sight of her. Did he think she was going to leave him here to die?

Breaking the contact, she focused back on the man in front of her. She felt worry fill her stomach when she looked up at his head. Anna hadn't realized how tall he was. He had to be at least 6'3. Beginning to panic, Anna stood there frozen. Was she even able to swing her stick high enough? What if she didn't hit him hard enough? All the worrying questions began to fill Anna's brain.

She looked back over the man's shoulders to see Luka. The man's hands were still tightly wrapped around his neck. Luka's own hands were around the man's trying to pry them off. Luka looked back at Anna pleading with his eyes. Anna could see the fear in them. *Dammit, Anna. Do something!*

"Anna please." Luka's voice was barely a whisper.

Anna manoeuvred the stick so it was back towards her shoulder, ready to swing. But Anna's arms stood frozen when she noticed the man loosening his grip on Luka's neck. *Shit. He knew she was here.*

He slowly turned back toward Anna. "Couldn't stay away, huh? You just had to come back and save your little friend."

Anna could feel her face drop as her heart began pounding. *Keep it together, Anna.*

She kept her eyes on the man in front of her. She could hear Luka behind him gasping for his air back. The stick in her hands seemed to suddenly weigh more. Was she going to pass out? *No. Keep it together, Anna.* She tightened her grip around the stick once more, ready for action. But when the man leaped toward her, she couldn't find the strength to move.

Twenty-six

Before Anna could process, she was on the ground. Gathering her strength, she opened her eyes. She needed to knock this guy out and get the hell out of here. But, before she stood, she noticed she was no longer holding the stick. *Fuck.* She looked up, expecting to see the man standing over her with it in his hands. But, when she looked up, her jaw dropped. That's not what she saw at all. Above her stood Luka, face beat red, with the large stick in his hands ready to swing at the old man. When did he have time to grab it? Anna didn't really care, she was just glad Luka had more power over that man right now.

Looking away from Luka, she saw how close the tall grubby man was standing to her. She could see his hands beginning to lower their way down for what Anna assumed was an attempt to grab her.

"Anna, move!" Luka shouted.

Anna leaned backwards creating more space between her and the drug filled hands in front of her. She moved her hands to the side and placed them on the ground. She kept a low crouch and used the strength of her hands to get up and move herself to the side. The second Anna was out of the way she prepared herself for the crack of the skull, like the one from last night. But, it didn't come.

"No, fuck!" Luka shouted.

Anna looked up to see the man had spun around and was now pulling one end of the stick. Luka on the other end was using both hands in attempt to secure it back.

Unsure of what to do, Anna found herself back over next to them. She lifted her foot and kicked it out directly at the back of his knee. He flinched and let out a small groan. He still kept a grip on the stick, but his grip loosened slightly.

"Luka, pull it." Anna yelled.

"I'm trying. This guy's a lot stronger than you think."

The man gathered his strength back and belched out a laugh. "You're damn right I am. You messed with the wrong guy, kids."

Before Anna knew it, the guy pulled the stick from Luka's grip and tossed it to the side. Anna watched as he grabbed Luka by the collar.

"No!" She screamed.

She knew she should have ran and gotten help, but she couldn't leave Luka. She felt the man's other hand grab her arm. She flinched at the strength of his grip. She could already feel herself bruising.

"Let go of me!" Anna yelled. "Help!"

She hoped that Jordan or Owen would hear her cry for help. She wanted to call out their names but couldn't risk putting them in danger.

The man began dragging the two closer down toward the water. Was he going to drown them? *No. Please.* Anna tried with all of her strength to squeeze out of his grip. "Help!"

"Would you shut up?" The man hollered. "No one is going to hear you out here."

Anna hoped that wasn't true. Where the hell were Jordan and Owen? They wouldn't leave without her and Luka. Which meant they were probably still on the other side of the wharf. Part of her hoped they were for their safety. But she still wished they were close enough to hear her now.

Once the man got to the concrete, one of them in each arm, she turned toward the red shack. Anna noticed it was open. It was too dark to see, but from the little light letting her see in, there looked to be a few piles of cocaine. The man drug the two to the open door.

Realizing his plan, Anna began to scream. "No!"

The yelling seemed to anger the man more. He pushed Anna forward first, throwing her into the dark shack. She landed on her ass. She quickly tried to get up, running for the door. But, she was knocked back down by the weight of Luka crashing into her.

She got up again, headed for the door. But, right as she reached it, the door slammed in front of her face. She heard the man twist the outside handle, locking them in. Leaving her and Luka in the pitch black.

Twenty-seven

Jordan was shocked when her father began walking the other way. "I thought he heard us."

"Me too." Owen whispered. "So where's he going?"

Jordan shrugged. "Maybe the sound echoed. He could think we're over that way."

Owen nodded. "That means we need an escape plan. Now."

"We should wait until he he gets up toward those trees a little farther." Jordan suggested.

"Then we'll make a run for the car." Owen agreed.

"What?" Jordan raised her voice quietly. "No. We need to find Luka and Anna."

"That's too risky, Jordan."

"Well we can't leave them here, Owen." Jordan looked ahead and noticed her dad was now out of sight.

"We wont leave them," Owen began. "We'll just get up there to safety, then you can call Anna."

Jordan was hesitant. She wanted to go searching for them right now. That's what Anna would do, wouldn't she? She does want to be a detective after all.

But, Jordan also knew the risks. She didn't want to run into her father here. Things could get very dangerous. Especially if he has killed before.

"Fine. He's gone. Let's move." Jordan sighed.

Silently, Owen began following Jordan from the safety behind the tree. Once they were off the concrete and up the gravel path, Jordan stopped.

"I'm really worried about them." She admitted.

"Relax. They've been here before. They dodged that same man last time, and my crazy brother before he was killed. They'll be fine." Owen assured her.

Jordan took a deep breath. She wanted to believe him. But something in her stomach just didn't feel right. "I don't know, Owen."

"Let's just get back to the car and then you can call Anna and tell her that they need to come back and be careful."

"What if it's too late?" Jordan hated to even think that.

"You think he found them?" Owen asked.

"I don't know." Jordan shrugged. She wanted to cry. She almost wished that she hadn't suggested they come here. But she needed to be sure if the man Anna was talking about was her dad. She needed to know if he had anything to do with this. She felt bad for making this personal, when really this was supposed to be for Owen.

"I'm sure they're okay. Let's go." Owen placed his hand lightly on her back, guiding her up the hill.

They continued walking up the gravel, hoping her dad couldn't hear their footsteps.

"I see your car." Jordan announced.

"It's still there?" Owen sounded as shocked as Jordan was. "Did he hurt it any?"

"Doesn't look like it." Jordan said as she reached the driver's side of the car. "Maybe he really didn't see it."

"Or he did." Owen suggested. "And that's how he knew we were here."

"I'm surprised he didn't do more." Jordan brushed a hand through her hair. "I mean, how did he not know we were that close to him?"

Before Owen could answer they heard a scream.

Owen jumped. "What the hell was that?"

Jordan felt goosebumps trickle up her spine. "Anna."

The scream was followed by a loud slam of a door. Jordan couldn't tell exactly where it was coming from, but she knew it was down by the water.

Jordan began trying to even her breaths out. "He found them."

"You stay here." Owen told her. "I'll go."

"Are you out of your mind?" Jordan questioned. "I'm going with you."

"It could be dangerous. I think it's safe up here."

"I don't care, Owen." Jordan began walking forward. "I'm going to save my friends."

Owen let out a sigh before jogging up to her. "Okay, but we have to be careful. We don't know where he is now."

"I thought I heard a slam." Jordan said. "Good chance it was the door of his little shack."

Owen nodded. "So he's probably by the water."

The two began walking back down the gravel road in silence, hearing nothing but the crunch of their footsteps. The sound of a cough in the distance startled Jordan. She ducked behind a tree.

"Did you hear where that came from?" She asked, peeking from behind the tree.

"By the boat dock I think." Owen guessed. "Come on."

Coming out from behind the tree, Jordan slowly crept down the hill toward the boat dock next to Owen. As they got closer, Jordan tried to peek through spaces between trees to spot her father ahead of time.

"Do you see him?" She asked again.

Owen shook his head. "No. Maybe he left on the boat."

Jordan hoped that was true, but with no sound of a motor, she had an awful feeling it wasn't. The last thing she wanted was to face her dad, but at the rate this day was going, she wouldn't be surprised if she did.

They continued down slowly until they reached the concrete. It was a blessing that they could no longer hear their feet hitting the gravel, but now there were limited trees to hide behind.

"Dammit!" A voice boomed in the distance.

Jordan jumped. She felt Owen place a hand securely on her back.

"Do you see him now?" Jordan whispered.

Owen shook his head. "Maybe we should hold back for a second."

Ignoring him, Jordan continued forward. There were only a few thin trees left in front of them. But, each time one came into view, Jordan would do her best to camouflage behind it.

"Keep going." Owen whispered. "Just be careful."

Jordan continued on, moving down toward the dock. She slowly crept up behind the shack. Once she was behind it, she swore she could hear banging.

"What is that?" Jordan asked quietly.

Owen listened carefully. "I think it's coming from inside this shed."

Jordan placed her ear up against the side in an attempt to listen more closely. She heard something that sounded like shuffling.

"Something is moving in there." She told him.

"You don't think it's-?"

Owen didn't even have to finish the question. Jordan had a feeling she knew exactly what was going on. "I told you he found them."

"We have to find a way to get them out without him seeing." Owen said softly.

Jordan nodded. "You distract him while I go open it and get them out."

"Are you sure?" Owen sounded nervous. "What happens when we get them out?"

Jordan shrugged. "We all make a run for it and never look back."

Owen sighed. "Okay."

Jordan watched as Owen began to walk forward toward the dock where they assumed her father would be.

"Be careful." She whispered. "Don't make me save you too."

Owen turned around and laughed silently. Jordan felt comfort in his smile. It made her feel like everything was going to be okay and they were going to make it out of here alive.

Jordan waited patiently for any sound coming from down toward the dock so she knew when to spring into action.

"Hey!" Owen's voice yelled.

"Who the fuck are you?" Her father's loud voice boomed.

It made Jordan feel sick to her stomach. She couldn't help but feel like she should have gone forward and distracted her father. She really hoped Owen didn't get hurt today.

Putting her thoughts aside, she began moving toward the front of the small red shack. When she got there she heard mumbling. *Luka and Anna.* She felt relieved to know they were in there and alive.

The low voices seemed to get quite loud. It sounded like the two of them were yelling at each other. Jordan felt a smile creep upon her face picturing the two trapped in the dark screaming at each other.

She took a step back and examined the door. It had a large horizontal handle. Jordan wasn't exactly sure how it worked, but it looked like it was a simple manoeuvre. Taking a guess, she twisted the handle down and pulled it forward. *Click.* The low voices inside came to a stop. She couldn't help but feel proud of herself for a moment. She could still hear the echoing voices of Owen and her father in the distance. Jordan grabbed back onto the handle and pulled the door forward. She whined at the creek the door made when she pulled it open. Her father most likely heard that. Once the door was open she noticed Owen and her dad had stopped yelling. *Fuck.* He heard her. He was coming.

Twenty-eight

The afternoon sun attacked their faces as Jordan pried open the door.

"Jordan?" Luka's jaw dropped.

"Oh thank god." Anna sighed. "I can't believe that guy trapped me in here. Not even that, but with him."

Jordan held back a laugh. "Come on, guys. We have to go."

"Jordan, this is the happiest I'll ever be to see you." Luka joked.

"Thanks?"

He nodded.

Anna and Luka stepped out of the dark shack and began to look around.

"Where's Owen?" Anna asked.

"He was distracting my-" She stopped herself. "That guy. Owen went to distract that guy while I got you guys out of there."

"We need to find him and get the hell out of here." Luka insisted.

"Hey! Come back! I'm not finished talking to you." Owen's voice yelled in the distance.

"I should have known there were more of you." Her dad yelled.

"Shit." Jordan whispered.

The sound of footsteps began approaching them.

"Just start going straight." Luka pointed. "We'll stop up there and loop back around for Owen."

With no argument, Jordan and Anna began following Luka up toward the trees. Jordan tried her best to keep her footsteps as soft as possible.

As they walked past a large stick Anna pointed. "Look there's our stick. Maybe we should grab it again."

"Really, Anna?" Luka scoffed. "Neither one of us could keep hold of it last time."

Anna kept silent and nodded.

"What the hell are you talking about?" Jordan asked.

Luka waved it off. "Don't even worry about it."

"You know I brought it to save you." Anna barked. "It's not like I have a gun."

"Well it didn't work, did it?"

"Guys," Jordan butted in. "Can we please focus on finding Owen?"

Anna nodded. "You're right. I'm sorry."

"Thank you." Jordan's voice was cold.

Jordan felt worry in her stomach knowing that Owen was still back there. Why hadn't she just ran back for him right after she freed Luka and Anna?

"Okay, stop here." Luka whispered. "We'll give it a minute and see if that guy goes over that way. Then, we'll head back and find Owen."

The three stood behind a bush waiting to hear Jordan's father's footsteps. She couldn't stop worrying about Owen. She began rubbing her hands together and biting her lip. She needed to find Owen.

"We need to find him." She said, impatiently.

"Let's go." Anna nodded.

Without second thought, Jordan began creeping forward. Anna kept close to her side. Once they got back down the gravel hill, they came back upon the water and the little red shack.

"I don't see either of them." Luka's voice was low.

Anxiety began rising in Jordan's stomach. "Where the hell is he?"

Anna placed a hand on her shoulder. "We'll find him."

Jordan bit down harder on her lip. "Do you think he hurt Owen?" She wouldn't be surprised. Her father was a violent person, especially when his deals weren't going well. She felt bad for suggesting they come here. She should have known how angry her father would get seeing people snooping around his property.

"I'm sure he's fine." Luka spoke up. "We'll find him."

Jordan sighed. She wanted to believe those words, but she just wasn't sure. But one thing she did know is she wasn't leaving without Owen.

Moving behind small trees, she scanned around for movement.

"Guys." Anna stopped walking. "What is that?"

Jordan looked over to where Anna was pointing. Near the water she could see something blue lying half behind the truck.

"Fuck." Luka mumbled.

Owen. Was he unconscious? Jordan couldn't tell, but it looked like it.

"Oh my god." She cried.

She began jogging forward, no longer looking around for her father. She no longer cared where he was or if he was coming for her. All she knew in that moment was that she needed to save Owen. She felt like she owed it to him. She did send him to distract her father after all.

She reached Owen before the other two did. He lay on his side with his eyes closed. *Was he breathing?* Jordan couldn't tell. She felt her hands shaking.

She reached her hand forward and shook his body. "Owen."

No movement.

Luka joined her on the other side. "Owen, wake up."

"Oh my god." Anna gasped.

Luka looked up at her. "Watch for that guy."

Jordan kept her hand on Owen's side."Owen, come on. Please."

To some miracle, Owen let out a groan.

Jordan and Luka looked over at one another with the same relief in their eyes.

"Owen," Jordan repeated. "Open your eyes."

His eyes slowly blinked open. When he lifted his head Jordan gasped.

"Owen. What happened?" Jordan asked.

She couldn't rip her eyes of the bruise around his eye that was closest to the ground. "Did he hit you?"

Owen sat up fully. "I'm fine."

Luka lent out a hand. "Here."

Taking a deep breath, Owen grabbed it. Luka helped him up as Jordan kept her hand on Owen's shoulder.

"Anna, see anything?" Luka asked.

She shook her head. "No. But we should get moving. It's only a matter of time."

Jordan reached up and brushed the light brown around Owen's eye.

He flinched. "I'm okay."

Jordan shook her head. "I'm sorry."

"Jordan," Owen's hand found her waist. "I'm okay. You don't have anything to apologize for."

If only he knew. Jordan wanted to crack right there and tell them all that the dangerous man up ahead was her father, but she couldn't find the words.

Owen seemed to take her silence for understanding. "Let's get out of here."

Jordan kept an arm around Owen's back as they walked. Luka stayed to the front, being the lookout. The breeze blew through their hair as the woods stayed quiet. The only sound was their four footsteps.

"We're almost there." Anna said, hopeful.

Jordan almost felt relief. Almost. But it was stopped short when she saw that same familiar face pop out from behind a tree in front of them. He gave them a smile.

Twenty-nine

Jordan gripped her fingers tighter around Owen's side. She leaned into his side as close as she could get. Half of her was scared and leaned into him for comfort. But the other half wanted to protect him from her father. She wanted to protect all three of them. She couldn't help but feel like this was all her fault.

"Gotcha." Her evil father smiled.

Luka stayed in front, shielding the group.

"That stick might help now, wouldn't it?" Anna whispered.

Luka sighed. "You guys go to the left and run."

"Luka." Anna protested.

"Just go, Anna. I'll be right behind you."

Lightly, Jordan grabbed Anna's arm and began pulling her to the left. Jordan knew they still had to go forward, even if they were going to the left side. She felt nauseous that her father was about to see her face.

Hesitant, Anna gave in.

Owen stood in front and led her and Jordan back up the grass. As they began walking, Luka made his way up toward her father.

Jordan tried her hardest to keep her eyes straight ahead. But she couldn't help but focus to the side, wondering what her father's next move would be.

Jordan could see Luka walking into this fight empty handed. She couldn't let him. She was not about to watch her dead beat father kill Luka.

Once the three reached the top and were far enough away, Jordan pulled away from Owen. She began to take a few steps back toward the way they came from.

Owen reached for her. "Jordan."

Jordan pulled her arm forward, dodging his grip.

"Jordan," he repeated. "What the hell are you doing?"

Anna turned to see what all the fuss was about. "Are you out of your mind?"

Jordan sighed. "Can you guys just trust me for a second?"

"Not if it involves you getting killed, no." Owen huffed.

Jordan rolled her eyes and turned toward the direction of her father. Just looking at him made her sick. He was never good to her.

"Hey, Randy! Eyes up here." She shouted.

Her father's head shot up in her direction fast. She felt her stomach flop as they made eye contact. She almost felt like crying. His eyebrows furrowed as he dropped his arms to his sides. It was far away but Jordan swore she saw sadness replace the anger in his eyes.

"Luka, run!" Jordan yelled.

Paying no attention to Luka, Jordan's father kept his eyes on her. "Jordan?"

She felt her cheeks heat. She couldn't imagine the faces behind her. She couldn't imagine what they all thought of her right now. But more than anything, she felt overtaken by a wave of sadness. She wished this man in front of her wasn't her father. Either that, or simply that he was a better man.

Luka dashed up the hill, grabbing Jordan's arm in the process. "We need to go."

The four ran to the car faster than ever before. Jordan and Anna quickly got in first, jumping over to their side. Once they were all in the car, Owen locked the doors.

"You think that's going to help?" Luka scoffed. "That man looks like he could beat these doors in with his fists."

Owen shook his head as he grabbed the keys from his jeans pocket, quickly starting the ignition before throwing the car in drive. He took no time before stepping on the gas pedal, headed for the road.

Jordan leaned her head back against the seat and closed her eyes. She pictured her father's face as he looked over at her. She wondered what was going through his mind right now. Did he feel bad for the life he had? For never being there for her? She hoped he did. She hoped he regretted his shitty life after seeing her. But, she knew how her father was. His addiction and dealings mattered over anything else. Including feelings and family. She wondered how her mother put up with him for so long. Though, picturing his sad eyes she couldn't help but wonder if he was softening in his age. She shoved the thought to the side, not wanting to deal with that right now.

When she opened her eyes she noticed Owen looking over at her. She closed them again, this time out of embarrassment.

"You want to tell us what the hell happened back there?" Luka asked.

Jordan looked back to see Luka and Anna also staring at her. But, she noticed a realization in Anna's eyes.

"Oh my god." Anna threw her hand over her mouth. "I knew I had seen him before."

"Who is it?" Owen asked, keeping his eyes on the road.

Jordan took a deep breath. "That-"

Anna flung her hands in the air. "It's her father!"

A smile creeped to Jordan's mouth. "Thanks, Anna."

She shook her head. "I can't believe it. I should have figured that out."

"I'm sure you would have, detective." Jordan tried to soothe her. She knew how much Anna dreamt of being a detective one day.

"Wow." Luka scratched his chin. "You look nothing like him."

Jordan smiled. "I hope not."

"Wait." Owen looked over at her.

The smile on Jordan's face faded.

"My brother worked for your father?"

Jordan swallowed hard. "Yes. I'm sorry."

"He also beat you up." Luka reminded him.

"I'm also sorry about that." Jordan reached out to touch Owen's arm.

"You don't have to be sorry for any of this, Jordan. None of this is your fault."

Jordan smiled. She really hoped Owen felt that way. But, she would understand if this all changed his perspective of her.

"Speaking of," Luka butt in, "Should you really be driving? I'm not about to die at the hands of Owen Bentley."

Owen laughed hard. "Under no circumstances am I letting you drive my car."

Luka fell back against his seat and groaned. "Just be careful."

Owen rolled his eyes.

"Well that really sucked." Anna sighed.

"Not completely." Jordan grinned. "Do you still have it?"

Owen nodded. "It's in my sweater pocket."

Jordan reached over into Owen's pocket, grabbing the small ring. Anna and Luka kept their wide eyes on her. They looked as curious as the kids in *Charlie and The Chocolate Factory*.

Jordan held the small emerald ring between her index finger and thumb. "We did find something."

Luka jolted up. "That's Chelsea's."

Owen nodded. "Exactly. So what the hell was that guy doing with it?"

Thirty

Owen was about a block from the deli when he got a phone call. With one hand still on the wheel, he reached his other into his front jeans pocket. He could feel his three friends in the car eagerly watching him.

"Hello?"

"Owen Bentley?" A deep voice asked.

"Speaking."

"It's detective Carmen."

Owen felt his anger already beginning to rise even though nothing had happened yet. "Detective. What can I do for you?"

"Well, if you happen to be free right now, we have some more questions for you."

Owen sighed. "We've already talked."

"I'd like to speak with you again." He explained.

"Is this really necessary?" Owen asked as he felt an hand lightly brush his arm. He looked over to find Jordan looking back at him, eyes full of worry.

"Owen, please." The officer sighed. "It's just a few questions."

Owen felt his fingers grip around the steering wheel. "Fine."

"Glad to hear it. Are you free now? Maybe you could make your way down."

"You'll have to give me a few minutes." Owen told him.

"Sure thing." The officer said. "See you soon."

Owen hung up without saying another word. He felt his body full of anger as he pressed the gas pedal a little harder. He was sick of being questioned about his sister's murder.

"Owen." Jordan's voice snapped him back into reality. "Slow down."

Taking a breath, Owen let his foot off the gas pedal. "Sorry."

"What was that about?" She asked.

He shook his head. "One of the detectives just wants to talk to me again."

"Again?" Anna repeated.

He nodded. "They talked to me this morning. I'm surprised they want to talk to me again so soon."

"What were they talking to you about?" Jordan questioned.

"They were questioning me."

"As a suspect?" Jordan and Anna asked at the same time.

He nodded.

"What the fuck?" Jordan's voice was filled with rage. "They think you killed your brother?"

Owen shook his head. "I explained how I had nothing to do with that. But, that's when they started drilling me about Chelsea."

"Why the hell would they think you killed your sister?" Luka asked.

Owen shrugged. "Look, I don't know, guys. They'll realize they're wasting their time soon enough."

"You're damn right they will." Jordan leaned back in her seat. "Idiots."

"If anything I thought they would question Luka more, not you." Anna said.

Luka turned to look at her. "Thanks." He said, sarcastically.

She slapped his arm. "You know what I mean."

"Still. That hurt a little." Luka joked.

"Why would they want to question you again?" Jordan asked, getting back on the subject.

"I don't know." Owen admitted. "But this better be the last time."

"I'm going with you." She announced.

"No you're not."

"Yes-"

"Jordan." He stopped her. "You know that will cause nothing but more problems. I can handle this myself."

She sighed as she crossed her arms. "Fine."

"Not that I don't want to help you out," Anna leaned up between the two front seats. "But I have a shift at the deli in fifteen minutes."

Owen laughed. "Relax. That's where I'm going to drop you guys before I go."

"What about your uniform?" Jordan asked her.

Anna shrugged. "I'll grab an extra from the shop."

The rest of the drive there was silent, even though it was only a couple minutes. Anna was the first to step out of the car, making sure she wouldn't be late.

"You're sure you can drive with that eye, buddy?" Luka asked him.

Owen waved it off. "It's not too swollen yet. I'll be alright."

Luka nodded. "Call us if you aren't. Don't be too risky."

Jordan stayed glued to her seat as Anna and Luka headed inside. She looked over at him with furrowed eyebrows. Owen couldn't tell if she was worried or angry. He figured she was a little bit of both.

"I'll be fine." He told her. "It's no big deal."

"But it is!" She yelled. "They can't just accuse you like that."

He placed a hand on her leg. "I"m innocent and I will prove it. You have nothing to worry about."

"Why didn't you tell me about the first time?"

He shrugged. "I didn't want to worry you, like I have right now."

She sighed, defeated. "Okay, fine. But you better call me."

He smiled. "I will."

He watched Jordan until she was inside of the deli before speeding off.

When Owen got to the station, he felt lost. The place was full, both with officers and people just like him being questioned. He looked around the room attempting to find the officer he had spoken to his morning.

"Can I help you?" A officer with short brown hair, who Owen had never seen before asked him.

"Uh, yeah actually." Owen nodded. "I'm looking for officer Carmen."

Before the officer in front of him could speak, he heard a loud voice from behind him. "He's with me, Lenny."

Lenny, the officer in front of Owen, pointed behind him. "There he is, kid."

Owen quickly made his way across the room over to the familiar officer.

"How are ya?" He asked.

"Holding up." Owen admitted.

Carmen nodded. "What happened to your face?"

Owen reached up and rubbed a finger across the bruise. "Don't worry about it."

The officer furrowed his brows. "Well now I'm worried."

Owen sighed. "A guy from university hit me at a party. It's no big deal."

"Now why would he do that?"

"He thought I was looking at his girlfriend." He lied.

"Were you?"

"No."

The officer stared at him for a moment. "Interesting."

Owen was already growing tired of this. "Can we get on with this?"

"Sure. Right this way."

Owen began following him out of the main area and down a long hallway. Owen's mind was coming up with thousands of ideas of where this officer was going to take him. But, when they came upon the interrogation room, Owen could honestly say he was surprised. Sure, he knew he was here for questioning, but he thought this was a bit extreme.

"Right in here, Owen." Officer Carmen pointed into the direction of the room with his brown file, letting Owen enter first.

Hesitant, Owen stepped foot into the room. He walked in just a few steps before stopping in the middle of the floor. He turned around to look at the officer.

"Have a seat, Owen." His voice was stern and sent a shiver up Owen's spine.

Owen walked over to the table, taking a seat in one of the chairs. The officer followed behind, taking a seat across from him. Owen was beginning to feel anxious. He couldn't understand what he was doing here.

"Forensics updated me with the little they have." The officer said.

Owen felt nervous, but eager to know more. "What did they tell you?"

"Whoever hit your sister over the head was strong. It was a good blow. Just the one hit killed her."

"We already knew that." Owen sighed.

"Right, but it lead us to some new information." The officer explained. "They're saying whoever killed your sister was most likely a man, given the strength."

Owen nodded. He couldn't help it, but Jarid came to his mind.

"They also gave us a better timeline." He said.

Owen stayed silent, waiting for the officer to continue.

"She was found on the shore Friday morning at 8am and the forensics say she was killed twelve to fifteen hours before that. So, she was killed anywhere between 5 and 8pm Thursday night." The officer told him.

"Do you have any leads on who could have killed her?" Owen asked.

The officer narrowed his eyes at Owen. "Well, that bruise around your eye is telling me I might have one, yeah."

Owen raised his eyebrows.

"Come on, Owen. You expect me to believe your little story about some guy from your university punching you at a party?"

"Yes." Owen gritted his teeth.

"You could've at least said it was a bar fight." The officer rolled his eyes.

"You know what?" Owen shouted. "I'm getting real fucking sick of this."

"Then tell me the truth, Owen."

"I am!" Owen slammed his palm against the table. He was so angry he barely felt the pain. "I didn't kill my sister."

"You're sure that's the story you're going to stick to?" He asked.

"It's the truth."

The officer stayed silent and nodded.

"Then tell me one last thing." The officer said, finally.

"And what would that be?"

"Where were you Thursday April sixteenth between the hours of 5 and 8pm?"

"I had a football game that night. I was at the university." Owen told him.

"What time was your game?"

Owen leaned back in his seat. "6:00."

"So where were you at the hour of 5:00?" The officer asked.

Owen glared at him. "I was at home at my mom's house."

"And can anyone confirm that?"

"Yeah, my mom." Owen grumbled.

"You better hope so, kid."

Owen shook his head and scoffed, looking around the dark interrogation room feeling more anger than ever.

Thirty-one

Anna looked up when she heard the chime of the deli door bell. She looked up to see Owen walking in with his head down. He had his hands in his jeans pockets as he looked up and nodded at Anna. She gave him a small smile. She watched as he went over to the booth Jordan and Luka were sitting in. Curious to find out what happened, she jogged from behind the counter over to the booth.

"I'm taking fifteen, Mindy." She announced.

Mindy nodded. "No worries, An."

Anna quickly flashed her a small smile before sitting down beside Luka.

"Cute uniform." Luka smirked.

Anna rolled her eyes as she looked down at her two piece blue and white striped uniform. "Thanks."

Jordan turned to Owen. "How'd it go?"

He shrugged. "Just like before."

"They loaded you with questions?" Luka assumed.

Owen nodded.

"Yeah," Luka shook his head. "That's how mine went too."

"What did they ask you?" Anna asked him.

"A bunch of stupid questions." Owen answered. "And for an alibi."

"An alibi?" Jordan repeated.

"Yeah, for the night Chelsea was killed." He explained.

"They're so pathetic." Jordan scoffed. "They're wasting their time."

"Well," Anna began. "That's why we're on the case."

"Speaking of," Jordan looked down at her lap. "I'm really sorry I suggested we go back to the wharf. I should have known how angry my father would get when he found us."

Luka shook his head. "Don't be sorry. Anna and I had been there once already."

Anna looked over at Luka. Jordan and Owen had no idea what really happened the first time they went to the wharf.

"Yeah, but nothing bad happened to you guys that time." Jordan sighed.

If only you knew, Anna thought.

She looked back to Luka who was meeting her gaze. He had a look in his eyes Anna didn't recognize. Guilt? Regret? She really couldn't tell. Was he about to slip up and tell them what he had done to Jarid? Anna felt the need to save him.

"Still," Anna started. "It makes sense that since things wen't differently for Luka and I that you thought it might be easy this time."

Anna couldn't fully bring herself to lie to Jordan. It was true that things were way different for her and Luka the first time they stepped foot into that place.

Luka let out a sigh and nodded. Anna swore she could see his suit of armour reattach and that flat look returned in his eyes.

"I at least should have gone to distract him instead of you." Jordan turned to Owen.

"No." Owen shook his head. "I wouldn't have been able to live with myself if I let this be you." He pointed to his eye.

"I am curious though. How would your dad have reacted had it been you that went down there to keep him occupied?" Luka asked.

Jordan shrugged. "I like to think he wouldn't have punched me."

Anna nodded. "I caught a glimpse of sadness in his eyes when he saw you on the hill before we left."

"Yeah, me too." Jordan sighed. "Maybe he's starting to feel regret in his old age. I still hope we never have to see him again, though."

"I second that." Luka raised his bottle of soda before taking a sip.

"Yeah, let's never go back there. I've had enough of that place." Anna stated.

Owen reached in his pocket and pulled out the ring. "I think we've got what we needed anyway."

"I still can't understand why her ring was there." Luka pondered.

"Maybe she was there." Jordan suggested. "I just can't come up with a reason for why."

"I'm going to go out on a limb and say she wasn't." Anna said.

"What do you mean?" Luka asked as all three of her friends looked over at her with curious eyes.

"Well, where did you guys find the ring?" Anna asked.

"At the edge of the water." Owen answered.

"Right, okay." Anna nodded. "Even if she was there, what would she be doing by the water?"

The three stayed silent, coming to a blank.

"What are you saying, Anna?" Jordan questioned.

"I don't think Chelsea was there *alive*."

"What?" All three of them asked.

"Think about it. She was found on the beach." She began. "But, they say she was killed hours before that."

"So you think her body was brought to the wharf?" Luka began putting the evidence together.

"That's exactly what I think." Anna nodded. "They were trying to load her onto the boat and her ring slipped off. Nobody noticed, so it stayed there. They were all too worried about getting her into the water."

"All for her to wash up." Jordan shook her head.

"Yeah, their plan clearly didn't work." Luka sighed.

"I don't think it was thought out well enough." Anna suggested. "I think they panicked and were trying to do what they could before daylight."

Luka nodded. "Well done, detective Harvey."

Anna couldn't help but smile. "That's just my take."

"It makes sense, though." Owen said. "When you guys were there the first time, you never came across it?"

Anna shook her head. "It was dark."

And someone was being murdered so there wasn't much time to look.

"Right. So it could have easily been there since the night Chelsea was killed." Owen concluded.

"Yeah." Jordan agreed. "You guys were only there last night."

Anna nodded. She was beginning to feel anxious about last night being brought up.

"And Jarid's body was found this morning," She continued. "Do you think no one would have noticed it since Thursday night? That was five days ago."

Anna was trying her best to breathe evenly. She just wanted to get back to work and avoid this conversation. How had her and Owen not come to the conclusion of how close the two events of Jarid being found and her and Luka at the wharf were?

"It's a good possibility." Luka shrugged. "Do you think your dad would have noticed it?"

"I don't know a whole lot about him." Jordan admitted. "But I do know enough to say he's a very messy person. So the odds of him continuously passing by a ring without noticing it are pretty good."

"So the odds of your theory are looking good then, Anna." Luka smiled at her.

Before she could say anything, she saw a realization in Jordan's eyes. It was as if she could physically see her gears turning. *Here it comes.*

"Hang on." Jordan leaned her arms on the table. "Jarid's body was found this morning, which means he was most likely killed the night before."

Luka nodded, clearly oblivious to Jordan's conclusion. "Yeah, the updated article said he was killed around twelve hours before his body was found, just like Chelsea."

Jordan looked up at Anna with wide eyes. "That would mean Jarid was killed the same night you guys were at the wharf."

Anna could feel her heart in her throat. Here comes the conversation she had been trying to avoid.

Thirty-two

Anna had stopped breathing. She wasn't even sure her heart was still beating. Did Jordan think they had something to do with it? No, she couldn't, could she? Would she believe her best friend had something to do with a murder? Even if she technically did.

Her thoughts came to an end when Luka discreetly put his hand on hers on the seat beside them. It was behind the table so Jordan and Owen wouldn't see.

She felt a certain calmness from Luka's touch. Which felt really ironic in this situation.

"You're right." Luka said.

Jordan nodded. "It must've happened shortly after you guys left."

Anna finally let out a breath. *Oh Thank God.*

"That's a scary thought." Luka shook his head.

"Thank god you guys got out when you did, then." Jordan shuttered.

"That could have been us." Luka turned to Anna.

She looked up at him knowing the irony of what he had just said. It really could have been them, had Luka not killed Jarid instead.

"You guys said you saw him get on the boat?" Owen checked for clarification.

Luka continued to speak for both he and Anna. "Yeah, he got on just before we left."

Anna closed her eyes. She hated that lie. How many times was she going to have to hear Luka say that? She wished this whole thing would just end.

"So then comes the question of who killed Jarid." Owen sighed. "I can't ignore the similarities between his and Chelsea's case."

Anna held her breath again.

"Me either." Jordan agreed. "Especially how they were both killed and then dumped into the water."

"And they both were killed from a blow to the head." Owen added.

"But," Jordan began. "When the killer dumped Chelsea in the ocean, it looked like they were in a hurry, like Anna pointed out. So why did Jarid end up the same way?"

"Maybe his was unplanned too." Luka said, flatly.

Anna looked over at him. She wondered what was going through his mind right now.

"Okay." Jordan sighed. "So are we saying that we think both Jarid and Chelsea were dumped into the ocean at the wharf?"

"That's my guess." Anna nodded.

"We need to look for more similarities between the two cases." Jordan suggested.

Anna looked over at Luka. "I agree. That way we can figure out if we're looking at two different murderers or not."

Jordan nodded. "But I have a feeling we're not."

Anna furrowed her brows.

"Come on." Jordan scolded. "What are the odds that both victims are siblings? This is why I've been extremely worried about you." She turned to Owen.

"I told you, I'm fine." He snapped, waving it off.

"You should just stay alert." She told him. "You could be the next victim."

He nodded, knowing he wouldn't be able to stop her worry. "I will."

Anna stared at Owen silently as she thought about what had just been brought to her attention. What were the odds of two siblings being murdered five days apart?

"We need to do some more digging before we come to anymore conclusions." Anna inquired.

Jordan groaned. "This is so difficult."

Luka turned to Anna. "Yeah, and you want to do this for a lifetime."

She shrugged. "What can I say?"

Owen reached over and placed a hand on Jordan's leg. "We should all go get some rest. It's getting late."

"No, I really want to figure this out." She argued.

"Cases aren't solved in a day." Anna pointed out.

"Not unless you're really good." Luka laughed.

"I think even the best of detectives can't solve a case in a day, Luka." Anna sighed.

"Exactly." Owen nodded. "I'm exhausted."

"And bruised." Luka reminded him.

Jordan gave him a weak smile. "Yeah, you should get some rest."

"I've got to get back to work anyways." Anna sighed. "Besides, we found enough for tonight."

Luka nodded. "Exactly. It's not like we came back empty handed."

Owen held the ring up in front of him. "I'm keeping this by the way."

"I never planned to take it. You should have it. I found the bracelet I gave her anyway."

Anna sat back down in her seat fast after remembering what Luka had told her this morning. *The bracelet.* The one Luka had found on the shore. Something about that still didn't sit right with Anna.

Jordan took a drink from the glass in front of her. "What do you mean you found it?"

"Yeah," Anna jumped in. "You still haven't finished explaining that to me."

Luka threw up his arms in defence. "What's there to tell?"

"Why were you at the shore?" Anna barked.

"It's a beach, Anna. People go there." He responded.

Owen glared at Luka with his one eye that was still working. "The shore where Chelsea's body was found?"

"Yes, okay?" Luka looked overwhelmed as he slouched back in his seat. "But you guys make it seem a lot worse than it really is."

"You better start explaining then." Jordan's voice was stern.

"If you guys calmed down and let me, I would." He complained.

Owen kept his attention firmly on Luka. Anna could tell what he was thinking. He was walking down that same path of believing Luka had killed his sister.

"As you all know, Chelsea was on her way to my house the night she was killed." Luka began.

"That's a bit suspicious, don't you think, Anderson?" Owen asked, interrogating him.

Anna's chest suddenly felt like it weighed more than it really did.

Luka closed his eyes and let out a sigh. "Just give me a chance, Owen."

Jordan took Owen's hand in hers, while she kept her eyes on Luka.

"When she didn't show up, I text her only a couple times before I fell asleep. If I'm being honest I half expected her to show up in the middle of the night."

"But she didn't." Anna stated.

"Right." Luka nodded. "I figured she would at least call in the morning. I assumed it would be to end things, but still."

"Why?" Anna questioned. "Were things not going well between you two?"

Anna hated to admit it, but only part of her was asking that question as a detective. The other half of her was just curious about Luka's old relationships. She had heard through the vine that his and Chelsea's relationship was casual. She could feel herself beginning to grow jealous. She knew she had to stop. She needed to focus.

"I wouldn't say that." Luka shook his head. "Sure sometimes we fought about dumb things. Like how I told her she should get out of the house when Jarid comes over. She never listened to me, though."

"He was still her brother, Luka." Anna said.

Owen let out a loud sigh as he crossed his arms. "He was still dangerous. You had a fair point on that one."

"Thank you." Luka nodded.

The anger returned in Owen's eyes. "Get back to the story."

"The next day I still hadn't heard from her. I started to get worried." Luka looked down at the table as his eyes filled with sadness.

Anna was beginning to think Luka hadn't hurt Chelsea after all. Either that or he was really good at faking his emotions to hide the truth.

"I stopped by your mom's house." Luka turned to Owen. "She told me that Chelsea had left last night and didn't return home yet."

The other three in the booth couldn't rip their eyes from Luka. They were more than eager to find answers. Especially Anna, this being her first case and all.

"I thought maybe she had gone to one of her friends's houses or something." Luka let out a loud sigh."Until I started hearing sirens across town. I immediately got a terrible feeling in my gut."

He stayed silent for a while, trying to gather his thoughts.

"It was later that night when I went to the beach." He told them. "Once I had heard the news, I didn't believe it. I thought maybe if I went there I would either wake up from a horrible nightmare or it would give me clarification that she was really gone."

Anna saw the anger in Owen's eyes disappear and replace with confusion. She could tell he wanted to feel sorry for Luka, but wasn't sure if he was telling the truth. She could see it in Luka too. His eyes looked heavy. They looked genuine. Her detective skills were telling her that everything Luka was saying was true.

"Anyway," Luka snapped himself out of his sadness. "I began walking round, trying to clear my head when I saw something shiny in the sand."

"It was her bracelet." Anna finished for him.

He nodded. "Yeah. I bought it for her two weeks ago." He reached into his pocket and grabbed his wallet. Once his wallet was open, he reached in the large pocket and pulled out a small silver bracelet. It wasn't overly fancy, but it was shiny.

"Luka," Jordan gasped, leaning over the table to get a closer look. "It's beautiful."

He didn't say anything. Instead he kept his eyes steady on the bracelet.

"Look," He finally said, looking them all in the eye one by one. "I know you guys think I killed Chelsea. Sure we weren't in some long term relationship, but I could never hurt her. I know I act like I don't care sometimes. But truthfully, I don't know how to process it."

Anna wanted to hug him. But her thoughts of Luka's arms around her were debunked by her detective side bombarding her with questions.

"Hang on, that would mean you found the bracelet after her body was removed from the beach." She realized.

Luka nodded. "Right."

Anna could tell Luka had no idea what she was getting at. He was too wrapped up in his feelings right now.

"Why was the bracelet not on her?" She asked.

Luka furrowed his brows, forming wrinkles on his forehead. "I- I hadn't thought of that. I don't know."

"Are you thinking someone took it off her?" Jordan asked.

Owen ran a hand down his face. "But why leave it behind?"

"Maybe they didn't mean to." Anna explained. "Maybe whoever killed her wanted to take it in for money or something, but when they returned to the crime scene to get it, they dropped it."

"That's a good theory." Luka nodded.

"Perhaps whoever killed Chelsea is sicker than we thought and when she washed up they went back to see her body." Anna continued.

"So potentially, that could be evidence." Jordan pointed to the bracelet.

Anna nodded. "I know it's a long shot. But, Chelsea's killer's fingerprints could be on that bracelet."

Thirty-three

"We need to get this checked out." Anna decided.

Anna couldn't tell if Luka was just really tired and emotional or if he really just didn't know what was going on half the time. Either way, his obvious question didn't surprise her. "You mean like, get it checked for fingerprints?"

"No," Owen said sarcastically. "We're going to see if it's really hers."

Luka was about to make a snappy remark back, when Anna butted in. "Yes, Luka. We need to see if there are any strange fingerprints on it."

He shrugged. "What if they're just mine and Chelsea's?"

"Than at least we'll know that." Jordan chimed in. "It's better to know."

Anna couldn't agree more. This could be a big break in the case. She could have finally figured something out for real. During a real murder. But, she also knew she had to prepare herself for let down. For all she knew there were no other fingerprints on this bracelet.

Luka sighed. "I guess. But let's do it tomorrow."

Anna wanted to scream at him. Tomorrow? They needed to figure this out now. She couldn't tell why he wasn't willing to give it up, but assumed it was because it was Chelsea's.

"You'll get it back." She told him.

He looked over at her and shrugged. "I know. It's no big deal."

"Then we should go take it in now." She insisted.

"Luka, you want to find out who killed her as much as I do, don't you?" Owen asked, narrowing his eyes to look at him.

"Yes, of course." He answered. "But I really need to go check on my mom. We'll take it to the station first thing tomorrow. I promise."

"How is she, anyway?" Jordan asked, gently.

"She's holding up."

"I miss seeing her at the bakery everyday." She smiled softly.

Luka returned a saddened smile and nodded.

Anna wanted to protest, but she couldn't argue about his mom. She knew she wasn't getting any better. Luka's family wasn't sure how much time she had left.

Before anyone could say anything else, Luka's phone rang. Furrowing his brows, he picked it up. "Hello?"

Anna looked over at him.

"Yeah, that's me." He said. "Yeah, I can come in."

Anna looked over at Jordan with a questioning look that she returned.

"Yeah, alright. Bye." Luka grumbled.

"What is it?" Anna was the first to speak.

Luka turned to Owen. "I'm assuming your alibi checked out?"

Owen shrugged. "Why?"

"Because now they want to talk to me."

Anna's jaw dropped even though she didn't feel surprised. "What the hell?"

He shook his head. "It's fine. I'm sure they'll just ask me some dumb questions like they did with Owen."

Jordan nodded. "You must be their newest suspect if Owen is off the list."

"Fuckers." Anna spit out. "They sure know how to waste time."

"That's why we need you." Jordan smiled.

Owen pointed a finger in Anna's face. "Yeah. So stay in university, detective."

Anna laughed. "Will do."

"Alright." Luka groaned as he stood. "I guess I should head over."

"Did you want any of us to come?" Anna asked.

Luka gave her a funny look. "You need to get back to work, slacker."

She rolled her eyes. "Relax. I will."

"I'll be fine." He told her.

"Keep us updated." Jordan shouted as he walked out the door.

Anna leaned her head back against the seat, still avoiding work. "I really hope that bracelet gets us somewhere."

Owen nodded. "Me too."

The quietness of the deli was overtaken by the sound of two teenage girls walking through the deli door.

"I know he didn't kill his sister. He was just forced to help clean up her body by his asshole boss." One of them whispered, but the deli was quiet enough that Anna could still hear.

Anna whipped her head around to see who they were. She recognized the girl with long brown hair. She had seen her once when she came into the deli with Jarid, right before they had followed him.

"I can guarantee it was his dirty boss that killed him. Jarid always talked about him and how shitty he was. He said he roughed him around a lot and was never fair to him. I mean, he was literally arrested once for charges that should have been put on his boss."

Anna couldn't rip her eyes off the girl. She wasn't surprised to hear that Jarid was arrested in the past. He looked like he'd spent a few nights in county jail before.

"She's talking about Jarid." Owen whispered.

"And my dad." Jordan nodded.

Tuning them out, Anna kept her eyes on the girl. Part of her wanted to go up to her, but she knew she couldn't do that. She knew what really happened to Jarid.

"I recognize her." Jordan stared at the girl, trying to figure out who she was. "She was here that night you guys followed Jarid to my dad's wharf."

Owen nodded. "And you and I heard her saying a bunch of suspicious things."

Anna turned to them. "I think she and Jarid dated."

Owen's eyes went wide. "I can't believe he got a girlfriend."

Anna shrugged. "Look at her. She's too young to know any better."

"And too young to be dating your twenty four year old brother." Jordan shook her head.

"I guarantee her parents definitely didn't know anything about it." Anna looked back toward the girl.

"Jarid probably knew she would be easy to get because of her age, unfortunately." Owen sighed.

Jordan's voice was light and filled with sadness. "What a shame."

Once the two girls got their pizza, they sat down at one of the booths beside the window facing the main road.

Jarid's girlfriend looked her friend straight in the eye. "I can guarantee I know exactly what happened to him. I know that horrible coward of a boss killed him. And I'm going to prove it."

Thirty-four

I was sitting in my usual chair in the garage scrolling through *Facebook* when I saw the article. "**Another Body found on Edgar Cove Beach**." I was shocked at first. Who else had used my dumping spot? Not that it was a regular thing for me. Chelsea was my first kill. And she will be my last. I never had any intentions on killing. I was just forced to kill her under unfortunate circumstances. She was just at the wrong place at the wrong time.

I thought back to Chelsea's bracelet. It wasn't anything too special. It was beautiful, though. I was surprised Luka had decided to spend any money on the girl.

After I had dumped her body at the wharf, I remembered the bracelet. When I had grabbed her, I grabbed her wrist. I knew I had most likely left my fingerprints on it. I was hoping it would have washed off in the water, but I had a nasty gut feeling it didn't considering the size of it. It was a bracelet she could clip onto her wrist, leaving little to no room to slip around or fall off. I rushed back to the dock, stealing it off her wrist before either of us had a chance to dump her body.

Once her body was found Thursday morning, I had gone to the beach to look at the scene like many people from town did. But unfortunately while I was there, It slipped out of my pocket on the way out.

I was so focused on blending in and putting on the sad act, I hadn't realized it wasn't secure in my pocket like I thought it was. I was too scared to place it anywhere but on me, so I kept it in my pocket for safety. But, apparently it wasn't safe anywhere.

I clicked on the article to see what it was about. It talked about some Twenty-four year old Jarid Bentley. Bentley? Hang on, isn't that Chelsea's last name? After a quick google search, it was confirmed. Jarid was Chelsea's *brother*.

I hadn't expected this. Two siblings found on the same beach? Both murdered? It looked like things were looking up for me after all. It would have been good enough if the two weren't siblings. Just someone dumping another body down that way was enough to save my ass. Everyone will think they're connected. The police will have to look into the most recent murder. Hopefully that guy will be caught and given charges for both murders. Hopefully whoever this other guy is, saves my ass.

Thirty-five

Luka pulled up to the same familiar building. Flashbacks of that afternoon he was brought here in the back of a police car flashed through his head. He remembered how claustrophobic and sick he had felt in the backseat, much like he felt now. He wasn't sure why. It was just another questioning. It shouldn't be a big deal.

Taking a deep breath, He slipped the bracelet out of his pants pocket and back into his truck dash. He walked up to the front doors. Once he stepped in, he was greeted by the same officer who had driven him here last time.

"Luka Anderson." He greeted. "Good to see you."

Luka nodded. "Officer Marvin." He couldn't say the same. Truthfully, Luka didn't think it was good to see Marvin. This was the last place he wanted to be.

"Let's head on down here." Marvin said, turning his back to Luka as he lead him down the hall.

Luka walked behind him through the hallway, down a long corridor. The corridor was fairly empty aside from the odd door to a room and the pictures of retired officers hanging on the wall.

Once they reached the small interrogation room, Marvin stopped at the door. He turned sideways, letting Luka enter first. Once he was in Marvin followed as he carefully shut the door behind him.

"Have a seat." Marvin told him.

Luka didn't say anything as he walked around to the other side of the table to take a seat. The chair scratched the floor as he pulled it out before sitting.

"So," Luka began. "What do I owe the pleasure?" He asked, sarcastically.

Marvin pursed his lips as he sucked in a breath. "I just had a few more questions for you, Luka."

Luka nodded. "Ah, a second round."

Luka wasn't sure why he was acting out. He assumed it was because he didn't want to be here and was annoyed he was asked to come back in.

"If you cooperate we can be done faster, you know."

Luka rolled his eyes. He wanted to continue to piss off Marvin, but decided to let it go if he wanted to be out of here fast.

Marvin took the time to explain that they were much closer to the exact date and time that Chelsea was murdered. Luka couldn't help but suck in a breath.

"Why are you telling me this?" Luka asked.

"I thought you'd be happy about that information."

"I am. But I still don't see why I had to come here to find that out from you."

Marvin placed his arms on the table, folding his hands together. "So you want to get straight to the questions then."

Luka shrugged. "Sure."

"Where were you Thursday night between 5 and 8pm?"

Luka sighed. "In my room."

Marvin raised his eyebrows. "You were at home?"

"Yes." Luka nodded. "She was supposed to come over to my house. I've told you that before."

"Right." Marvin tapped his chin. "And you were home for all three hours?"

"Yes." Luka grumbled. "I didn't go anywhere that night."

"Not even outside to check if Chelsea showed up?" He asked.

"No. At the time I didn't really care if she showed up or not." Luka admitted.

"Why's that?"

Luka leaned forward so that his elbows were on the table. "You saw the texts. We were fighting."

"That's right." Marvin's eyes widened as he remembered. "You seemed pretty angry at her."

"I just wanted her off my back."

"Well, she is now." He put forth.

Luka sighed as he looked at his lap. "This wasn't what I meant. I never wanted this to happen."

"But it's real ironic, isn't it?" Marvin looked directly into Luka's eyes.

Luka looked to the cold concrete floor as he shifted in his chair.

"Well," Officer Marvin began. "Can anyone vouch for you being home that night?"

Luka rubbed his hands down his face. "My mom was home."

"Your mom?"

Luka nodded.

Officer Marvin laughed. "Of course. The only person who can confirm where you were is your mom." He shook his head and leaned back in his seat.

Luka furrowed his brows. "Is that an issue?"

Officer Marvin shrugged. "I just think it's funny."

"Why's that?" Luka gritted his teeth.

"I don't know many mothers who wouldn't back their son up on something like this." He told him. "Especially if it's a cop asking."

Luka couldn't help but laugh. "So you're saying you don't believe me."

Officer Marvin looked Luka directly in the eye, making Luka shiver. "I'm just saying, I'll be keeping a close eye on you."

Luka slammed his right palm against the table. "I didn't kill Jarid, okay?"

Officer Marvin stared at him silently, making Luka realize what he had just said. Not knowing how to fix things, he immediately started rambling. "Chelsea. I didn't kill Chelsea."

"Did you know Jarid, Luka?" Marvin asked, crossing his arms.

Fuck, He thought. He knew he had messed up now.

"No." Luka answered. "Not really, anyway."

"It's a yes or no question."

"I only met him once." Luka stammered.

"Once is enough to decide to commit murder." Officer Marvin pointed out. "In fact, some sick people murder people they don't even know."

Luka tried to act normal, but couldn't help his shaking leg underneath the table. "I didn't kill anyone."

"I almost believed you before." The officer clicked his tongue. "But now I don't know what to think."

"So where were you last night?" Officer Marvin grinned.

Luka took a deep breath as he thought about what he was going to say. He could say he was home again, but that wouldn't make him look any better.

"I was with a friend." He shrugged.

The officer raised his eyebrows. "Does this friend have a name?"

Luka's mouth moved faster than his mind. "Anna Harvey." He blurted.

Officer Marvin nodded. "And she can confirm you were with her?"

"She can." Luka closed his eyes regretting his decision. Anna had already had to witness what he had done, she shouldn't have to cover for him too.

"Well, Luka." Officer Marvin started. "You better hope your friend is as good as you think she is."

Luka knew he needed to get out of here before he did any worse damage. Without permission, Luka stood up and stormed out of the interrogation room.

Thirty-six

I parked my car on the side of the road across from the police station. I was quick to turn off the lights and cut the engine. Once my car was silent, I looked toward the police station parking lot as I watched Luka pull into a parking spot and cut his own engine.

I knew Luka had what I wanted. That bracelet. I needed it back. I know my fingerprints are on there. Normally it wouldn't occur to Luka to ever get it checked for that sort of thing. But, I couldn't help but notice he has some new friends who are most likely a little smarter than he is. I figure it's better to be safe than sorry.

As I was driving home from town I saw his truck parked at the deli. I decided to sit and wait to see where he was headed. I knew eventually I would get an opportunity to get it back. I think now might finally be that time.

I sat there patiently waiting for him to leave his truck. He seemed to be taking a long time.

"Come on, Luka." I muttered to myself.

As if on cue, the driver door finally opened. Luka stepped out of the truck and looked around, as if he could feel my eyes on him. I leaned back in my seat a little, making sure he couldn't see me. But, I knew it was dark enough out that he couldn't.

He began walking toward the building with his dark hair blowing in the wind. Once he got to the front doors, he looked behind him.

Once he was inside I waited a few more moments before springing into action. I stayed in my vehicle until I felt it was safe. I looked around to make sure there were no cars coming before hopping out of my vehicle. I was sure to keep in the shadows until I crossed the street into the parking lot. Luckily, there was no one out here right now.

I walked directly up to the driver's side door of Luka's truck. I reached the handle and gave it a pull, but it was locked. *Shit*. I should've known. I knew I didn't have much time and needed to figure out what I was going to do. Without thinking too deeply, I threw my elbow into the driver's window, smashing it. I turned my head away from the truck, avoiding the flying shards of glass.

Once it was open I stuck my hand in and opened the door. I climbed into the truck and sat in the driver's seat. Pulling out my phone, I began to look around. I knew there was no guarantee he had left the bracelet in his truck, but I was feeling hopeful tonight.

I checked the console first, finding nothing but fast food napkins and a phone charger. I figured the only other place he could keep it here would be the glove compartment. Still hopeful, I pulled it open. I fumbled around with what was inside. Some more napkins, a Kleenex box, his truck papers. Finally, the bracelet brushed my fingers. I felt a jitter of excitement rush through my body as I picked it up, putting it under my phone flashlight to look at it. The silver shined under the light. It was exactly what I had been looking for.

Realizing where I was, I hopped back out of Luka's truck. I checked my surroundings before shutting the door gently. Cuffing the bracelet tight in my palm, I ran back across the street to my own vehicle. Once I was inside I locked the doors. I opened my palm to stare down at the bracelet in the dim moonlight shining through the window. As I looked down at it I couldn't help but grin.

Thirty-seven

Anna set the deli's broken mop down to text back Jordan when the door flew open. She could tell by how fast the little bell up top jingled, something was going on. When she looked up she spotted Luka scanning the place. His face was pale and his eyes were wide.

"Luka?" Anna kept her voice soft.

Luka whipped his head her way and began jogging toward her. "Oh, thank god."

Anna stopped mopping and gave him her full attention. "What's wrong?"

"The bracelet." Luka blurted. "It's gone."

Anna stared at him for a moment, trying to understand him. "What do you mean it's gone?"

He shrugged. "I don't know, Anna. It's just gone."

"Where did you leave it?" She asked him.

"I put it back in the glove compartment." He explained. "Somebody smashed my truck window in and stole it."

"Somebody smashed your window?" She shouted.

Luka looked around to see if there was anyone in the deli to hear them. Luckily, there was not. "Yes. It happened when I was inside the police station."

Anna's eyes went wide. "In the police station parking lot? That's risky."

Luka nodded. "I know. But whoever it was got what they wanted."

Anna's detective instincts began to kick in. "Did you notice anything else missing?"

Luka thought for a moment. "No. Just the bracelet."

Anna set the mop back in the bucket and leaned it against the counter.   "Interesting. Clearly they were strictly on a search for that bracelet then. The only question is why."

Luka shook his head, defeated. "I really don't know."

"How would they even know the bracelet was there?"

"They must have guessed."

"Wow." Anna sat on one of the stools in front of the counter. "That's a risk."

"A big risk." Luka agreed.

"How would they even know you had it?" Anna set her chin in her palm.

"I don't know, Anna." Luka cried. "All I know is I want it back."

"Do you think there would be any footage?"

"From the police station?" Luka asked for clarification.

Anna nodded. "Do you think they'd look for us?"

"Not while I'm a suspect." Luka reminded her.

"I take it your questioning didn't go well then?"

"Well my truck got broken into, so no."

Anna rolled her eyes. "I meant the actual questioning, Luka."

"I know." Luka looked to the ground. "I fucked it up."

"What do you mean?"

"I slipped up."

"What?" Anna choked out.

"I said Jarid's name." Luka kept his voice low even though they were the only two in the shop.

Anna froze as she kept her eyes on him. "What did you say?"

"I told them I didn't kill him." He whispered.

"But did they ask about him?" Anna was afraid of the answer.

Luka stayed silent but shook his head.

Anna stood from the stool and began to pace around the shop. "Luka, that's bad."

"I know." He admitted. "But it's not like they have anything on me."

"But now they'll look into you." She rubbed her hands down her face.

"They can't prove anything."

"That's not the point, Luka."

"I know." Luka began to pace around. "The point is I need to find out who took that bracelet."

"And get a new truck window." Anna reminded him.

"Right." He sighed. "That too."

"Did anyone know you kept it in your truck?" Anna asked.

"No one even knew I bought it except for Chelsea when I gave it to her."

"Oh boy." Were the only words Anna could find.

"I don't know what the hell is going on, Anna." She could have cried at how desperate his voice sounded. "I want that bracelet back."

"And we'll get it back." She did her best to make her voice sound certain. But there was no guarantee.

He nodded.

"They'd have to be desperate for it to break into your truck in the middle of the police station parking lot." Anna pointed out.

"That's what makes me think it was the killer." Luka's voice was casual.

Anna stared at him. "What?"

"I think whoever killed Chelsea stole that bracelet."

"Why would a murderer break into your truck?"

Luka threw up his arms. "I don't know. Do you have any better conclusions?"

Anna thought for a moment. "No." She paused. "You may have a point."

Luka's eyes widened in surprise. "Really?"

Anna rolled her eyes. "Don't worry, I'm surprised too."

Luka threw up his middle finger at her.

"It makes sense, though. Who else would want that bracelet that bad?" Anna realized. "It wasn't worth much was it?"

Luka shook his head. "God, no."

"You sound like a great boyfriend." She said sarcastically.

Luka shook his head, but smirked.

Anna spun back around on her stool. "That would mean whoever killed Chelsea tailed you to the police station."

"I know!" Luka whisper yelled. "That's why I'm so freaked out."

"We don't know it was her killer, though."

"But I know it was, Anna." He looked deep into her eyes. "I can feel it in my gut. We need to find Chelsea's killer."

Anna nodded as she grabbed her phone out of her uniform pocket. "Okay."

"What are you doing?" Luka asked. There was a hint of worry in his voice.

"Texting Jordan." She answered. "This is a big deal. We all need to be together to figure this out."

Luka didn't say a word but kept his eyes on Anna eagerly.

She began typing a message to Jordan when she heard Luka let out a loud sigh. She looked up to see an uneasy expression written on his face. "What's wrong?"

"I don't think they'll believe me."

"What are you talking about?"

He sighed again. "Owen and I always seem to be walking on thin ice. Maybe he really doesn't think I'm the one who killed Chelsea anymore. But this could change his mind."

Anna set her phone down on the counter and looked up at him. She was trying to understand what he was saying. "You think because someone stole her bracelet, that Owen will suddenly believe you're a murderer again? How does that even go together, Luka?"

"I don't think he'll believe someone took it." He closed his eyes.

Anna could feel his fear from across the room. If there was one thing she knew, it was that she believed Luka. If someone else didn't, that was their own problem.

"I think your shattered window will be enough evidence." She pointed out.

"Or he'll think I made this all up." He shook his head. "That I broke it myself to look more believable."

Anna squinted her eyes. "You're being a bit dramatic."

"Come on, Anna. Think about it." He sighed. "What are the odds of the bracelet being stolen right after you guys said we should hand it over to the police? Especially when Owen knew the last thing I wanted was to give it to someone else. Not that that part matters, anyway. Considering it's in the hands of somebody else now."

Anna stayed seated on the stool silently. She could see Luka's point. She hated for Luka's sake that he and Owen were on icy terms. But, she could understand why Owen would hate everyone until he found out who killed his sister.

"We'll convince them." She finally said. "We will make them understand that you are telling the truth."

He looked at her as if she were speaking a language he didn't understand. "What?"

"Just from the fact that you don't have the bracelet with you and
the panic expression on your face, I can tell you're telling the truth."
Anna said. "Not to mention the broken window."

"So?"

"So they will too, Luka."

He chuckled, unconvinced. "Jordan maybe. I don't know about
convincing Owen though."

Anna sighed. She was getting annoyed at the fact that Luka had
to think people wouldn't believe him, when this situation could have
endangered him had it gone wrong. "Fine. You don't have to if you
don't want to. But I will."

"What do you mean?"

"I'll fight for you. I will make sure that they believe that somebody
really broke into your truck and stole Chelsea's bracelet from you."

He looked stunned. He looked as though he hadn't heard Anna
right.

"Why would you do that?" He stared at her.

"I believe you, Luka."

She swore she could see his cheeks starting to blush in the dim deli
lighting.

"Kiss me." Was all he said.

She genuinely thought she heard him wrong. There was no way he
had just said that.

"What?"

But she didn't, as his deep voice said again, "Kiss me."

Thirty-eight

Anna hadn't slept all night. In fact, she had barely gotten through the rest of her shift at the deli. Between the few customers and texting Jordan, she had attempted to distract herself. But, it didn't work. Too much had happened. Chelsea's killer had broken into Luka's truck. Luka had kissed her. *Luka had kissed her.* She still hadn't fully processed that last one yet. She wanted to tell Jordan about it each time she sent her a text, but she knew she couldn't yet.

After they had kissed, Anna had promised him she would tell Jordan that she and Owen had to meet them at the deli after classes.

Luka had seemed to relax more once she had explained to him that she believed him and no matter what, she would help him find that bracelet. And Chelsea's killer.

Once the early afternoon hours had arrived and they were all finished with classes for the time being, they all made their way to the deli. Luka had offered they meet up at the bar, but Anna knew if she started drinking now, she wouldn't make it to her class tonight at six.

Anna was the first to arrive, ordering a strawberry milkshake, while she scrolled through *vsco* as she waited for her friends to get there.

To her surprise, Luka was the next to arrive. His hands had a little grease on them from just finishing up a car from his mechanic class. If she was being honest, she was surprised to see him. She didn't think he would show up at all. She thought maybe he wanted her to tell Jordan and Owen about what had happened, just in case things do go south.

"Hey." His voice seemed jittery. "You're here early."

She scooched over, allowing room for him to sit next to her. "You are too. I'm really glad you're here." She could smell the oil on his clothes.

He flashed her a genuine smile. "Thanks. Me too."

She noticed him exhale deeply. "Are you sure you're okay? You seem a little on edge. And like you could use a shower."

He chuckled lightly. "I'm okay. Just a lot going on. As for the shower, I definitely could use one, yeah."

She gave him a soft smile, hoping it would calm him down. To her avail, it seemed to work. Anna couldn't help but notice the way his eyes focused on hers. She wondered if he had thought about their kiss since it happened. She couldn't stop thinking about it.

"Everything will be okay." Anna reached over and grabbed his hand. "I'm on your side."

He let out a sigh of relief as he curled his fingers, squeezing her hand tightly. She took it as a silent "Thank you".

The doorbell above the door rang as Jordan and Owen entered.

"Hey, guys." Jordan said as she scooted into the seat across from Anna and Luka. "You said you had some news?"

Anna nodded. "Big news."

"Let us in on it then." Owen told her as he rubbed his hands together.

Anna looked over to see where Luka stood on all of this. She hadn't expected it, but he was already looking over at her. He didn't look scared, but his eyes were asking her to do the talking for him.

"Whoever killed Chelsea isn't over it."

Jordan furrowed her brows. "What do you mean?"

"The bracelet Luka had yesterday, It's gone."

"What do you mean it's gone?" Jordan asked.

"I mean someone took it." Luka answered. He began sucking his bottom lip out of nervousness.

"Hang on," Owen lifted up his arm to stop them from talking. "You're telling me someone stole the bracelet you gave Chelsea?"

Luka nodded. "They stole it out of my truck."

"The one piece of possible evidence we had?" Owen's neck began turning red.

Anna knew this is what Luka expected. While she believed Owen had every right to be frustrated considering it was his sister's case, she hated how he constantly blew all his anger toward Luka.

"I know, okay?" Luka sighed. "This is bad."

"How do we know you're not lying?" Owen barked.

There it is.

"Really Owen?" Anna could feel her body getting tense. "Go look at the busted window in his truck."

Luka nodded. "It's not hard to see that there's no longer any glass on the driver's side."

"The bracelet had value to you. It makes sense you wouldn't want to give it up." Owen shrugged. "That's all I'm saying."

"But it's something we needed to give up." Anna couldn't tell if Jordan was saying that to stay on Owen's side, or if she didn't believe someone stole the bracelet.

"Look, guys." Luka began. "I really do not have that bracelet anymore, okay? I wish I did."

Jordan and Owen didn't look convinced.

"Look at him." Anna pointed to Luka. "Can't you see it in his eyes? The hint of fear and sadness? He obviously doesn't have the bracelet."

Jordan's eyes studied Luka's face. Anna could see a realization form in her eyes as she sighed. She believed him.

One down, one to go.

"Why would he lie about this?" Anna turned so she was directly talking to Owen. "Clearly someone broke into his truck. The missing window is enough to prove that, Owen."

Owen sighed. "I know. But why would someone steal it? How would they even know it was in there?"

Luka shrugged. "Clearly someone was desperate."

"I believe you." Owen let out a shaky breath. "I'm sorry, man. Things are just so frustrating. It's like we're getting no where in Chelsea's case."

Luka nodded. "I know."

"But we're getting somewhere now." Anna brought forth. "Who else would be that desperate to steal that bracelet in the middle of the police station parking lot than Chelsea's killer?"

Owen leaned back in his seat. "That's true."

"How would they even know you were there?" Jordan asked.

"They must have tailed me."

"Luka, they could have killed you." Jordan's face filled with fear.

Luka nodded. "Yeah, I haven't really processed that part yet."

"That must not have been the guys plan." Anna suggested.

"Or girl." Jordan said. "We really don't know who we're looking for."

Anna nodded. "That's true."

"Either way, they obviously got what they came for." Jordan looked at Luka. "They probably won't come back for you."

Anna nodded in agreement. "They have what they want."

Owen's voice went stern. "Now we just need to get it back."

Thirty-nine

They all left the deli to go take a look at Luka's broken window. Luka led the three out the front door and down the alleyway to where his truck was parked.

"That's a broken window alright." Owen nodded.

"Who the hell would do this?" Jordan moved closer to the truck.

"Like I said," Luka began. "Whoever killed Chelsea."

Anna walked over so she could get a closer look at the truck. "There doesn't seem to be any other damage. Just a broken window."

"Yeah well that window is gonna cost me." Luka sighed. "I need to run over to my dad's auto shop and get him to order a new one in for me."

"Want to go now?" Anna asked.

Luka furrowed his brows. "You guys want to come?"

Anna shrugged. "Why not?"

"I've got nothing better to do." Jordan piped up.

"Unless you're hiding something." Owen joked.

Luka flipped up his middle finger at him. "Get in the truck."

Laughing, they all hopped into Luka's truck. Anna sat in the passenger seat, per usual. Luka couldn't help but feel a smile creep to his lips at the thought of her wanting to sit next to him.

Luka drove them straight to his dad's auto shop. He really hoped his dad wasn't busy. He needed a new window. He knew he could only get away with not having a window for so long. Besides that, it was getting annoying, considering how much time Luka spends on the highway.

He pulled the truck into the shop and saw that no cars were being worked on right now. *Perfect.* That meant his dad was inside. He took off his seat belt and began reaching for the door handle.

"Did you want some company or did you want to go in alone?" Anna asked, placing a hand on his arm to stop him from moving.

"Uh," he began, honesty not sure. He looked back at Jordan. "Your mom does work here, if you want to come in." *She does a lot more than work here.* Luka really hoped *that* wasn't going on right now.

Jordan shrugged. "Sure, if you don't mind."

He shook his head. "It might be better anyway. You could talk to her so I can get my dad's full attention." *And keep him off your mom.*

Jordan didn't seem to ask any questions about the way he worded things and began getting out of the truck.

"Yay. A little Luka and Jordan team up." Anna joked.

Luka noticed Owen look at Anna with a questioning look. He could tell he was jealous. Feeling cocky, he enjoyed it.

"Let's go, Jordan."

When they entered, Luka noticed his dad standing at the front counter with his back to them. At first he assumed he was talking to Jordan's mom, Meghan, but quickly noticed she wasn't sitting in her usual seat.

"Hey, dad." Luka called out.

Chad was quick to turn around. "Hey, son." He took immediate notice to Jordan standing next to him. "Hey, Jordan. How are you?"

She gave him a friendly smile. "I'm fine, thanks."

Luka noticed the shocked expression on his dad's face from seeing Luka bring Jordan with him. He quickly shook his head as to tell him nothing was going on there. What his dad didn't know is Luka was much more focused on Anna.

"What brings you in?" His dad asked, setting his pen down on the papers in front of him, turning his full attention to Luka and Jordan.

"I just wanted to ask you something."

"And what would that be?"

"I was wondering if you could order me in a new window." He told him.

Chad nodded. "Oh, that's right. I meant to do that today after you told me what happened last night."

"So you'll be able to?" Luka asked.

"I'll order it today and install it as soon as it comes in."

"Thanks, dad."

Chad leaned his body against the counter behind him. "Have you reported this to the police yet?"

Luka shook his head.

"You should get on that. They could have camera footage."

"That's a good point, actually." Jordan piped up.

Chad nodded again. "Thanks, Jordan. I hope you'll consider it, Luka. This is a big deal, you know."

"I know." Luka sighed.

"Good. Anything else for you two?"

"That's it I believe." Jordan smiled.

Right as they were about to turn, Jordan's mom walked out of the back room. "Oh, hey, Honey." She waved.

Jordan looked up at her mom. "Hey."

"What are you doing here?"

Jordan gestured in Luka's direction. "Luka just stopped in to ask his dad something. I'd figured I'd come in and say hi to you while he did."

Her mom smiled. "Well, I'm glad you did."

Jordan carried on the conversation as if everything was normal. But things were not normal. Jordan must have been too focused on her mother's face while she was talking and didn't notice what was nearly sending Luka over the edge as he stood beside her.

Luka couldn't tell if he was crazy or not as Meghan reached an arm up to push some hair out of her face. Was he seeing things? Was he too obsessed with getting Chelsea's bracelet back? But, he decided he wasn't crazy. There was no question what he was seeing in front of him.

The gold that sat around Meghan's wrist looked all too familiar.

Forty

Jordan exited the auto shop first with Luka behind her. As they began walking back towards the truck, she felt satisfied. She was glad Luka was getting his truck all fixed up. She was also happy that she ran into her mom. Now if she didn't go over this week, it wouldn't matter.

"Your dad has a really good point about telling the police. Maybe the idiot who broke into your truck was caught on camera."

Luka stopped walking and stood in front of her so she would have to stop walking too. "Did you really not see that, Jordan?"

Jordan looked at him with her face full of confusion. "What the hell are you talking about?"

"The bracelet your mom has on. It looks a hell of a lot like the one I just lost."

Jordan could feel her anger rising. "Are you suggesting my mom broke into your truck and stole Chelsea's bracelet? And for what, so she could wear it?"

If she was being honest, she hadn't even noticed her mom was wearing a bracelet.

Luka shrugged. "I don't know. Nothing is adding up."

"I'll go in there right now and ask her about it if that will make you happy."

Luka nodded. "That would be great actually."

Jordan hated how snarky his voice sounded. Her mother was a lot of things, but a thief wasn't one of them. Breaking into Luka's truck is the last thing her mother would ever do.

Jordan opened the door and saw her mother sitting at the front desk where she left her.

She looked up from her seat. "Hey. Did you forget something?"

Jordan forced a laugh. "I just couldn't help but notice your bracelet."

Her mom lifted her arm and used her other hand to rub a finger across the gold.

Jordan stared down at it. *The gold. Holy shit. Luka was right.* That bracelet looked too much like the one Luka had showed them at the deli.

"Someone gave it to me." She smiled.

"Really?" Jordan asked, feeling very curious. "And who would that be?"

Her mom's cheeks turned pink. "Someone special."

Jordan leaned onto the front counter toward her mom. "Someone I'll meet?"

Jordan already knew the answer. Jordan either didn't meet her mom's boyfriends, or she met them at the wrong time.

Her mom shrugged. "Maybe sometime."

There it was. The same answer every time. She wasn't disappointed, it was what she expected. But she still couldn't wrap her head around that damn bracelet. Did her secret boyfriend manage to buy some bracelet right as Jordan and her friends were looking for Chelsea's? The odds were slim but the idea is what kept her sane. Her mom could not have done this. Jordan still cared about her mom, even if she sucked sometimes.

"Well, either way," Jordan shrugged. "The bracelet is beautiful."

"It is, isn't it?" Her mom smiled. "Thanks, Honey. I wish he would tell me where he bought it, though. I would love to see more of their jewellery.

Jordan chucked. Of course she would. Her mom was very materialistic. "He didn't tell you where he got it?"

Her mom shook her head in disappointment. "I'll just have to ask again."

What the hell?

Jordan nodded. "You do that. I'd love to know. I'm in need of some new jewellery."

Her mom didn't say anything but smiled.

"Well, I need to run. My friends are waiting for me."

Her mom nodded. "It was good to see you. You know, since you're never home."

As Jordan turned she couldn't help but roll her eyes. She gave her mom a quick wave and exited the building, making her way back to the truck.

"You were in there for so long!" Luka whined as she opened the door.

"Sorry." Jordan said, sarcastically. "I was getting answers for you. You should be thanking me."

"What did she say?" Luka barked.

Jordan shrugged. "She said it was a gift."

Luka's eyes widened in disappointment. "Someone gave it to her?"

"I guess so."

"Do you believe her?" Luka asked.

Jordan was never extremely close with her mom like some kids are, but she did know her well enough from her mom practically having to raise Jordan on her own. Her dad always put drugs before her.

"Are you calling Meghan a liar?" Owen's fiery eyes stared at Luka.

"Woah," Luka looked surprised. "You're on a first name basis with the mom I see." He winked at Jordan.

"Owen, relax." She sighed. "Yes, I believe her. She said whoever she's currently dating gave it to her, but wouldn't say where he bought it."

"Or didn't buy it." Anna reminded.

"True." Jordan nodded. "I'll admit it looks suspicious. But I really don't think my mom knows anything about it."

"Do you know who your mom is seeing?" Owen asked. "That would help us find this guy."

Jordan shook her head. "No idea. She likes to keep things quiet."

"So that could leave anybody." Owen sighed.

Luka put his head in his hands, clearly frustrated.

This was one of those times Jordan actually wanted to know who was in her mom's life.

"Or not." Anna's voice sounded suspicious. "Luka, remember what you told me when you stopped by my apartment?"

"You were in our apartment?" Jordan sounded surprised.

Luka and Anna completely ignored the question. Jordan had been having suspicions about those two lately.

"Oh my god." Luka looked over at her. "Anna, it can't be."

"Would either of you care to inform us about what's going on?" Jordan leaned up between the seats. She was growing frustrated now.

Anna sighed. "Remember a while ago when I suggested your mom and-"

"I caught your mom making out with my dad." Luka cut her off, getting straight to the point.

"Wow, okay. Way to rip off the bandaid, Luka." Anna scolded.

Jordan didn't move. She wasn't even sure she was breathing. "What?"

"Your mom and-" Luka began.

"She heard you the first time, Luka." Anna slapped his arm. "She's just trying to process."

"How long have you guys known?" Jordan looked up at them.

Anna turned in her direction, placing a hand on her knee. "A couple days. I just wanted to protect you."

"No." Jordan was in denial. Her mom wouldn't do this. Not to Luka's mom.

"Wow, okay." Luka pretended to be hurt. "If you don't want to be step siblings, just say that."

Anna pinched her fingers on the bridge of her nose, clearly having enough of him.

"My mom wouldn't do that. She wouldn't sleep with your dad knowing full well your mom is at home sick." Jordan couldn't bring herself to understand.

"But she is." Anna said in a soft voice.

Luka shrugged. "Yeah well, apparently my dad would go out and sleep with other women knowing my mom is at home sick."

"I swear to god, I will never forgive her for this." Jordan was growing infuriated. She could feel her blood beginning to boil. It was taking everything in her not to go in there and rip her mother apart.

"Not that this is something we should forget about," Anna started, "However, what about who gave her that bracelet."

"Well, it wouldn't have been Chad, right?" Jordan asked. She honestly didn't know what to believe anymore.

Luka sighed as he leaned his head back against the seat. "I sure hope not."

"Would your dad break into your truck and steal that bracelet for Meghan?" Anna asked, catching all three of them off guard.

"No." Luka shook his head immediately. "Absolutely not."

Jordan could tell Anna wasn't convinced, but she didn't say any-thing else.

Jordan was beginning to feel overwhelmed. How were both her parents connected to this murder?

Forty-one

Anna looked over at Luka, who was staring out the windshield lost in his thoughts. She knew he was overwhelmed. Considering what happened, she didn't blame him. The truth is, they all were. So much had happened since Chelsea's death.

"We should go to the police station, Luka." Anna said to him.

Her voice seemed to snap him out of his thoughts. "Why?"

"To see if there's any footage of whoever broke into your truck."

Luka stayed silent, but sighed.

"Why are you so worried about it?" Jordan asked. "This could help us."

"Or not." Luka replied.

Owen leaned forward. "What do you mean?"

Luka shrugged. "It was dark. Plus I was parked in the back row. I just have a feeling this is going to lead us no where."

"It's worth a shot." Anna insisted.

He looked at her for a while before nodding. "Okay."

Pleased with herself, Anna leaned back in her seat. As much as she wished she could figure this out herself, she knew they were going to need a little help from the local police.

Luka started his truck before spinning out of his dad's auto shop. The truck stayed silent as he cruised down the side roads until they came upon the station. Once they found a spot, Luka cut the engine, but stayed still.

"Are you coming in?" Anna asked.

"You're coming, right?"

She nodded. "Of course."

Luka began to unbuckle his seat belt. "Okay, good."

Anna turned toward the back seats where Jordan and Owen were sitting. "You guys stay here. We'll be right back."

Jordan nodded. "Sure."

Without another word, Anna hopped out of the truck. She shut the door behind her and made her way to the front doors of the station. Before opening the door, she looked behind her at Luka. "Are you okay?"

"I just think they still consider me as a suspect in Chelsea's case."

Anna furrowed her brows. "Maybe the idiots do. But you didn't kill her. This could help you prove yourself innocent." She paused. "Not that you should have to."

Nodding, Luka followed her into the police station.

Once Anna was inside, she looked around. The room was filled with a handful of police officers. The lights were dim and hurt Anna's eyes a little, but she continued to scan around. She knew she would be in an area like this one day.

Cutting into her thoughts, an officer came up to them. "Hi there."

Anna gave a small smile. "Hello."

"What can I do for you?"

"Well," Anna began. "My friend here has a truck that was broken into in the parking lot just outside last night. We just thought maybe you guys would have some footage of the parking lot you could take a look at?"

The officer knit his eyebrows together. "It happened right here in the parking lot?"

Anna nodded. "Yes, sir."

"Well, then. I could take a look for you. What kind of truck do you drive?" He turned to Luka.

"A black *Dodge Ram*." Luka answered.

The officer put his hands on his hips as he nodded. "I can see what I can do for you."

Anna turned to look at Luka with wide eyes. He didn't return the happy expression. She could tell he was nervous, considering he is technically still a suspect. She could understand why he felt the way he did, but it made her feel sad for him.

"You kids take a seat." The officer gestured at the seats against the wall. "I'll take a look at what I can find."

Anna smiled. "Thank you."

As the officer walked away, Anna couldn't help but notice the way Luka looked around the room.

"This isn't about you being a suspect in Chelsea's case, is it?" She asked. "It's about your slip up during your interrogation."

"Of course it is, Anna." Luka's voice was a hoarse whisper.

Anna felt taken back by the roughness of his voice.

He closed his eyes and sighed. "I'm sorry. I just- sometimes I wish we never followed Jarid that night."

Anna reached over and put a hand on his arm. "Me too."

"You don't understand." Luka shook his head. "What I did to Jarid it...it haunts me."

Anna looked around the room to make sure no one could hear them. "That makes sense, Luka. But you know he would have killed us."

Luka hesitated before nodding. "I know."

Anna moved her hand to his back and began rubbing it back and forth. "It's okay to feel this way. But you have to remember you did save us."

He looked over at her and smiled. "Thanks, Anna."

She smiled back. "You know I'm here for you, right?"

He pulled her hand forward so that it was curled in his own. "I know."

She squeeze his hand. "Then we'll be okay."

It was at least forty minutes before Anna saw the officer they talked to come back into the room. She had text Jordan and updated her that they were waiting.

As the officer approached them, he scratched his head. "Why don't you kids come into my office?"

Anna squeezed Luka's hand again before standing. "Sure."

The officer turned and led them down the hall. "I'm detective Shaw, by the way."

"I'm Anna. My friend here is Luka."

The detective kept walking, but turned his head to look at Luka. "Luka, huh? That name sounds familiar."

Luka cleared his throat. "I was in here last night actually." He let out an awkward laugh.

The detective nodded. "Can I ask why you were here?"

"I was answering some questions about Chelsea Bentley."

Anna was surprised at how honest he was being. Part of her wanted to tell the officer to mind his business. But, she knew if they wanted his help they had to be nice to him.

"Luka Anderson." Detective Shaw said. "Now I know who you are."

Luka pursed his lips as he nodded, clearly not knowing what to say.

Anna was relieved when they reached the detective's office. Now they could focus on the matter at hand.

"Have a seat." Detective Shaw stood behind them, shutting the door.

Anna and Luka each sat in the chairs across from the detective's desk as he sat in his own chair.

"I did a little digging while you were waiting out there." He began. "I think I may have found what you're looking for. However, I'm not sure it'll be much help."

Anna furrowed her brows. "Why's that?"

"Take a look." The detective picked up the iPad in front of him and turned the screen so it was facing Anna and Luka.

Anna leaned forward eagerly as she watched the footage play in front of them. She watched as a dark figure began walking toward Luka's truck. Once he walked over to the driver's side of the truck, he was no longer in view of the camera. It was a few moments before the figure came into view again, as he jogged back the way he came from. As he was running, Anna looked closely, trying to take note of any details about him, but it was too dark to see.

Once the figure was out of sight of the camera, Anna leaned back in her seat. "Now I see what you mean."

Luka looked over at Anna. "Well that won't help us."

"Did you notice anything missing from your truck?" Detective Shaw asked.

"A bracelet."

The detective scratched his chin. "Interesting."

Luka nodded as he moved around in his seat. "Thanks for looking."

Anna could tell by his body language that he wanted to leave. He was getting too worried now that the officer knew who he was. He didn't want to be questioned about Jarid. Anna didn't want him to be either.

"We could have forensics take prints from your truck." He offered.

"I think I saw in the footage that he had gloves." Anna lied. "Don't worry about it. Luka can always get a new bracelet. Thank you for all your help."

The detective looked skeptical, but nodded. "No problem. If you find out anything else, come back to us for help."

Anna nodded. "We will." That was a lie too. Anna was starting to feel as uncomfortable as Luka looked.

"And Luka." He turned to him with a smirk. "Stay out of trouble."

Luka let out a nervous chuckle. "Uh, yes sir. Thank you."

Feeling chills run up her body, Anna was quick to open the door and lead the way out. She made a silent vow to herself to never go back there.

"What the hell happened back there?" Anna questioned once they were outside. She felt the cool air hit her face, making her feel like she could finally breathe.

"I don't know. But we're getting the hell out of here."

Without further question, Luka started up his truck and drove them away from there as fast as he could.

Forty-two

The group of unlicensed detectives made their way to the local bar. The room was loud, but the four friends that sat in the booth at the back stayed quiet. They were all trying to process not only what had been seen at the auto shop, but everything that had happened so far.

"You know," Luka was the first to break the silence as he took a swig of his beer. "It's really starting to feel like we're detectives now."

Anna let out a small laugh. "I don't think we've seen half of what they've gone through. We're just winging things, doing our best to find answers."

"Yeah, well we've found a ton of answers, I just can't tell which one is right." He sighed.

"Me either." Jordan leaned back in her seat, holding her bottle of beer to her chest.

She was growing tired of this investigation. This was supposed to be Anna's thing. Even though Jordan wanted to help her, this case proved to her that being a detective was not for her. She wanted nothing more than for Owen to find closure for his sister, and maybe even his brother too. But, it seems ever since they began trying to solve this mystery, Jordan's life has fallen apart. She struggled enough learning her dad may have been responsible for at least one of Owen's siblings deaths, but now that her mom was caught up in all of this, she felt lost.

"I should go home and get Ruby." Luka joked. Then we could be a real *Scooby gang*. Well, Ruby gang, if you want to get technical."

Anna slapped his arm. "We are not bringing your dog into this."

They all laughed. It felt good to laugh after all that had happened in just the last few days.

"What are the odds of my mom having a different boyfriend now and buying the bracelet she has at a terrible time?"

"You mean what if this is all a coincidence?" Luka asked, his voice filled with disbelief.

Jordan shrugged. "Maybe."

They all looked at her, letting her know the answer. She knew already, but she thought maybe if she put it out there, it would feel true.

"The odds are really slim, J." Anna's voice had more sympathy.

"I know." Jordan's voice was low as she pulled her knees into her chest, still holding onto her beer.

Luka stared at Jordan for a long period of time without saying a word.

Jordan stared back at him. "Yes, Luka?"

"Is there any way you could figure out who your mom is seeing?"

Jordan gave him a puzzled look. "What are you talking about? You're the one who told me she was seeing your dad."

"Yes, I know. But there's no way my dad was the one who gave her that bracelet. He's too cheap."

"Well, it was stolen." Anna reminded him.

"My dad wouldn't do that." Luka glared at her. "There had to be someone else."

"So you're calling her mom a whore?" Owen forced himself into the conversation.

"What? No. That's not what I'm saying." Luka put up his hands in defence. "I'm just suggesting maybe someone else gave your mom that bracelet."

Owen opened his mouth to speak, when Jordan placed a hand on his leg to stop him. At just her touch, he obeyed.

"I get it." She said. "You don't want your dad to have done this. If I'm being honest, I don't either." Jordan thought about how sick Luka's mom was and how no one really knew how much time she had left. If Chad was responsible for any of this, Luka would have no family except for his three sisters.

"Maybe you're not wrong, either." Jordan continued. "Maybe she is seeing someone different now."

"Maybe she's seeing your dad again." Anna said. She immediately put her hand over her mouth, showing she regretted her decision.

"I hope not." Jordan glared at her.

Luka shrugged as if he was considering it. "Would your dad tail me and break into my truck and steal a bracelet?"

"He would break into nearly anywhere and steal pretty much anything, so, yeah."

"Wow." Owen whispered.

"He'd probably have someone else do it for him, though." Jordan explained.

"Someone like Jarid?" Owen asked.

"Have you had too much to drink?" Luka looked over at him.

Owen furrowed his brows. "No, why?"

"Your brother is dead, Owen." Luka reach over and patted his arm.

Owen rolled his eyes. "I know. But maybe he's replaced Jarid already."

Jordan hadn't thought of that. "That's true. He could probably use the extra hand to help him. Without Jarid his business would be slow. He'd need to have someone new by now."

"I'm not going back to that place to find out." Anna stated.

"How else are we going to know?" Luka asked.

"You're kidding, right?" Anna pleaded.

"What if we just drove in, looked from the vehicle to see if there was anyone new there and turned around and left. No one would even see us." He began compromising.

"We thought no one would see us last time." Anna reminded him. "That didn't exactly workout, did it?"

"My still slightly black eye says no." Owen answered.

"Look, Anna." Luka began. "You're the detective here. Don't you think it would be a good idea to at least see if he had someone new working for him?"

"We don't even know Jordan's dad was the one who had your bracelet stolen." Anna argued.

"You're the one who brought up the idea." Jordan reminded her, getting frustrated. Jordan did not want to go back to that place. She did not want to see her dad again.

"Exactly. Plus, we have no evidence of anyone in my truck, Anna. At this point anything we do is a guess." Luka sighed, trying his best to convince her.

She stared at him silently. She clearly agreed with him, but didn't want to go back to that place either.

"We're not taking your truck." Owen said, refusing to take no for an answer.

"Fine." Luka sighed. "We'll take your tiny ass car."

Owen rolled his eyes. "At least we won't get caught in it."

"Having a loud truck is all fun and games until you get caught up with a detective." Luka looked over at Anna.

Jordan smirked at the way Anna's cheeks blushed. "Okay, lovebirds. Are we going or not?"

Anna looked over at Jordan to protest what she had just said, but Luka had downed the rest of his beer and stood up, ready to go. Jordan couldn't help but smile when Anna silently gave her the finger.

By the time they were on their way back to the wharf, it was nearly 5pm, but with spring coming closer to an end, the days were getting longer. This left the group a little over an hour before sundown.

As they proceeded closer to the gravel road, Jordan could feel her stomach beginning to swirl. She couldn't tell if she was just nervous to be back there with the possibility of running into her dad once again, or if it was her gut telling her she wasn't going to like what she saw tonight.

She glanced up to the driver's seat at Owen and immediately felt a little relief. Owen felt like comfort to her. She hoped there would never be a time he wasn't in her life.

Now that Owen's eye was slowly going back to normal, he had just a small black and purple ring around his eye. Meaning he could finally drive so they didn't get caught by the deafening sound of Luka's truck.

Right as they pulled up to the gravel road and were beginning to turn, Owen stopped the car right in the middle of the road. "Are you guys sure about this?"

Luka let out a sigh. Jordan couldn't tell if it was out of annoyance or if he was nervous. "Yeah, I'm ready."

"I'm just saying," Owen began, "Last time we were in here, we almost died."

"I refuse to leave the car this time." Jordan announced from the backseat.

Anna's voice piped up from the seat beside her. "I second that."

Luka had taken the passenger seat this time, just in case they did get spotted. Jordan was thankful, but she also hated it because of how far he put his seat back. She had to turn her knees to the centre console and was extremely uncomfortable.

Owen nodded and stepped back on the gas, turning the car down the path. Jordan looked over at Anna, who returned the same expression full of terror.

Anna reached over and grabbed Jordan's hand.

Jordan gratefully took it, giving it a squeeze.

"I'll try to park near the same spot I did last time." Owen announced.

"Hang on." Luka said, leaning closer to the windshield.

Anna leaned up between the seats. "Do you see something?"

He didn't say anything at first, as Owen stopped the car. He kept looking ahead at something the others weren't seeing.

"Luka." Anna grumbled. "Talk. What do you see?"

"I don't know yet." He admitted. "Owen, can you drive just a little closer?"

Owen nodded and proceeded to drive up the gravel path.

"Right here is good enough." Luka told him. He began leaning close to the windshield once again.

"Okay, enough of this." Anna scowled. "We're a team here. What do you see, Luka?"

"I just can't tell if I'm right or not." He told her.

"About what?" Jordan asked, trying to see over Anna's head.

"All I see is an *suv*, man." Owen said, shrugging it off.

"Exactly. It looks familiar." Luka nodded.

"You've seen it before?" Owen asked.

Jordan leaned farther ahead and finally spotted the parked red *suv*.

"Luka, do you know how many people have that same vehicle? That could be anyone." She grumbled, leaning back in her seat.

Luka sighed. "But it doesn't look like just anyone's. I recognize that dent in the back end."

"A name, Luka. We need you to give us a name. Who's *suv* do you think it is?" Anna's tone was quickly growing annoyed.

He shook his head. "No, I know who's *suv* that is. It's my dad's."

Forty-three

Luka stared at the *suv* while tuning out the voices of the others in the car. Why the hell would his father be here? Last time he checked, he and Jordan's dad were not friends. As he stared at the red *suv* parked in front of them, he found himself coming up with a million reasons as to why his *suv* could be here. None of them were good things.

"Luka!" Anna's voice was the first to cut into his thoughts.

He quickly turned his head to look back at her. "Yeah?"

"Are you sure that's your dad's car?"

He nodded. "I'm positive. He got that dent in the back from backing into my grandfather's jeep a couple months ago."

"And he didn't fix it?" Jordan asked. "The guy is a mechanic."

Luka shrugged.

"What would your dad be doing here?" Anna questioned.

Luka rubbed his eyes, clearly stressed. "I really don't know. I didn't think he even knew this place existed."

Jordan nodded in agreement. "It's very secluded. My dad clearly doesn't want anyone around here."

"That means your dad would have had to call Luka's dad to come down here, Jordan." Anna told her.

Jordan's eyes were wide and full of confusion. "You're right. He wouldn't let unwanted visitors stick around."

"You saw the way he reacted to us." Owen reminded them.

"Exactly. If your dad was an unwanted visitor, he would probably be getting beaten up by now." Anna looked at Luka.

"Or at least kicked out." Jordan agreed.

Luka turned to face Jordan. "Why would your dad call my dad to come down here?"

Jordan looked defeated. "I really don't know. I'm sorry."

Luka sighed, disappointed. He wanted answers. What was his dad doing here?

"But we'll find out." Anna spoke soothingly.

It brought Luka comfort how Anna was always willing to help him. Throughout this entire case they were trying to solve, it really felt like Anna cared about him.

"We're going to get caught if we keep sitting here." Owen pointed out.

"Your dad's vehicle sitting there isn't going to make you want to go in, right?" Anna's voice pleaded from the backseat.

Truthfully, it did make Luka want to go in and see what the hell was going on. He didn't care what would happen to him or the consequences. He wanted to go down there and cuss his dad out. He felt completely overwhelmed and useless. His sick mother was sitting at home, while his dad was out doing mysterious things, one being cheating, and there is nothing Luka can seem to find to stop him.

He knew he couldn't confront his dad about him and Meghan. His dad would just get angry and he had no proof. The town wouldn't believe him either because his dad is such a big shot and well liked. Besides that, he didn't want to worry his mom and make her any worse.

But, he knew all he wanted right now wasn't safe. He couldn't endanger his friends. Especially Anna. Part of him believed if he went down there she would be worried about him and the last thing he wanted to do right now was stress her. But even if he hadn't come to those conclusions, just the plead in Anna's voice made his heart shatter. It made him want to drop to his knees and do anything for her.

"No." He finally said. "I'm not going down there."

He could hear Anna's sigh of relief. If he was being honest, it made him happy. It was proof Anna really did care about him.

"Back up." Luka told Owen. "Park over there in that long grass. I want to see if my dad comes out."

Owen blinked at Luka. "In the long grass?"

Luka nodded. "Yeah. No one will see us."

"What about my car, man?"

Luka shrugged. "You guys didn't want to bring my truck."

"It's louder than a train, Luka." Anna reasoned.

Luka looked back and smiled at her. He felt his insides get warm when she smiled back.

Owen let out a sigh and put the car in reverse. "Fine."

He backed up until they hit the long grass. He then turned to the right and parked them beside two tall trees.

"Good." Luka said, approvingly. "My dad won't see us here."

As if on cue, a tall man began walking toward the *suv* up ahead. He wore ragged old jeans, a sweater and a ball cap.

"That sure looks like your dad, Luka." Anna whispered.

He nodded. "It definitely is. I recognize his walk."

His dad had something shiny in one hand as he made his way to his vehicle. He looked down at it before looking around him carefully.

"What the hell is he doing?" Jordan asked.

After deciding no one was around, Luka's dad quickly shoved the shiny object into his jeans pocket before getting into the driver's seat.

"Did anyone see what he had in his hand?" Anna asked.

Luka shook his head. "No. But i'd like to find out."

His dad started the *SUV* and began to drive out the gravel road towards them. They were toward the side of the road and were most likely not going to get caught, but Luka wanted to take precautions anyway. "Everyone get down."

They all ducked behind something in front of them, whether it was the dash, a seat or the steering wheel.

Luka ducked his head behind the dash, but kept it up just high enough so he could still see his dad coming.

Right as his dad reached the spot directly in front of them, he stopped the vehicle. Luka felt his stomach turn into a hurricane. Had he seen them?

"Luka." Anna whispered from the back. Her voice was full of worry.

He reached a hand back in her direction, not caring if Owen or Jordan saw. Without hesitation, Anna squeezed it.

He continued to watch his dad. He was now looking down at something neither of them could see. Luka assumed it was his phone. After a few seconds, his dad looked out the window directly at the car they were sitting in. Luka closed his eyes and hoped with everything in him that he wasn't about to get caught by his dad today.

After a few shaky breaths and some luck, his dad turned on his high beams and started onto the main road.

Forty-four

Anna looked down at her hand that was intertwined with Luka's. She kept it in her firm grip but lifted her head up to see his dad had finally made his way onto the main road and hadn't spotted them. She squeezed Luka's hand one last time before letting go. She noticed Jordan staring at her with raised eyebrows. Not knowing what to say, Anna simply shrugged.

"Follow him." Luka's voice boomed from the front.

Owen nodded and reached forward in attempt to start his car. The car whirled over before letting out a rattling sound.

"What the fuck, Owen?" Luka barked.

Owen tried again, but the car kept making the same sound. "It won't start."

"Yeah I got that, genius." Luka let out a sigh.

"What do we do now?" Anna asked. She could feel herself growing worried. Even if Luka was by her side, she could not be stranded at this place.

"We can't stay here." Jordan hissed. "We need to get the hell out."

Anna took notice to Luka as he began looking ahead where his dad had came from when they first saw him getting in his *suv*.

"I have a plan." He said as he began reaching for the door handle.

"Is it a good one?" Anna questioned. She didn't like the idea of him getting out of the car.

He paused. "...I have a plan."

Anna whined. "Oh god. We're going to die here."

"Hey," Luka looked back at her with hopeful eyes. "We're not going to die here, okay? But I need you to trust me."

Anna did her best to try to stay calm. The truth of the matter was, she did trust Luka. She had no idea why, but she did. "Okay."

"I will be right back." He told them. "Nobody move." He grabbed the door handle and began to exit the car.

"Luka-" Anna began to protest, but he was already making his way down to the wharf.

"What the hell is he doing?" Owen asked, still trying to start his car.

Anna didn't take her eyes off Luka. She could see him as he made his way down the gravel road toward a small blue civic.

"Wait, he's not going to-" Jordan didn't even get to finish before Luka had walked over to the driver's seat and opened up the door.

Luka hopped into the blue civic and turned on his phone flashlight. Anna saw him lean down to the floor.

"What is he doing?" Anna asked. There was nothing more she wanted right now than to get out of here.

"Trying to start it with the wires." Owen spoke. "The keys must not be in it."

"I don't want to know why you know that." Jordan quipped.

Owen looked back at her and dropped his jaw a little, as if he just realized how casually he said that. "Hey, I've seen movies."

"Yeah, *movies*." Anna mimicked. "Sure, that's definitely why."

Their joking was cut short when headlights lit up the trees in front of them.

"Oh my god he did it." Jordan sounded amazed.

Anna hated to admit it, but she almost felt proud of Luka. Though if it were under different circumstances, she would feel much different.

The car made a loud revving noise, one that Jordan's dad and whoever else may be down there, definitely heard. Luka had quickly stepped on the gas and brought up the car so it was directly in front of Owen's. He made a wave signal, telling the three to hurry to the car.

They all quickly got out and ran toward the car. Anna ran the fastest so she could be in the passenger seat, Owen and Jordan threw themselves in the back. Luka had quickly locked the doors.

"Just so you know," Anna began, "I'm not on board with this."

"Oh, really?" Luka asked sarcastically. "Could've fooled me."

Anna noticed a man beginning to run toward them in the side view mirror. "Luka, drive!"

Without second thought, he stepped on the gas as fast as he could.

They all kept quiet until they were well down the main road.

"What do you guys think the odds of still catching my dad are?" Luka asked.

Anna blew out a breath. "That's hard to say. We're a few solid minutes behind him now."

Luka looked disappointed, but nodded in agreement. "Thanks to your car." He looked at Owen through the mirror.

"I'm never going to get that car back, you know."

"Good." Luka joked. "It nearly ruined our lives."

"Am I the only one still trying to process that Luka just hijacked a car?" Anna asked, still not coming to terms with what just happened.

Luka shrugged. "I saved us, didn't I?"

"Yeah, but you just knew what to do." Anna said, disbelieving. "It was so causal."

"My dad is a mechanic." He responded.

"And he showed you how to hot wire a car?" Owen asked, clearly knowing that was a poor excuse.

"Okay fine. I may have done it once or twice." He admitted.

"What the fuck?" Was all Anna could manage. What kind of person was Luka?

Owen couldn't stop laughing.

"Relax, they were all returned." Luka shrugged it off.

Anna leaned her head back against the seat. "Fuck!" She felt like she was at her breaking point.

"What?" Luka looked at her worried.

"This has really been the worst week of my life."

"How's that?" He asked calmly.

"Well, I've been trying to find a killer but it seems like each turn leads down a different road and we're getting no where, I've almost been killed multiple times, I'm riding shotgun in a stolen car, with of all people Luka Anderson next to me, and on top of all that, I never got to have my afternoon coffee today."

"Oh," Luka nodded. "I know what you mean. I can't get by without coffee either."

Owen began cackling from the backseat. Half of Anna wanted to slap them all, but the other half of her wanted to laugh along with them.

Anna sighed as she reached for the dash. "Who's car is this, anyway?" She began to dig around in the dash until she found a blue piece of paper. "Oh my god."

Luka furrowed his brows as he looked over at it. "What is it?"

"This is Jarid's car."

They all stayed silent for a moment, trying to process.

"Great." Anna let out a fake laugh. "Not only is the car I'm in stolen, but it's also a dead guys."

She continued rummaging around in the glove compartment, when she came across a key. It was the key to start the car. "Luka, the key was in here the entire time!"

Luka's cheeks turned red. "I didn't have time to check, okay?"

Anna let out a loud groan as they came to a stop at the red light. As she looked out the windshield she recognized that same red dent in the bumper just two cars ahead. "Luka, your dad."

Luka looked ahead eagerly until his eyes fell upon the *suv*. "Let's see where he's going."

Once they caught up to him, Luka couldn't keep his eyes off the red *suv* in front of him. He kept a good distance between them so he wasn't obvious.

He hadn't noticed the grip he had on the steering wheel until Anna had placed a gentle hand on his knee, making him relax.

His dad looked to be taking the main road back into town. Anna could feel it in her stomach that whatever mysterious thing Luka's dad was doing tonight had already happened and she wasn't about to get any answers. Sure enough, his dad turned onto the exit ramp that led to downtown Edgar Cove.

"It looks like he's just going home, Luka." Jordan sighed from the backseat.

"Yeah, I'm going to go out on a limb and say whatever he's been doing tonight has already been done and now he's going home to pretend like it never happened." Anna agreed.

"More like drink it off." Luka sighed. It was true. If he couldn't find his dad, there was always a good chance he was in the garage drinking.

Luka continued down the street following his dad feeling extreme disappointment. His dad turned down Rand road, which was the road they lived on.

Anna moved her hand to Luka's arm. "I'm sorry. I was really hoping to find some answers tonight."

Luka sighed into her touch. "Me too."

"You're not going to follow him in, right?" Owen asked. "We could get caught."

Luka shook his head. "No, relax."

Right before Luka's neighbours house there was a small gravel patch on the side of the road that was wide enough to park a car. His neighbour did use it sometimes when he had a bunch of people over and all the cars wouldn't fit in the driveway, but tonight he was lucky enough it was empty.

Luka pulled the stolen car onto the gravel on the side of the road and turned the headlights off.

Owen's worried voice piped up from the backseat. "Are you sure he won't see us?"

"He'll probably assume it's just our neighbour."

Anna's arm slapping made him jump. "Look."

Luka looked ahead to see that his dad was now out of the *suv* and standing in front of the garage. The outside light above the garage door was enough light for them to see him clearly. His dad once again pulled that same shiny object out of his pocket.

"What the hell is that?" Anna asked.

Luka shook his head, frustrated. "I still can't see."

His dad stared down at the object for what felt like a long time. Finally, he lifted his head up and looked around him carefully.

"He's doing that again." Luka couldn't understand.

"He's checking to make sure no one is around." Anna clarified.

"But why?" Luka shrugged. "What is that in his hand?"

"Whatever it is," Jordan began, "He wants to make sure nobody sees it."

"Yeah." Anna agreed, still watching Luka's dad. "It's definitely something special to him. Or at least something he doesn't want anybody to touch."

Anna couldn't stop focusing on how paranoid Luka's dad was. He looked around once more before glancing up at the upstairs window.

"That's his and my mom's room he's looking at." Luka told them.

"Maybe he doesn't even want her to see what he has." Anna suggested, intrigued.

Anna felt an uneasy feeling in her stomach as she stared at Luka's dad.

Chad finally stopped looking around and reached for the garage door handle before entering.

When his dad disappeared inside, Luka sighed. "We need to figure out what that is in his hands."

Anna nodded in agreement. "I have a feeling it's going to lead to something."

Jordan's face filled with worry. "Something we're not going to like."

Forty-five

Anna kept her eyes on Luka as he stared at his house. Luka decided to wait a little while until his dad was in bed before going into the garage to find that shiny object his dad was holding just hours ago.

It was nearly 10pm and Luka had offered to drive the other three home, but they all decided they wanted to be apart of this. Especially Anna. She knew between her wish to be a detective and how she cared for Luka, she wasn't going to leave.

"We've been sitting here for a really long time." Owen whined.

"I know. But we can't risk getting caught." Luka grumbled.

"There aren't even any lights on, Luka." Jordan pointed out.

"I-" Luka sighed. "Okay, fine. But we need to be careful. We can't get caught."

"And we won't." Anna sighed. "Let's just go."

Anna reached for the handle and slowly exited the car. The crisp air touched her skin, making her shiver.

Luka walked in front of them as he began to lead them across the road to his house. When he got to the end of the paved driveway, he turned to them. "We need to be extremely quiet."

Anna was starting to grow annoyed. Luka was clearly paranoid and she just wanted to get on with the search.

They all nodded before Luka led them up the driveway. When they got to the garage door he pulled his set of truck keys out of his pocket. He quietly rummaged through them until he came across a small gold key that he shoved into the lock of the garage door, unlocking it. Luka opened the door slowly.

Anna was growing impatient. She needed to get inside. She couldn't shake the feeling that they were going to make a serious breakthrough tonight and she wanted to get started.

Luka reached around the side and flicked on the lights.

Anna squinted at how bright they were. She looked around, taking in the room. It didn't look much like a regular garage. The way the place was set up, there wasn't really any room for a car. Luka's dad had a couch and a few chairs set up in a circle with a small table in the middle. She noticed a mini fridge to the side and an ashtray full of cigarette butts. There was a large red four wheeler parked directly in the middle of the floor. Anna came to the conclusion that they definitely didn't use this as a car garage, but more as a hangout area.

"We don't even know what we're searching for." Jordan reminded them.

"It looked to be a small to medium size silver object." Anna shrugged. "Just look for anything remotely close to that."

The four separated and each took a corner of the garage.

Anna had the corner with the tool supply counter. She rummaged through each drawer and shelf looking for anything out of the ordinary. Most of the tools she found were silver, but none looked quite like what Chad was holding.

"I'm not seeing anything." Luka sighed.

Anna felt her heart shatter a little at the saddened look on his face. She needed to find whatever Chad had tonight. For Luka.

"How do we know what we're looking for is even in here?" Jordan's voice piped up as she closed the drill kit she was looking inside of.

She made a good point. There was no evidence saying whatever Chad had, he left in his garage. For all they knew, it was hidden in the house somewhere.

"We don't." Luka sighed. "We just have to hope."

Anna refused to give up. She was going to find whatever Luka's dad was hiding tonight.

She continued looking through the drawers on the counter before moving to open the cabinet doors. The first one was filled with oil filled gloves. It was easy to assume they were Chad's. The second had a tool bag full of tools in it with Luka's name on the bag. But the third and final cabinet was where she found what she didn't know she was looking for.

Anna's jaw dropped when she laid her eyes on the object in front of her. She tried to gasp, but nothing came out. She looked behind her to see if anyone else could see what she was seeing, but the three of them were still in the process of searching the other corners of the garage.

The garage light reflected off the shiny silver object in front of her. *A wrench*. The open end of the wrench was covered in dried blood that dripped down the middle of it. It sat at the front of the shelf behind the cabinet doors. She assumed Luka's dad had decided not to hide it, but instead had other plans for it later. She needed to decide what to do fast.

She finally found her words, "Guys."

Anna kept her eyes on the wrench in front of her while she listened as her friends began to walk over to where she was crouched down in front of the cabinet.

"What is it?" Luka's voice was eager.

Anna pointed to the wrench in front of her. "Just look."

Owen's voice boomed. "What the hell is that?"

Luka was quick to put his finger to his lips. "Quiet down!"

Owen widened his eyes apologetically.

"Is that blood?" Jordan asked.

Anna couldn't bring herself to talk, instead she nodded.

They all stood in silence staring at the object in front of them.

"Luka..." Anna's voice was low.

"I've never seen that before in my life." He panicked.

"We didn't think you did." Owen told him.

"We know." Anna began to reassure him. "But your dad has."

"Your dad was holding a bloody wrench." Jordan said, as if she was just realizing what was going on.

"And is now hiding it." Owen added.

"I wouldn't call this hiding. It's practically in the open." Anna pointed out. "Anyone could open up this cabinet door and see it sitting there."

Anna could see goosebumps form on Luka's skin.

"Why would he do that?" Luka asked. "That sounds pretty dumb to me."

"Maybe not." Anna sighed. "He probably plans to come back for it."

"He most likely has a plan for what he is going to do with it." Jordan agreed.

"Why would he bring it home then?" Owen questioned.

Anna shrugged. "Maybe he just needed to wait for the right time to dispose of it. Besides, coming home when he did and going to bed would make everything look normal."

"Do you think that blood is Chelsea's?" Jordan asked.

"No!" Luka was quick to answer. "My dad isn't a murderer, you guys."

"Then how do you explain the wrench sitting in front of us that is covered in blood?" Jordan barked.

"I-I don't know." Luka stuttered.

"That's blood, Luka. Clearly your dad has been up to something." Owen shook his head.

"Maybe it isn't his." Luka began to pace around the garage. "Maybe he was disposing it for your dad, Jordan."

"Really, Luka?" Owen turned and walked a few steps the other way.

"Come on, you guys." Luka pleaded. "We saw him with it at the wharf."

Anna nodded. "That is true."

Jordan sighed. "But why would my dad give it to your dad? Why wouldn't he dispose of it himself if it was really his?"

Luka sighed, clearly defeated. "I really don't know."

Anna finally snapped out of the shock and realized she needed to do something. They needed to find answers.

"We need to take this to the police." She decided.

"What?" Luka asked in disbelief. "What if we get caught by my dad?"

"Luka." Anna sighed. "Do you want to figure out what is going on or not?"

He stood silently with his hands on his hips before nodding.

"Then we need to get this to the police now." She told him.

"Fine." Luka said, beginning to crouch down to pick up the bloody wrench.

"Luka, no!" Anna hissed. "If you touch it your fingerprints will be on it. That will make it harder for the police to figure things out."

Luka was quick to pull his hand away and step back.

"Do you have a small bag?" Jordan asked.

Luka began to run around the garage in search for a bag. With some luck, he found an old brown paper bag behind one of the chairs. Anna guessed Luka's dad had got it from the liquor store.

"Will this work?" He asked.

Anna nodded as she reached out a hand. "Good enough."

Anna took the bag from Luka's hand and pulled down her sleeve so her fingers wouldn't touch the wrench. Once she grabbed the wrench she quickly set it into the brown bag.

Anna was growing nervous. She was now holding a bag that had a possible murder weapon in it.

"We need to go."

The other three quickly began following her toward the door. But they all came to a sudden stop when they heard footsteps making their way down the stairs.

"Do you hear that?" Luka asked.

Anna nodded. "Your dad is coming."

Forty-six

Anna sucked in a sharp breath. She could feel herself stop breathing. This was one of those moments when she wondered if she really was cut out to be a detective. She wanted to let out a breath but was too scared. She needed to think fast. Luka's dad was on his way down here and who knows what would happen if he caught them with a possible murder weapon. Would he hurt them? Would he deny it all? Anna had no idea and she had no plans to stick around and find out.

"We need to hide." Luka announced.

"What?" Anna scoffed. "What we need is to get out of here. Fast."

Jordan nodded as she dashed toward the door. "Agreed. Let's go."

She could tell that Luka was about to argue, so she grabbed his arm and began pulling him toward the door. Once they were out she let go and ran toward the civic as fast as she could.

They all started running down the street, the cool air smashing against their faces. Once they were close, Luka pointed the keys toward the car, unlocking it.

Luka was the last to get in, slamming the door. "You have the wrench?" He turned to Anna.

She nodded, lifting the bag so he could see. "Yes. Now, go!"

With no hesitation, Luka stepped on the gas.

As they sped past the house, Anna noticed they had left the garage light on. *Shit.* Luka's dad would for sure know someone had been there now.

"We left the light on." She told them.

"So?" Luka asked, still speeding. "At least we made it out alive."

"He'll probably just think he forgot to turn out the light." Owen suggested.

"No." Anna shook her head. "The first thing he'll do is look for this wrench."

"And notice it's gone." Jordan added.

"Exactly. Then what?"

Luka shrugged. "It's not like he'll know it was us."

"You better hope he doesn't." Anna glared at him.

Once they were off Rand road, Anna felt herself relax. She unclenched her fists, releasing her tight grip on the brown bag.

The police station was just ten minutes down the road, but at the speed Luka was going, they got there in five.

"He didn't tail us, right?" Luka asked as he pulled over to the side of the curb.

Anna looked out the back windshield. "I don't see him."

Luka nodded as he cut the engine. "We're doing the right thing, aren't we?"

"Yes." Anna confirmed.

"That could be connected to Chelsea or Jarid's death." Jordan said.

Anna held back her words. She knew the weapon in her hand had nothing to do with Jarid's death, but it could be connected to Chelsea's.

"It's better to know, Luka." Jordan tried reassuring him.

"You want to find answers for Chelsea, don't you?" Owen began to push him.

Luka took the keys out of the ignition, but didn't move.

"Luka?" Anna called his name.

He didn't answer. He kept his eyes straight ahead, staring at the police station doors.

Anna felt her heart sink. She knew he was contemplating if he was doing the right thing. She knew Luka didn't want to go behind his dad's back, but in this case they didn't have a choice. The last thing that both Luka and Anna wanted was for his dad to be a murderer. Anna hated to admit it, but from the way things seemed to be going, that was looking more and more like the case.

"Luka." She repeated.

He shook himself out of his trance and looked over at her, "Yeah?"

Anna reached over and held his hand. "Are you ready?"

He shook his head as he chuckled. "Not at all."

But without any second thoughts, the four of them stepped out of the car and headed into the police station, with the brown bag in Anna's hand.

Anna held the brown bag tightly in one hand and Luka's in the other. Once they reached the door Luka stopped moving and looked over at her. Her heart broke when she saw his eyes. They looked heartbroken. She knew he was having second thoughts, but she couldn't let him back out now. She was taking this wrench in with or without him. But, she hoped with everything in her that it was with him.

She gave his hand a final squeeze before reaching for the door handle. To her surprise, Luka followed.

The station wasn't very busy. There were a few officers sitting at their desks, some on the phone while others had their nose shoved in the files in front of them. Anna hated how dim the lights were, they reminded her of the lights at the hospital. She had only been here a minute and her head was already beginning to hurt from them.

An officer sitting at the desk closest to them looked up at them and gave them a small smile. "Hey there. What can I do for you?"

Luka looked over at Anna, begging her to speak for him.

She smiled at Luka before turning to the officer. "We found something that we think may be relevant to Chelsea Bentley's case. Even if it's not, it's definitely relevant to something."

The long haired officer raised his eyebrows. "May I see?"

Anna nodded as she handed the paper bag over to him. "Of course."

The officer's jaw dropped when he opened the bag. "Hey Mitch!" He yelled to an officer behind him. "You need to see this."

Luka looked around the station as he fidgeted with his hands.

The officer named Mitch was quick to jog over, taking a look into the bag. "That's blood."

The first officer nodded. "We need to get this to the lab." He turned back to Anna. "I'm going to need to run this down to the lab. But, I'm going to need you kids to take a seat right over there until I get back."

Anna looked behind them to where the officer was pointing. She saw a line of chairs over in the far corner.

She nodded, letting the officer know it was okay to leave them.

They made their way over to the seats and sat down. Anna couldn't help but notice Luka fidgeting in his seat as if he was uncomfortable.

"Luka." Anna whispered. "Are you okay?"

He shook his head. "What's going to happen when they find my dad's fingerprints on that?"

"They will have to look into things." Anna told him.

Luka leaned his head back against he back of the seat and sighed.

"If your dad really didn't do anything, they'll prove that." Owen said, trying to be helpful.

"Exactly." Jordan nodded. "And if it was my dad, they'll prove that too."

Luka looked Jordan dead in the eyes. "What if it was both of them?"

"Do you mean what if they worked together?" Anna asked, trying to understand.

Luka nodded. "We saw him with it at the wharf and then he took it home. Clearly something was going on between our dads."

"I've been thinking the same thing." Jordan's voice was low. "Maybe now we will finally find out."

"I hope so." Luka sighed. "Because I don't like this at all."

They sat in silence for a few moments before Anna came to a very important conclusion. "We're going to need a story, you know."

"What do you mean?" Luka asked.

"They're going to ask us where we found that wrench." Owen sighed.

"So we tell the truth." Jordan shrugged. "That we found it in your dad's garage."

Luka shook his head, defeated. "Yeah, I guess."

"Luka, you need to be one hundred percent certain on this." Anna scowled.

He raised his hands in defence. "I am. I'm sorry."

"What about before hand?" Owen asked. "What if they ask us how we knew where to find it?"

Anna nodded. "That's exactly why we need to discuss this. I say we should not mention anything about the wharf and just say that we were all hanging out in your garage when we came across it in the cabinet."

"Right." Jordan agreed. "We could say we were looking for something when we came across it."

"Fireworks." Luka blurted.

"What?" They all asked.

"We will say we were looking for fireworks. That way if they really did want to check, the police will actually find some sitting in my dad's garage. He loves fireworks."

Anna wanted to protest, but when she saw the officer coming back towards them, she figured Luka's story was a good idea.

"Okay, folks." The officer stood directly in front of them. I'm going to need to ask you some questions. Separately."

Forty-seven

Luka recognized both the officer and the room he was walking into. The officer in front of him was named *Officer Baldwin*. He had questioned Luka before to chat about Chelsea's death. Luka figured things would go the same tonight as they did that day. He knew officer Baldwin would most likely try to blame him at first, before letting Luka get to his truthful story. That's what happened during Chelsea's questioning at least.

"I believe we have met before." Baldwin smirked. "Luka Anderson, isn't it?"

Luka sat down in the chair at the investigation table and sighed. "Officer Baldwin."

Baldwin nodded. "Now let's talk about that possible murder weapon, shall we?"

"Yes, sir."

"Where exactly did you come across it?"

Luka didn't say anything for a moment. He didn't want to give up his dad. Sure, he wanted his dad punished for cheating on his mom, but a murder charge is extreme if he didn't kill anyone. But, the flashback of his dad holding the wrench before entering the garage flashed through his mind. He knew he needed to tell the truth.

"I found it in my dad's garage."

Baldwin's eyes widened. "Now that's interesting."

Luka closed his eyes and shifted in his seat.

"You found it in your dad's garage." Baldwin said in a tone as if he didn't believe him.

Luka nodded. "Yes."

"So you're telling me that blood covered wrench belongs to your dad?"

Luka gritted his teeth. He wanted to take it all back. "Yes."

Officer Baldwin shoved his hands in his pockets. "Now how did you come across that?"

Luka shrugged. "We were looking for fireworks."

Baldwin laughed as he threw his head back. "Fireworks, huh?"

"Yeah, we just wanted to have some fun."

"But quite the opposite happened."

Luka nodded. "When we opened up one of the cabinet doors it was just sitting there."

Baldwin squinted as if not believing him. "He didn't try to hide it?"

Luka shrugged. "I guess not."

Baldwin pulled his hands out of his pockets and crossed them. "I see."

Luka stared at the officer waiting for him to ask something else.

Instead, he sighed. "I hope you're telling me the truth, Luka."

Luka furrowed his brows. "I am."

Baldwin nodded. "So you're sticking to your story?"

"It's not a story." Luka shook his head. "It's the truth."

Baldwin stayed silent as he stared at him.

"I swear on my life that before tonight when we found it, I have never seen that blood covered wrench before."

Baldwin locked his eyes with Luka as if he was trying to find the truth in them. "So you're saying it's your dad's?"

Luka nodded. "We found it in his garage, anyway."

He wanted to tell him the truth. That he saw his dad with the wrench. But he knew he couldn't do that. He knew that would lead to more questions he couldn't answer.

Baldwin nodded one last time before walking back over to the table and setting his hands on it, leaning toward Luka. "Alright then. Some of our lab techs will have a look at that wrench and see what they can find and we will go from there."

"Thank you."

"You're free to go, Luka. But, don't go too far."

Luka nodded even though he could feel his body fuming. "Yes sir."

He may have cooperated in there, but he only did it to get Baldwin off his tail. If he was being completely honest, he wanted to go back and throw a few punches. But, he knew he couldn't mess up Chelsea's investigation. She deserved justice.

Forty-eight

Anna had been the last to be questioned. It had gone nearly exactly how she assumed. She had told the officer she had found the wrench in a cabinet in Luka's dad's garage. She had also told the officer that she was the one who opened the cabinet door and found the wrench. But, once it rolled off her lips, she realized she may have made a mistake. For all she knew, anyone of them could have said they were the one who found it. The last thing they needed was for the police to think they were lying. Anna was trying to solve a murder, not go down for one.

As she was walking back towards her friends who were sitting in the same chairs they were sitting in before the questioning, her eyes met Luka's. He looked both worried for her and extremely stressed about the whole situation. She knew he was definitely feeling both. She wanted to be a detective, not a profiler, but she still somehow found it easy to read Luka.

"How'd it go?" Jordan asked, getting up to meet her half way.

Anna shrugged. "Good I think. But we've done all we can do here."

Jordan nodded and reached for Anna's hand, giving it a squeeze.

Luka was quick to stand. "So let's get the hell out of here."

"You do remember we're still driving a stolen car, right?" Jordan whispered.

Anna sighed. "Shit."

"Which gives us more reason to leave." Owen began. "We need to get that car gone before someone realizes it's not ours."

Luka nodded. "I'm with Owen on this one. We need to get rid of that car."

Jordan nodded. "Considering we did just leave it on the side of the curb in front of the police station for the last hour."

With no protests or questions, the four began walking back to the stolen car.

Once they were in the car Luka started the ignition and began speeding down the road. As he pulled away from the curb the car made a screeching sound and Luka laughed.

"Really, Luka?" Anna asked, shaking her head. "We're in front of a police station."

"And trying not to get caught with a stolen car." Jordan added.

"Would you guys relax?" Luka rolled his eyes. "I'm just trying to have a little fun."

Anna could tell he was acting out because he didn't know how to deal with his emotions right now. This entire thing about his dad having possession of a blood covered wrench was starting to get to him. Luka was already about to lose a mom, he knew he didn't want to be responsible for him and his sisters losing their dad too. Anna wanted to help him, but she didn't know how.

"Where are we going to dump this thing anyway?" Owen asked.

"We can't take it back to my dad's wharf." Jordan put forth, "We've pushed our luck enough with that place."

Anna raised her hand. "I second that."

"Don't worry," Luka told them, "I have a better idea."

Anna furrowed her brows. "Last time you had an idea you stole a car."

"We're not going to steal anything this time." He grumbled.

"You keep saying *we* but it was *you* who decided to steal this car, remember." Anna reminded him. "You gave us no warning."

Luka ignored her remark and continued driving down the road. But Anna could see in his eyes he knew she was right. Though she couldn't deny stealing the car probably saved their lives.

"So where are we going?" Owen asked, leaning on the centre console.

"You'll see." Luka said. "But we have to make a small pit stop first."

Anna looked over at Luka, but he kept his eyes on the road ahead. She wanted to protest, or at least ask for more context. But she could see Luka had his mind set on a plan for this stolen car and there was nothing she could do to change it.

She could feel in her stomach she wasn't going to like what happened tonight.

The car stayed silent as Luka continued down the road. Anna kept her eyes on Luka a majority of the ride, waiting for him to say something - anything. But, he kept his eyes straight ahead and didn't say a word.

Anna could feel herself growing nervous. She didn't know why, but the nervousness in her gut was enough for her to keep her head on straight and be prepared for anything tonight.

Luka pulled into the parking lot of the bar and parked the stolen civic behind his jacked up dodge.

"Luka what the hell are we doing here?" Anna barked.

"Relax." He answered. "We're not staying here. Even though I could use another beer."

Jordan nodded sarcastically. "Well we don't exactly have time to sit and chat over beer right now."

Luka rolled his eyes. "We're going to need my truck to get home."

"So you're going to let me take your truck?" Owen asked.

"What? No." Luka looked at him as if he just killed a man. "No one touches my truck."

Anna rolled her eyes. She never understood men's personal feelings for their toys.

"You're going to make me drive the stolen car?" Owen's eyes went wide.

"Well I'm not driving it." Anna announced.

"Me either." Jordan shook her head.

Luka sighed. "Could you guys just listen for a minute?"

Anna bit her lip apologetically. "Sorry. Continue."

"Thank you. Now here is the plan." Luka turned in his seat so he was facing all three of them. "Owen is going to drive the car-"

"Dammit!" He shrieked. "I knew it."

Luka glared at him. "I am going to follow him in my truck."

Owen leaned his head back against the seat. "Fine. Where are we going?"

"Just drive to my dad's auto shop."

Anna furrowed her brows. "We're going to dump the car at your dad's auto shop?"

"Kind of." Luka thought for a moment. "It's hard to explain."

"Well you better explain." She grumbled. "Because I don't see how this is going to work."

"You just have to trust me, Anna." He looked directly into her eyes.

"Trust you?" She repeated. Flashbacks of Luka hitting Jarid over the head with a rock flooded in her brain.

"Yes, Anna. Do you trust me?"

She stayed silent for a moment. Did she trust Luka? She wanted to. She really cared about him. But trusting was an entire different concept. She knew she did, she just hated to admit it.

"Yes." She said finally.

He nodded. "Nothing bad is going to happen."

Jordan chuckled. "We keep saying that and then walking ourselves into danger."

They all nodded in agreement.

Anna knew Jordan was right. She wanted to get the experience of being a detective, but ever since she started this investigation, there has been nothing but bad things happening.

"You might be right." Luka sighed. "But this is a simple task. We're going to go to my dad's auto shop and leave the car behind the shop in the longer grass. No one will find it."

"You better hope not." Anna narrowed her eyes so she was looking at him over the top of her glasses. "Because our fingerprints are all over this car now."

Luka nodded. "I know. No one will find the car and no one will see us." He began trying to reassure them.

"Then let's get this plan in action." Anna said, eagerly.

Luka nodded. "Okay. Jordan, did you want to go with Owen?"

Without a beat she nodded. "Sure."

Luka turned to Anna and smirked as he mouthed, "Figures."

Anna rolled her eyes. "Let me guess." She pretended to think for a moment, placing a finger on her chin. "I'm going with you?"

Luka put his hands up in surrender pretending to play innocent. "Well, its only fair. That way there are two of us in each vehicle."

Anna scoffed. "Right."

But if she was being honest, she wasn't complaining.

"Alright. Let's go." Luka said as he began getting out of the car.

Anna was quick to follow behind him on the way to the truck.

Luka had left the driver's door open for Owen to get in. Jordan on the other hand had simply crawled between the seats up to the passenger seat and plopped down.

Anna grabbed the handle so she could climb up into Luka's truck.

Before turning on the loud engine, he looked over at her. "You ready?"

She nodded, but she honestly wasn't sure.

Forty-nine

Anna bounced her leg the entire ride there. She didn't know why. She wasn't sure if she was simply nervous or if she really just wanted to get rid of that stolen car. After all, she wanted to be a detective, not a criminal. Either way, she knew she needed to relax. She knew if she really did want to be a detective someday that she had to put away her fear and think with her head.

Luka looked over at her as he reached forward to put the truck in park. "You okay?"

Anna nodded. "I'm fine."

He stared at her for a moment, silently asking to get more out of her.

She laughed. "Relax. I just want to get that stolen car out of our lives."

Luka smiled. "Me too."

Luka had parked his truck beside the far side of the auto shop where no one would see them.

Owen and Jordan stepped out of the blue civic in front of Luka's truck, waiting for Anna and Luka to go over and meet them. With no other words they made their way over.

"So where are we leaving this thing?" Owen asked.

Luka looked far out into the darkness. He squinted a little as if he saw something interesting.

"Luka, what is it?" Anna focused all her attention on him.

"I have a better idea."

"Why can't we just leave it here?" Jordan's voice was filled with annoyance.

"We are." Luka smirked. "Technically."

"What do you mean *technically*?" Anna demanded.

Luka shrugged. "It'll just be a little beat up."

They all gave him a blank stare.

Luka kept the smirk on his face as he walked over to the civic. "Hop in."

The three remaining all gave each other a confused look. Anna could tell none of them wanted to get in the car with Luka right now since they didn't know his plan, yet they all complied and piled into the car.

Luka started the civic and began driving forward on the gravel towards a large object. Because of the dark, Anna couldn't make out what it was at first. But as they continued closer, the object came clear into sight. It was a car crusher.

"Luka..." Anna's jaw dropped. "You're not going to...?"

He shrugged. "Why not?"

Owen chuckled. "I mean technically there's no harm in it."

Luka smiled at him. "See, someone is on my side." Luka moved his hand back and gave Owen a high five.

"Seriously, you two?" Jordan scoffed.

"Come on," Luka sighed. "We need to get rid of this car and make sure no one finds it. What better way then to remove all evidence possible?"

Anna looked over at him, trying to hear him out.

"That way, if someone really did find it, it would be crushed so there's no way they could find out who's car it was." He finished.

Anna looked back to meet Jordan's eyes. She could see a small spark in them and a relaxation in her shoulders. Jordan was convinced. Anna knew that was three against one. Not that she thought it was a bad idea, because if she was being honest she did sort of agree with this plan, she just wasn't going to admit that to Luka.

Anna sighed. "Alright, fine."

Luka beamed. "Yeah!"

They all laughed.

"Okay," Luka began, "Is anyone here good at picking locks?"

Jordan looked directly at Anna. "Yeah, I know someone."

Luka gave her a smug look. "Really, you? The detective?"

Anna scoffed. "I have no idea what you're talking about."

Luka rolled his eyes and laughed. "I need you to pick the lock on this side door into the auto shop."

Anna smirked and lifted her hand to begin fumbling with her high ponytail.

"Sure thing." She said as she pulled out a bobby pin from the back of her head.

Luka shook his head, but kept the smile on his face. "Let's go."

Fifty

Luka led the way to the side door of his dad's auto shop as Anna followed behind him. He needed to get inside and get the keys to both the claw crane and the car crusher. His dad had opened this auto shop when Luka was fairly young, so he had been around it nearly his whole life and knew where pretty much everything was kept. He learned a lot about cars too, that's what sparked his interest in trucks.

"Okay," Luka said as they arrived at the door. "Do your magic."

Anna laughed. "It's not magic. It's actually quite simple."

Luka watched as Anna took the bobby pin in her hand and began bending it open so she could use one of the ends like a key. She started poking it into the hole and Luka couldn't take his eyes off her. He wasn't exactly sure what she was doing. All he could really tell was that she was manoeuvring it side to side. She looked very focused. She was crouched down so that her eyes were lined right up with the door knob so she could see what she was doing.

"It's a bit dark, you know." She glared at him. "You could stop staring and help me."

He was thankful for the dark as he felt his cheeks flush. She had caught him staring. Without a word, he quickly pulled out his phone and turned on the flashlight shining it down toward the door knob.

"Thank you." She muttered as she continued to work her lock picking magic.

This time, he didn't care if she caught him staring at her. Anna was impressive. A detective who can pick a lock to help him get into places? He couldn't help but feel slightly turned on.

Click.

"Gotcha." Anna chuckled.

Luka smirked at her. "Well done."

He pushed the door open and entered the auto shop. It was dark but Luka could tell where the large objects like the desk and the counter and things like that were. He began walking through the place trying to remember where he was going.

"Seriously," Anna scoffed. "What is with you and not using flashlights?" She quickly reached in her pocket grabbing her phone and turned on her flashlight so they could see.

Now with better vision, he headed over toward the secretary desk, which would be Jordan's mom's desk where she writes up the paperwork and handles the phone. It was also the place Luka had caught her making out with his dad. He tried to push that memory out and continue to scan the desk.

"If I recall," Luka started, "It should be in one of these drawers."

He opened each drawer in front of them and began moving things around in search for the keys. It wasn't until the third drawer he checked that he came across something.

He paused, staring at the object in front of him.

"What is it?" Anna asked.

Luka stayed silent as he kept his eyes on the fluffy pink pom pom ball that was used to attach to a set of keys. It looked too familiar.

"What are you staring at, Luka?" Anna's voice showed the frustration at him not answering the first time.

Luka moved his hand down and picked up the pink ball key chain. "This."

"A key chain?"

Luka nodded. "Yeah."

Anna stared at him waiting for a clearer answer, but Luka wasn't sure how to say it.

"Who's key chain is that?" She asked. "You're face has gone pale so I assume you know."

Luka could have guessed that about his face. He couldn't feel his body. He wasn't even sure he was breathing at this point.

He turned directly towards Anna, still holding the key chain with the tips of his fingers. "It's Chelsea's."

Luka turned his focus from Anna back to the key chain. He couldn't wrap his head around the fact that he had just found his dead ex girlfriend's key chain shoved in a drawer in his dad's auto shop. Why would his dad have it?

"What would Chelsea's key chain be doing here?" Anna asked.

Luka shook his head. "I have no idea."

Anna walked over and got a closer look at the pink ball. "She had good taste."

Luka nodded. Anna was right about that. Chelsea had always managed to pick what other people would see and then immediately go buy, whether it was clothes, shoes or even a key chain.

"What good reason would your dad have to have this here?" Anna furrowed her brows. "Because I can't come up with one."

"Me either." He wished he had an answer. One that could defend his dad. "I mean, it is in the secretary desk. That would be where Jordan's mom always is."

Anna thought for a moment. "Yes, but, it's in the drawer way over at the far end of the desk." She began scanning the entire desk. "I would guess Jordan's mom doesn't even use this drawer. What else is in it?"

Anna quickly began to dig through the drawer Luka had found the key chain in. It had random tools and car parts, some guest check pads that were filled with messy writing that she had guessed was Luka's dad's hand writing.

"See. This looks like a random junk drawer for your dad."

Luka closed his eyes, trying to stay calm. He couldn't understand why his life was going the way it is right now. His girlfriend had been murdered, his mom is dying and he can't stop finding connections between his dad and Chelsea's murder. He was pleading for something that would prove his dad's innocence, but he wasn't sure his dad was innocent anymore.

"Let's be honest, Luka." Anna's voice was soft. "We already found a wrench that was covered in blood in your dad's garage, now Chelsea's key chain is sitting in a drawer in his car shop. Something is going on with your dad."

Luka nodded. He hated to admit it, but Anna was right. There were too many signs. Too many connections. He needed to find the truth.

"Continue looking for the keys." He told her. "Then we'll go out and tell Jordan and Owen about the key chain."

Anna didn't say anything, but nodded.

Luka knew she wanted him to tell her she was right about his dad being involved in something awful. She was right, but he couldn't find the words to say that right now. Chelsea used to call him a coward, maybe she was right.

He continued through the desk drawers and cabinets of the auto shop office looking for the keys. Luka knew he wasn't very focused at the moment, but figured he should still be able to spot the keys even with his brain not fully focused on what was around him. He was right. It didn't take him long to spot the two keys sitting in the corner of one of the shelves.

"I found them." He announced. "Let's go."

Anna was quick to step in front of him, leading the way back to the car where they had left Jordan and Owen to be the look out.

When they reached the car the two were already eagerly waiting for them.

"Did you get the keys?" Jordan asked.

Anna nodded. "Yes, but Luka found something else too."

Jordan raised her eyebrows. "What is it?"

Luka held up the key chain in their direction. "Recognize this, Owen?"

Jordan stared blankly at it, not knowing who it belonged too. But, Owen looked from the key chain up to Luka.

"That's Chelsea's." He said. "She always had that on her car keys."

"Yeah." Luka sighed. "It was shoved in a drawer in there."

Owen's eyes turned cold. "Why would your dad have that?"

"I don't know." Luka began looking around in the dark. "But we need to find out."

Fifty-one

They had all decided they needed to crush Jarid's car they had stolen from Jordan's dad's wharf before they did more digging on Luka's dad.

Truthfully, Luka had forgotten he couldn't just start crushing the car, he needed to take a few things out first. Well, he could just start crushing it, but there would most likely be some complications. But, thanks to his dad for sparking his interest in being a mechanic and slowly teaching him over the years during summer breaks and week-ends, since he lived at home during college, he was able to learn exactly what to do in this situation. He had even crushed cars before.

Luka hopped back into the stolen civic and driven it to the bay, propping it up so he could get underneath. Once the car was set up in the right spot, he began tearing the car to pieces. He started with removing all the working parts such as the engine and body panels. Next, he moved onto removing the battery and air conditioning sys-tem, as well as the gas tank. Lastly, Luka removed all four tires.

Once he was done, he looked up at his friends who were sitting there watching him. He didn't say it, but he hoped he had impressed Anna with his skills.

"No one will see the light on and know we're here, right?" Jordan's voice was filled with worry.

"Relax." Luka chuckled. "We're at the end of this road. No one really comes down here unless they're coming to the shop, and I don't think anyone will be coming at this hour."

"No one except for us." Anna shook her head.

"Alright," Luka clapped his hands together. "Let's get this thing crushed."

Luka hopped in the seat of the crane and stuck the key in the hole, turning it on. Luckily, when he had helped his dad before, he learned how to operate this machine.

He reached forward and grabbed one of the large handles and began manoeuvring it so that the large crane arm was able to move toward the vehicle.

Jordan, Anna and Owen all stepped back toward the side of the auto shop so that they were out of the way and there was no risk of getting hit. Luka could tell from their eyes that they didn't exactly trust him. But, they could at least still watch him from where they were standing.

Once he moved the crane in the direction of the small blue civic, he opened the claw and lowered it down toward the car. Once the claw was over top of the car, he closed the claw, trapping the car. He used the handle to lift the car and move it toward the direction of the crusher. Once he was directly in front of it, Luka lowered the car and placed it in the middle, between the two sides on the crusher. He then opened the claw, releasing the car so it was inside the crusher.

He began backing the claw crane up, putting it back up on the hill until he needed it again. He then opened the door and hopped out onto the ground and began walking over to where his friends were.

"I'm not too bad, am I?" He smirked.

Anna rolled her eyes. "Yeah, yeah. You're not done yet."

Luka nodded. "You guys ready to see this?"

Owen's eyes brightened. "Hell yeah!"

Luka laughed before he walked over and began setting up the crusher. Once it was started and all in place, he let the crusher do it's work.

He knew from other cars he had done, this crusher took about forty-five seconds per car. Luka leaned back and watched the car get smaller and smaller, with a smile on his face.

Once it was flattened and much smaller than it used to be, Luka hopped back in the claw crane and picked up the car from the crusher, placing it in the large pile of cars his dad had out back that were waiting to be taken to the junkyard.

But, before he was able to drive away, one of the flattened cars beside the one he had just placed, stopped him. Luka looked through the windshield, trying to focus on the flattened car in front of him. The car was white, but the line of pink paint on the side stuck out to him. Luka's heart sunk. That car might have been crushed, but he could tell exactly who's car it was.

Yet another clue leading to his dad.

He needed to solve this. Fast.

Luka was quick to call over the others. They all came jogging toward him to the section of crushed cars.

"Look," He pointed. "That's Chelsea's car."

Owen was the one closest to the car trying to inspect it to see if Luka was right.

He nodded. "Yeah, it is. I recognize the line of pink paint at the bottom of the door she got done last year."

"That's how I realized too." Luka put his hands on his hips.

Jordan and Anna stood back a little, but were close enough to see the car.

"Why would your dad have Chelsea's car?" Jordan asked.

"And why would he crush it for that matter." Owen added.

"Because he needed to hide it." Anna explained.

"He killed her." Owen's voice was stern.

Luka hated to admit it, but he knew Owen was right. Whether he wanted it to be true or not, his dad had something to do with Chelsea's murder. He watched the goosebumps form on his skin, and not from the slight chill in the air.

"Either that or he knows who did it."

"It looks like he more than just knows who did it, Luka." Anna said. "If he isn't the killer, he at least helped."

Luka nodded. "Yeah." He looked down to the ground. He hated this. How did his dad get involved in a murder? Was he a murderer? Did he kill Chelsea all on his own? Or did he have help?

"Either way," Anna pulled out her phone, "We need to call this in."

Owen nodded. "Maybe they've got something on that wrench too."

Anna shrugged. "That could take some time. I wouldn't get my hopes up."

Owen sighed. "Yeah, you're right."

"But at least we can report the car being here, that way they can come investigate things." Anna tried to lighten things.

"Okay." Luka nodded. "Call it in."

Anna dialed the number of the station and put her phone to her ear.

Luka began to walk back to the car so he was right up beside it. It was flattened but he tried to see the inside as much as he could to see if there were any clues in there. He really couldn't see much, but from the small hole he could, he didn't find anything out of the ordinary.

In the background he could hear Anna in the distance explaining what they had just found. Once she explained the story briefly, she hung up the phone and began walking back toward them.

"Okay," She began, "They're going to send a couple people down here to take a look. They asked me if we could all wait here so that we could answer a couple more questions."

"Oh good." Luka's voice was filled with sarcasm, "More questioning."

"Relax." Anna walked over beside him. "Just be honest."

Luka remembered the truth about why they were here. "We can't be completely honest, Anna."

Anna sucked in a breath. "Shit."

Luka had assumed Anna forgot they had came here to crush a stolen car. There was no way they could mention the fact they were crushing a car, especially a stolen one.

"We're going to need to come up with a good reason for why we're here and fast." Jordan warned.

"Okay," Luka rubbed his face, "Well, it's my dad's auto shop. We could say I parked my truck around the corner there and we came to pick it up."

Anna thought for a moment. "Okay, that's not bad."

Before they could decide if that's what they were going to go with or not, a police car pulled into the driveway of the auto shop. Two officers stepped out of the vehicle and walked over to them. The officers nodded to them. Luka nodded back.

"We got a call about a car that could possibly belong to the murdered Chelsea Bentley?"

Anna nodded. "Yes, that's right. We spotted it right down here."

Anna began to lead the way and the officers followed. Luka, Owen and Jordan followed on the side.

Anna led them directly to the white and pink flattened car. "It's right here, officers."

The officers stepped in front of her and began to get a close look at the car, examining it.

"It sure looks like the description we were given." One of the officers said.

The other nodded. "This just might be it."

"So what's it doing out here?" the first officer asked his partner.

The partner shook his head. "That's something we've gotta figure out."

The first officer turned to the four college kids. "I'll talk to them for a little while." He told his partner. "You get forensics down here."

The partner nodded. "Will do." He then pulled his phone out of his pocket, dialed a number and walked off.

The officer turned back to the four. "I recognize you guys. You were in the station earlier."

Luka felt his stomach grow nervous. Did this look bad?

"Yes." Was all Anna said.

The officer nodded. "Alright then. Let's talk."

Fifty-two

Anna knew lying was never a good idea, especially to a detective. Even more so when you yourself want to be a detective. But, she quickly weighed the pros and cons and immediately knew there was no way they could come clean about stealing that car. They had to go with Luka's lie about picking up his truck.

"It's a little late to be out here, don't you think?" The tall brown haired officer began interrogating them.

Luka nodded. "We just stopped by to get my truck."

"And you spotted the car?" The officer was trying to piece everything together.

"Yes." Luka confirmed. "I just walked around the corner because I really had to take a leak, when I spotted the pink line that I recognized from Chelsea's car."

Anna cringed a little at his lie about going over to "take a leak", but at the same time she was glad he had come up with something that sounded very reasonable and true. If she wasn't studying to be a detective, she would have been impressed with his lying. But at the same time, she knew that could happen to her one day and she was going to need to get good at reading people and detecting lies.

The officer looked around. "Do you have any idea what Chelsea's car would be doing here?"

Luka shook his head. "I'm just as curious as you are, officer."

"Yeah well, last we checked she didn't have an oil change before she was killed." The officer sighed.

The four stayed silent, not knowing what to say.

"And this is your dad's place, you say?"

Luka nodded, but didn't say a word.

Anna could tell he was uncomfortable. He was being shoved with the idea of his dad being a murderer and the worse part was that it was looking more and more like he was.

"Well, we'll get everything figured out and we'll get some answers." The officer promised. "We've got forensics coming in here and they're the best of the best."

Anna gave the officer a small smile. "Thank you."

"No," The officer waved, "Thank you. If you hadn't found this and called it in, we'd still be stuck where we were on this case while waiting for forensics to get to that wrench."

"Have they got to that wrench?" Owen asked, curious.

The officer nodded. "Last I knew they were in the middle of pulling fingerprints and blood off it."

"Good." Owen sounded relieved as a small smile crept to his face. "Maybe we can finally find my sister's killer."

The officer was surprised to hear that Owen was Chelsea's brother and gave him his condolences as well as some hope that they were so close to bringing his sister justice.

After the four had given their statements, the officers told them they weren't needed here anymore and that they could take it from here.

"Forensics will be here any second. They'll take over the area. You kids head home."

Luka nodded and Anna thanked them before leaving the area.

When they were on their way to Luka's truck, they saw some people in white suits and gloves from the forensics team make their way in.

They all hopped into Luka's truck. He then started the engine and headed toward the road. "I'm not going home. I can't. He'll know. I can't look him in the eye right now."

Anna rubbed his arm. She felt terrible for Luka. He had to find out the hard way that his dad was a murderer and he was the one to turn him in.

"You did the right thing, you know." Jordan tried to ease him.

Luka sighed as he turned on his high beams. "I sure hope so."

"If your dad really is responsible for something awful, then he needs to be put away." Anna's voice was soft as she looked over at him.

"Especially if it has to do with Chels." Owen chimmed in. "She deserves peace. Even if that means sacrificing your dad."

Luka gripped the steering wheel as he began driving out the auto shop driveway. "I know."

Anna knew he would understand he did the right thing someday, he was just hurting right now. But once it wasn't so raw, everything would be okay.

"We can all go back to Jordan and I's apartment." Anna suggested.

"Yeah." Jordan agreed. "It feels like we haven't been home in forever."

Anna laughed. "Yeah, you're right."

Without another word, they headed over to the apartment complex at the edge of town.

Fifty-three

I could feel it in my gut that something wan't right. That I had been caught. I had no proof of that yet, but I could tell just by the change in the air and by my rapid heart beat, that someone was coming close to figuring out what I had done, if they hadn't already.

I had heard a noise that sounded like it was coming from the garage. It sounded like muffled voices and objects being moved. I was quick to get up from bed and make my way downstairs.

I hadn't been sleeping. Whoever was in here must have thought I was. But, I had too much on my mind. My eyes refused to close as my mind kept running, thinking about that wrench I had hid downstairs. I knew it wasn't hidden well, but I didn't think anyone would get to it before I did first thing tomorrow morning.

I felt my heart sink and my anger rise as I opened the garage door. I could already tell this wasn't going to be good. I didn't have any proof, but my gut was telling me it was Luka. I could tell when he came into the shop that he recognized the bracelet I had given Meghan. I had told her to not wear it while working, rather just during our dates and things like that, but she was too excited about it to listen. I could see the wheels turning in Luka's head that day, I just didn't think he would be smart enough to keep digging on me.

I began to scan around when I noticed the light in the garage was on. I was sure I turned it off before heading upstairs to bed. I had been right about the noises I heard. Someone had definitely been in here.

I continued to grow nervous as the seconds went on. I had something valuable in here. Not valuable as in money, but as in the price of my life. I hoped and prayed to any of the Gods above that it was still sitting in that cabinet. But I could feel it heavy in my chest that it wasn't.

Before making any moves I looked around, careful to see if there was anyone still in here. Once I concluded the area was empty, I went directly to the cabinet where I had placed the wrench. The plan was to get up early tomorrow and deal with it. But now I wasn't sure I still had that chance.

As I stepped in front of the cabinet, I took a deep breath. I told myself on the count of three I would open the door and I would see the wrench still sitting there.

1...2...3...

I opened the cabinet door.

It was empty.

It was fucking empty.

Fuck!

I wanted to scream but I knew I couldn't risk waking my wife and daughters.

I had been made.

Instead of screaming I opened my mouth, but made sure nothing came out. I then threw an empty *Olands* bottle against the wall. I watched it smash into tiny pieces. I couldn't help but notice how it brought me comfort.

I let out a long steady breath and pulled myself together quickly. There was no time to get angry and lose it right now. I needed to screw my head on straight and focus.

Someone had figured out what I had done. I bet with everything in me that it was my son. I remember when I had left Randy Ember's wharf, I had spotted a small car in the grass. When I looked over I couldn't see any movement. There looked to be no one in it. But, something told me otherwise. I didn't make any moves at the time, but it was all starting to come together now. I knew the car wasn't Luka's, but he had been hanging around some new friends. Perhaps he has been on to me for quite some time now.

I stressed for a moment about what he would think of me, considering I was his only mobile parent. What would he do if I ended up in jail once his mother died? If he is the one who found me out and plans to turn me in, he'll regret it. I know he will. But I quickly dismissed that thought and realized I had bigger problems.

I needed to get that wrench back before my life was ruined, if it wasn't already.

Chelsea's blood was still on that wrench I had used to kill her in the woods.

It only took me seconds to come up with a plan. I wasn't sure if it was a good one or not, but it seemed like the only option right now. I hadn't thought it through, but there was no time for that. I needed to take that wrench back. Hopefully before it was too late.

I quietly made my way upstairs to my wife and I's bedroom. When I got to the door, I stopped and peeked through the crack to make sure she was still asleep. When I was certain she was, I slowly opened the door, careful it wouldn't creak and startle her. I needed her to stay asleep right now, this was a life or death situation.

I knew I was in a hurry, but making sure I didn't wake Eleanor was more important right now. She could not see what I was about to do.

I quietly made my way over to our shared closet and pulled out my phone so I could use the screen as a light. I crouched down and pulled out one of the bins on the floor at the bottom of the closet. It was filled with a bunch of my things that I didn't want Eleanor to find.

I dug through the bin until I found what I was looking for. I held up the blue button down shirt that had a fake police badge on it. I had bought it a couple of years ago for a Halloween party. I knew this would come in handy again.

"Gotcha." I whispered.

I put the cover back on the bin and shoved it back into the corner of the closet.

I made my way over to my dresser and pulled out a pair of business casual pants an some dress shoes.

On my way out of the room, I checked one last time to make sure Eleanor was still sleeping. I was never more thankful that she was.

Without another thought, I made my way down the hallway to the bathroom and quickly changed into the uniform.

Once I was ready, I headed downstairs, grabbed the keys to my red *suv* and ran out the door.

I decided not to park in the parking lot of the station, thinking they could figure out it was me. I decided to park in the cafe's parking lot that was right next to the station.

I made my way out of the car to the station's front doors.

I was smart enough to know some people in here would probably recognize me, given it was a small town and all, but I decided my plan was to keep my head down and keep walking to where I assumed I needed to go and hoped no one payed too much attention to me.

Fifty-four

I entered through one of the side doors so that I didn't bring too much acknowledgement to myself. Once I was in, I scanned the place.

There were probably about twenty officers on the main floor. Some at their desks, some walking around with files in their hands, some eating donuts.

I looked around the walls to see if there were any signs that would lead me to where I was going. But, given that it was a police station and not a hospital, there were no easy to follow signs.

Scanning the room again, I saw a woman in a lab coat talking to one of the officers. She seemed to be showing him a file and explaining her findings to him. I figured this was exactly what I needed. I waited for their conversation to finish and then waited to see where she was going. The short red haired woman turned and made a left for a set of stairs. Assuming she was headed where I needed to go, I began following her.

I kept a good length of space behind her, careful not to catch her attention. She walked up the stairs and down a corridor before making another left. Once I took the left, I saw a handful of glass rooms filled with both men and women dressed in both suits and white lab coats.

I let the woman in front of me out of my sight and stood behind the wall, hiding myself. *Why was I growing nervous? This wasn't who I am. I'm a risk taker.*

I took a deep breath before peeking around the corner again. This time I found half a dozen men wearing the same uniform I was wearing. Some were talking to some of the lab and forensics team, but others were just walking through to where they were headed. I knew I needed to blend in like that too.

I realized I couldn't just walk around and look for the wrench. It would be too obvious. Not only that, but I wouldn't know where to look. I had to come up with a plan.

I didn't know much about forensics or labs, I was a mechanic. However, my wife has always watched crime shows ever since I've known her. I usually complained every time she put one on, but really I was just too pathetic to admit they were actually good. Besides, they taught me a thing to two.

I figured my best option was to talk to one of the people who were wearing a lab coat. All I had to do was figure out what to say.

I stood behind the wall for a few more moments, coming up with my lines. I knew a man by the name of Tim Collins was the sheriff in town. He practically owned the town. I figured he had to have an office in this place somewhere.

I decided I would find a lab tech to talk to and ask her for the wrench. I would tell her that Sheriff Collins would like to take a look at it.

I nodded to myself as I went over the plan in my head. I hoped with everything in me that it worked. I assumed the worst that could happen is that she could say no. Either that or she would ask me to go get Sheriff Collins. I figured if that happened I would leave the place as fast as I could.

Putting my fears aside, I came out from behind the wall and began walking up to a shorter woman who was standing by an office door in the corner of the lab. I had never seen her before, so I knew she wouldn't recognize me. When I got close enough she raised her head to look at me.

"Excuse me," I smiled. "I'm officer Walden. I'm here on behalf of Sheriff Collins."

She smiled back. "Hi, there. What is it I can do for you?"

"He's pretty buried in paperwork right now. But, he'd like to take a look at a piece of evidence that was brought in. It has to do with Chelsea Bentley's case."

She nodded. "The wrench?"

I fought back a smile. I knew right when I saw her that she would be gullible enough to believe me and give me all the information. "Yes."

"Sure. We're all finished with it." She told me. "I'll go grab it for you."

I cleared my throat. "Thank you."

She nodded before scurrying off to the other side of the room to grab me my murder weapon.

While she was gone, I scanned the room. I kept my hands in my pockets, trying to blend in. I stood still as I watched the officers and lab techs around me run around the room trying to finish everything at once.

"Here you are, officer." The woman's voice startled me.

I turned around to see her holding a bag that had permanent marker on it that read "**EVIDENCE**".

I took the bag from her. "You're sure the lab techs won't mind me taking this?" I teased. I knew she didn't know any better. Either way, I was taking this wrench home with me.

She chuckled. "Of course not. Just get the sheriff to bring it back to us as soon as he's done with it."

I nodded. "Will do. Thank you."

She smiled before shuffling away once again.

As I turned around to head back where I came from, I discretely shoved the bag into my pocket.

As I made my way down the stairs, one of the officers who I had seen talking to the red haired woman in the main area, looked over at me. I could see a glimpse of confusion in his eyes. That was my cue to get the hell out of here.

Giving him a friendly nod, I moved my feet forward, continuing down the stairs.

After I made the left corner, my gut told me this wasn't going to be as smooth as I thought it was going to be. Out of curiosity, I turned to look behind me. Sure enough, there was the same cop, discretely following, his eyes fixated on me like a lion and I was the prey.

Turning my head back to my feet as I escalated down the stairs, I picked up my pace a little. Once I was in the main officer area, I quickly turned toward the side door I came in.

As I reached it, I turned back one last time to see if I was still being followed. Once my hand hit the handle, I saw the same familiar shape I had seen following me moments ago.

Before he could catch a glimpse of me, I exited the door, shutting it fast behind me.

Once I was out, I didn't give a second thought before running back to my *suv*.

As I shoved myself into the driver seat, I stripped off the fake police button down so I was just in my grey wife beater.

I was quick to reach in my pocket to make sure I still had what I came for. I felt a wave of relief come over me when I felt the head of the wrench.

Starting the vehicle with a grin on my face, I headed back home.

I had convinced myself I had made it. That I had gotten back my valuable weapon before the forensics had a chance to touch it. *Wait,* I thought. *No, that wasn't what she had said.* As I gripped the steering wheel I remembered what the short woman had said to me. *"We're all finished with it."*

"Fuck!" I yelled.

Did that mean I had been made? *No,* I thought. My fingerprints weren't in the system. They could run the fingerprints they pulled off the wrench all they wanted, but they wouldn't find a match.

I relaxed my shoulders a little. Sure, Luka could have told the police it was mine when he took it in, if it was him of course. But, who was going to believe Luka?

I assumed if that was the case they would come to my house and question me on the matter, but I would simply deny everything and say my son just got it mixed up. That way, without proof there was nothing they could do.

"Yahoo!" I screamed as I turned the radio up so loud that the whole town could hear the words of *Midnight Rider* by *Allman Brothers Band.* I lowered the windows down all the way and let the breeze hit my face as I screamed with freedom.

I was going to get away with this.

Or, so I thought.

Everything changed when I was halfway down Davidson Boulevard and turned my head to look down the road where my auto shop was.

In the distance was flashing siren lights, but the sound wasn't on.

Quickly turning down the music, I slammed my car to a stop.

I looked down the road again, trying to see as far down as I could. I knew I couldn't see the auto shop from back here, but I could at least see the road in front of it.

I spotted two cop cars and one crime lab van parked on the side of the road in front of my shop.

"Shit!" I slapped my steering wheel.

What the hell is going on? What did they find?

The memories of me driving Chelsea's car to the back and crushing it flooded my brain. I thought the truck that picked them up to take them to the junk yard would get here before any of this happened. But I knew that was no longer the case anymore. There was no way they hadn't found the car yet. I'd been made.

I couldn't help but wonder how. How did the police know to look at my shop? Was this Luka's doing? I couldn't understand how he would've figured it out.

If it was Luka, I couldn't help but wonder if Jordan had something to do with this. Was she sleeping with him? Ever since she had came into the shop with Luka last week, I couldn't help but wonder how close the two really were, or if they had figured out about Meghan and I.

Lost in my thoughts, I kept my eyes down the road on the police vehicles. I needed to come up with a plan. Did I have a solid alibi? I knew that wouldn't matter once they found Chelsea's vehicle in the back. Should I leave town? I honestly didn't know, but I had to decide quickly.

Before I could come up with a solid conclusion, one of the police cars ahead turned on their headlights.

Had they seen me? I knew they probably knew my vehicle, everyone did.

When the cop car pulled away from the curb and headed down the street toward me, I slammed my foot on the gas.

I hadn't even realized I was driving. It was just a spring of the moment. But, once I got my head on straight, I focused my eyes back on the road ahead of me and attempted to out speed the cop I knew was somewhere behind me.

Fifty-five

Anna was sitting in her beanbag chair next to Jordan, who was sitting in her other one. Luka and Owen were sitting in the two recliners across from them.

Owen seemed to be very interested in something on his phone, while Luka seemed to be too caught up in his thoughts to have a care in the world.

Anna knew he was thinking about his dad. There was no way he wouldn't be. Of course he felt bad, it was his dad. But, she knew someday he would realize it was the right thing to do.

Anna hadn't realized she was staring at Luka until Jordan discretely cleared her throat so that only Anna would hear her.

Anna brushed off her thoughts about Luka and looked over at her, "Hm?"

"You're staring." Jordan whispered.

Anna chuckled as she felt her cheeks warm. "I know he feels bad."

"He probably feels lost. If we're right about this whole thing and his dad really did kill Chelsea, he'll be thrown in jail for a long time."

Anna nodded. "I hope so, anyway."

Jordan nodded in agreement.

"Still," Anna sighed, "Losing your dad would be a lot."

Jordan shrugged. "I've made it this far."

Anna couldn't help but laugh. "That's true. How do you think he plays a part in all this anyway?"

She shook her head. "I really don't know. But I hope we find out."

Anna stayed silent and looked back at Luka.

"You two have been spending a lot of time together, you know." Jordan acknowledged.

Anna looked back to her and rolled her eyes. "I could say the same about you and Owen, but I've kept to myself."

Jordan's cheeks turned red. "Fair enough."

Anna widened her eyes in a "yeah that's what I thought" expression.

"What's he like?" Jordan asked.

Anna snickered. "He's cocky, demanding, too smooth for his own good and has better hair than me. I mean look at that fluffy raven coloured magic."

Jordan grinned. "Definitely sounds like you like him."

"Nah," Anna waved it off, "He likes himself too much for me to waste my time."

"Right." Jordan winked. "Of course he does."

Before Anna could say another word, Owen gasped.

"Guys!"

The three looked over at him.

"What is it?" Anna demanded.

"A news article was just posted." He told them.

"What does it say?" Anna ran over next to him so she could see his phone screen.

"It says the wrench we brought in is missing." Owen explained, looking up at them with his face full of confusion.

"Missing?" Luka repeated. "What do you mean *missing*?"

Owen shrugged. "It says '*The newest piece of evidence in the case of the murdered Chelsea Bentley has been reported stolen*'."

Luka slapped the wall. "Dammit!"

"Luka," Anna shouted. "This is an apartment, there are people upstairs."

He didn't look apologetic. He didn't even look like he cared.

"How could the wrench have been stolen from the crime lab?" Jordan asked.

Owen's eyes returned that same look of anger. "I don't know."

"I can guarantee I know exactly what happened." Luka spoke.

The three turned their full attention to Luka.

"My dad heard us in the garage," He began, "He knew we were in there, I don't have any doubt. He also would have had the wrench on his mind, knowing it was out there. My guess is, he came into the garage looking for it only to find out it was gone."

"So what?" Jordan furrowed her brows. "He stole it?"

Luka shrugged. "If he killed an innocent girl, I wouldn't put thieving past him."

"That's a big accusation, Luka." Anna tried to piece together the situation.

"But it would make sense," Owen nodded. "What are the odds of an analyst in the lab losing it? Probably slim. If your dad figured out that someone knew what he did, I wouldn't put anything past him."

Luka looked at Owen like he was grateful for his backup. "Exactly."

"Let me see the article." Jordan said, stealing Owen's phone out of his hand before he had the chance to object.

Jordan put her undivided attention to the screen as she began reading. "It was reported by an analyst that a man had came up to her asking for the wrench, saying it was for the sheriff."

Luka leaned back in his seat. "So my dad lied his way through."

"And someone willingly gave it to him?" Anna asked in disbelief.

Once Jordan was finished reading, she smiled as she looked at each one of her friends separately.

Anna got a hopeful feeling in her stomach. "What is it?

Jordan looked directly at Luka. "Your dad is an idiot."

Luka nodded. "Yeah, but what does the article say, Jordan?"

Jordan began to read directly from the article. "We would like the guilty person to know that we have taken both blood and fingerprints from the weapon. Even though you may now have possession of it, we will still find you."

Anna couldn't help but laugh. "Oh my god."

Owen cracked a smile. "Damn right."

"He stole the weapon back after they had what they needed." Luka said, explaining it to himself. "They're going to get him."

Anna nodded. "Yeah, they are."

Luka smiled at her, making her feel warm inside. She was glad to see him smile.

"Well," She let out a sigh of relief, "If your dad really did kill Chelsea, which from seeing her car, looks like he did, they've got him on both the car and the wrench."

Luka nodded. "Yeah."

Anna could've swore she saw relief in his eyes that replaced the guilt and worry.

"I will say though, a wrench is an interesting murder weapon." She brought forth.

"He shoves all kinds of different tools in his pockets all the time." Luka explained. "I don't think it's something he means to do, just a force of habit. It must have happened to be in his pocket during that time."

"I just don't understand why he would have killed Chelsea." Owen shook his head. "What did she ever do to him?"

"I don't know." Luka responded. "But we're going to find out."

Their attention was pulled from each other to the loud noise outside.

"Sirens." Jordan exclaimed.

Anna quickly grabbed her bag off the counter. "Let's go."

They all ran out the door and piled into Luka's truck, headed for the sirens.

To Anna's surprise, Luka found the sirens easily and fast.

"How did you know to find them that fast?" Anna was amazed.

Luka shrugged, "Just follow the sound."

Anna nodded.

He turned to her. "And take random turns and hope for the best."

They all couldn't help but laugh.

"I hope this is what we think it is." Owen sighed.

"Me too." Luka agreed. "Chelsea has waited too long for her justice."

They continued following the sirens to Rand Road, where Luka lived.

"This is a good sign." Owen smiled.

Luka continued driving toward his house. "Let's just hope he's here."

When the house came into view, Anna saw that the driveway was completely full of cop cars. There were a few officers standing outside, but Anna assumed there were some inside searching for Chad too.

Luka pulled his truck to the side of the road and put it in park.

"Okay, Jordan and Owen, can you guys distract the cops a little?"

Jordan raised her eyebrows. "You want us to distract them?"

Luka nodded. "I want to get inside."

"I'm coming with you." Anna told him.

"I figured."

Jordan sighed, "Okay, fine. We'll distract them."

"But we're going to need to hurry up." Owen said.

They all silently agreed and began getting out of the vehicle.

"Oh my god." Jordan's jaw dropped.

Anna looked ahead to see what she was looking at. When she saw it, her own jaw dropped.

"What is she doing here?" Jordan scoffed.

She was talking about her mother. Down by the other side of Luka's house, there was a crowd of people beginning to gather around to see what was going on. One of those people was Meghan, Jordan's mom.

"Do you think she knows?" Luka turned to Jordan.

Jordan thought for a moment before shaking her head. "There's no way."

Luka didn't question it anymore, although Anna could tell he was still thinking about it.

"We'll hang back here for a minute." He said, holding a hand out to stop Anna from walking.

Jordan and Owen nodded before beginning to walk toward the driveway, up to where two police officers were standing.

Anna couldn't hear what they were saying from back where she and Luka were standing, but she guessed they were simply asking what was going on.

Luka grabbed Anna's hand, catching her off guard. "Let's go."

With her hand in his, she began to follow him.

He led her up the side of their lawn. It was a steep hill and Anna could already feel it in her legs. She knew there was no way his dad could get a ride on mower down here.

"What's the plan?" Anna whispered.

"We're going to go in the side door here and try to find my dad."

Not fully on board, Anna followed Luka into the house.

Fifty-six

I knew my plan was terrible. If I went through with what I planned to do, I wouldn't get away with the murder of Chelsea Bentley. But, by the looks of the cop cars outside in my driveway, I wasn't getting away with it anyway.

I wasn't going to deny it any longer. I had been made. Even if I had stolen the wrench from the lab, they could still most likely find a way to get me on it. Not only that, but I knew they had me on the car. I had no ideas of how I was going to explain the car to them. I may be a good liar, but there was no getting out of that one.

After I had murdered Chelsea I knew I had to do something with her car so the police wouldn't find it. I was lucky enough to own an auto shop and a car crusher. But I wasn't expecting anyone to find the car, that's for sure.

"Chad?" I heard Eleanor's faint voice.

"Everything is going to be okay, Honey." I tried to soothe her.

I didn't really believe myself. I knew things were not going to be okay. All of my secrets were going to be revealed.

There was a loud knock at the door.

"Chad Anderson, open up!" A raspy voice boomed through the house.

"Chad what is going on?" Eleanor's voice was fragile, but filled with worry.

I looked over at her as she stood in the doorway. I was surprised to see she made it downstairs as fast as she did.

"It's going to be fine, Dear." I heard the worry in my own voice.

Before I could make my way to the door, it was busted in.

"Chad Anderson." A tall cop pointed his gun at me. "Hands in the air."

To my own surprise, I did as I was told. I put my hands behind my head and dropped to my knees, letting the officer cuff me. When he stood me up, he turned me around to lead me toward the door. That's when I spotted Luka out of the corner of my eye. He looked shocked and maybe a little helpless. His jaw was dropped and his face looked frozen in fear. But I could see the disappointment in his eyes. He was disappointed in me.

He was quick to run to his mother's side, with some other girl beside him, following him over. She looked familiar. I remembered her from that day Jordan picked her car up from my shop. She was Jordan's friend.

"Let's go." The officer said as he pulled on my arm.

"Wait." Luka turned so he was looking directly at me. "You killed her didn't you? You fucking killed Chelsea."

I took a deep breath. "Yes, son. I did. But you were the one to turn me in, weren't you?"

He stared blankly at me. "You're damn right I did, you coward."

I pursed my lips and nodded, wanting nothing more than to get out of here.

Tears began to well in Luka's eyes. "Why did you kill her? I need to know why."

I looked out the front window to see a crowd of people underneath the street light, curious to see what was going on. "She found me out."

"She found you out?" Luka repeated. "What does that even mean?"

I look another deep breath. I knew Luka deserved to know the truth. I couldn't hold back the tears that began to fill my own eyes.

"That night she came to see you. When she got here," I paused and let out a sigh, "She saw Meghan leaving."

Flashbacks of that night ran through my mind. Chelsea pulling in the driveway at the same time I leaned through the open drivers window to give Meghan a kiss goodbye. I knew she had saw it happen. I could see it in the shocked look on her face.

"You killed Chelsea because she caught you cheating?" Luka was yelling now.

I could barely see through my watery eyes. But as I looked past Luka, I saw Eleanor begin to cry.

I couldn't find any words as I bent my knees to collapse on the floor, but the officer holding my arm yanked me back up. I knew there was no way I could make Luka understand.

"So what?" Luka began getting curious. "Meghan leaves and you drag Chelsea to the water?"

I shook my head as I sniffled. "You don't understand, Luka."

"No, I don't." He laughed. "How could I possibly understand?"

"Please." I begged as I tried to collapse to the floor once again, this time the officer let me drop.

"You're pathetic." Luka shook his head. "Answer the question."

"I hit her first," I began, sitting up on my knees. "I knocked her out. I went to drag her onto the woods when she regained her consciousness back and got loose. She tried to run, but I was catching up to her. That's when I found the wrench in my pocket. It couldn't have been there at a better time." I was still crying, but I could feel the smile creep to my face.

Luka shook his head in disgust.

"How'd she get in the water?" Luka's friend asked.

I stared at the floor for a moment, replaying what had happened in my head. "I had an old friend."

"Jordan's dad." She said, as if she knew exactly what I was talking about.

I thought for a moment. "Now that you mention it, yeah. I believe it is Jordan's dad." I looked up at her.

Her and Luka stared at me silently.

"I knew he had a boat." I continued. "I explained my situation and he said he could lend me a hand."

Luka sat down on the arm of the chair his mother was now sitting in and put his hands in his face. "You killed her because you're a lying, cheating coward."

"I knew she would tell you." I began crying again. "I couldn't do that to your mother. Or Meghan."

"Oh forget Meghan!" He shouted. "You hurt mom anyway."

"But I didn't mean to." I sobbed. "I just...I fell in love with Meghan."

Luka's face turned red. "You're sickening."

"I didn't mean for this to happen, Luka." I tried to get up, but the officer grabbed me again. "I didn't want to kill her. I didn't have another choice. I'm sorry."

"You had a choice." Luka argued.

I nodded, feeling defeated. I looked over at the officers beside me. They seemed to be just as disgusted with my story as my son was.

"Let's go." the officer said again, this time pulling me out the door.

Fifty-seven

Anna had suggested that she and Luka get some air. She knew he didn't want to leave his mother, but she told him that they would go right back in and see her.

When they got outside they explained everything to Jordan and Owen. They were just as disgusted as she and Luka felt. Killing someone because they caught you cheating and you didn't want to get caught? That was an all time low.

Jordan shook her head. "Chelsea was killed because of another one of my mother's flings."

Anna shrugged. "He said that he loved her. I mean, he did kill for her and all."

"I'd bet she didn't feel the same way." Jordan sighed. "I'm going over to talk to her."

Without another word, Jordan made her way over to where her mom was standing. Anna could almost see the fumes of anger coming off her.

Owen made his way over to the front deck and sat down.

"You okay, Buddy?" Luka asked.

Owen looked down at the ground, but nodded.

"We'll give you some time alone." Luka said, before placing a hand on Anna's back guiding her away.

"I think I found something!" A voice yelled in the distance.

"What is it?" Another voice yelled.

Anna and Luka looked to the direction of the commotion.

"I found a rock in the garden out back." The first voice yelled again. "It has stains of blood."

Anna could see the yelling was two officers talking to each other. She felt her heart sink when she saw the rock in his glove covered hand.

"I washed it off and put it in my mother's garden."

That was the rock Luka had killed Jarid with.

"Luka." Anna's voice was a whisper.

"Relax." He shushed her. "They'll find Jarid's blood and think it was my dad."

She couldn't help but look over at him confused.

"You're going to let your dad go down for that?"

He shrugged. "He killed an innocent girl. That son of a bitch deserves to."

Anna stared at him for a little while longer. She couldn't fully wrap her head around what he had just told her. Luka was going to let his dad go to prison for a second murder. One that he didn't commit. But at the same time the officer already had that rock. There was nothing they could do now. Anna didn't want to lose Luka.

"It'll be our secret, okay?" He whispered in her ear.

She felt a smile creep upon her face. "Okay."

Things were better this way.

Epilogue

Anna opened the doors of her boyfriend's auto shop. The smell of oil and gasoline smacked her in the face.

Luka looked up from his desk and smiled at her. "Hey."

She smiled back. "Hey. I brought you some take out for lunch. Something you can eat with a fork so you're not getting the dirt from your hands all over your food before eating it."

He laughed before leaning forward and giving her a kiss on the head. "You didn't have to do that."

"Well, I figured if you keep eating sandwiches with oil on the bread, you're going to die. You might not believe me, but I'd like for you to stick around."

Luka smiled at her as he pulled the food out from the bag. "You're right. I don't."

Anna rolled her eyes. "What're you reading?" She asked, noticing the paper in front of him.

"The front page." Luka told her, showing her the front page of the newspaper.

Anna's stomach dropped when she saw a picture of Chad on the front page in an orange jumpsuit. Flashbacks of the day he was arrested and confessed flooded her head.

Luka shook his head in disappointment. "I can't believe it's been six years already."

Anna nodded. "Me either. You know, I've been hearing rumours that Meghan has been going to visit him."

Luka leaned back in his seat as he pulled his plastic fork out of the bag. "Wow."

Anna nodded.

Six years ago to the day, Chad had broke down and told Luka what really happened to Chelsea. Anna could never wrap her head around how he made himself believe he did the right thing.

He didn't confess to the murder of Jarid Bentley at first. But, given the bloody rock in his garden, the police kept pushing him. After a year in prison, things started to get to his head and he ended up confessing. It took Anna a few months to accept that Luka had let it happen. She knew it was wrong, but Chad deserved to rot in prison.

Chad was facing life in prison. They said after ten years he could apply for parole. But, when Luka had gone to visit him once, Chad had told him he wasn't interested. He said this was just where he belonged now.

Luka had only gone to see him once. It was the one year anniversary of Chelsea's death. He wanted to remind him of how terrible of a person he was and make him feel awful, but Luka said his dad couldn't wipe the grin off his face the entire time. Knowing it was pointless, Luka got up and left.

"How's your mom doing today?" Anna asked.

Luka smiled. "She's having a better day today."

Luka was still living at home with his mom. He knew someone had to take care of her, and he was more than happy to do so. Both of his younger sisters had moved out and gone to university. Since Luka's older sister hadn't lived at home for years, Anna had decided she would move in with him. She had always said she would try to get out of this small town, but decided this was where she belonged.

Luka had graduated college six years ago now, and was lucky enough to take over his dad's auto shop and make it his own. There were some people who didn't come here anymore since it was a small town and people assume Luka will turn out just like his father. But, there were other people who said Luka was the best mechanic in town. Anna was thankful for those people.

As for Jordan and Owen, they had both graduated university and college. Jordan became a nurse and Owen dropped out of university first year and decided to go to college to get a trade to become an electrician. After they graduated school, they both happened to land jobs right away and bought an apartment together.

"So," Luka smiled at her. "I heard you're about to get handed your first case?"

"My first *official* case." She corrected him. "I'm doing this one legally. Considering I finally have a degree."

"I'm really proud of you."

She smiled. "I can't help but wonder if this case will be anything like my first unofficial case."

Luka laughed. "I don't think anything could compare to that."

Authors Note

Thank you so much for reading my first ever novel, *First Case*. I had so much fun writing this book and getting to know each of the characters. If you have read this and you're from my small town and you know me personally, no you don't. I'm just kidding. Thank you for the support.